STRICTI

by

ROXANE BEAUFORT

CHIMERA

Strictly Discipline first published in 2003 by
Chimera Publishing Ltd
PO Box 152
Waterlooville
Hants
PO8 9FS

Printed and bound in Great Britain by
Cox & Wyman Ltd, Reading.

STRICTLY DISCIPLINE

Roxane Beaufort

This novel is fiction – in real life practice safe sex

Amelie listened and wondered and was disturbed by the tenor of the conversation. She strained her ears to hear what might be taking place around her, nerves stretched like bowstrings as she thought of Mervin selecting the instrument he would choose to chastise her. She heard rustlings and his footsteps and the sound of something swishing through the air. A whip? A cat-o-nine-tails? Her skin was stippled with goose bumps and her pussy ached, her nipples rising against the hard surface of the bench.

There followed a hush, the air loaded with anticipation. Waiting was a gruelling enough punishment on its own. Butterflies fluttered in her stomach and she panicked and struggled against those impossible bonds. Then there was a whoosh behind her, followed by a thwack.

'Ow!' he screamed as leather connected with her bottom and fire lanced her. 'Oh, ow!' She almost wet herself with the shock of it, so harsh, so brutal, so inescapable. Worse than when Thacker had whipped her – far, far worse.

Chapter One

'Good heavens, what ails you now, sister?' raged the tall, dark-haired aristocrat as he stalked the floral-patterned carpet with all the grace and ferocity of a caged tiger. 'Were I not such a tolerant person I would think you did this on purpose! You know I have guests for dinner tonight and, once again, you'll not be there to act as hostess!'

'I'm sorry, Mervin, I truly am, but this headache is dreadful,' whispered the pale young woman propped up by lace-edged pillows in the elaborate mahogany four-poster, watching him striding around. He had just come in from riding, wearing form-hugging breeches and a hacking jacket. As he moved he impatiently struck his leather booted leg with his crop, the crisp thwack making her spine tingle and her sphincter clench. 'I can't bear the light, Dulcie will tell you.'

Dulcie Higgins, the ladies maid, hovered in the background, daring to add her word. 'It's a fact, your lordship. Lady Millicent is extremely poorly.'

Mervin Bessborough swung round on her angrily. 'Who asked you to speak?' he demanded brusquely. He was a tall, commanding figure, strikingly handsome in an arrogant, domineering way, owner of Kelston Towers, an estate of hundreds of acres, and the nearby village of Kemble-on-the-Wylye.

Millicent adored him, her masterful brother, and never dared disobey him. She was twenty and he had inherited two years before when their father died. Up till that time Millicent had been, though never robust, a healthy young woman. There had been several personable suitors begging her hand in marriage, but she fancied none of them. Her father had not pushed her into making a decision, happy to keep her at home with him, but Mervin was different. He was the ringleader of a collection of male cronies whom Millicent instinctively disliked. There was one in particular he urged her to accept, Lord Nigel Balfour, the ugly, blustering heir to a dukedom, who stared at her in a manner that made her skin crawl. She had found that illness was an escape from his unwelcome attentions, but at the same time longed for a lover to woo and cherish her and introduce her to all those mysterious carnal matters of which she was ignorant.

She dreamed of passionate kisses and hands exploring her body, where she dared not touch, warned off by her strict nanny who found her innocently examining herself one day and said, sternly, 'Nice young ladies don't finger themselves down there.'

So, as she grew older, she burned and yearned, but for what she did not precisely know. Her body gave her clues, however. Her breasts ached, her nipples peaked and there was a throbbing centred at the apex of her cleft where a tiny nodule protruded from between the labial lips. She became wet – a slick, clear wetness that was unlike her monthly flux. But she remembered her nanny's edict and, though sometimes looking at her body in the mirror, secretly, admiringly, partly ashamed of the swelling breasts, rosy-hued teats, tiny waist, rounded hips and that smoky triangle of hair that surmounted her mound, she never, ever touched.

'Nigel's coming tonight and he particularly wants to see you,' Mervin continued, anger smouldering in his steely grey eyes.

Millicent shuddered inwardly and welcomed the pain in her temples which would prevent her having to endure Nigel's leering glances and damp, podgy hands that always seemed here, there and everywhere as he attempted to fondle her furtively. Though not exactly certain of what he wanted, Millicent guessed it to be something of an intimate nature, alarmed by yet curious of the swelling that appeared in the region of his flies whenever he was close to her.

She wanted none of this stress, retiring to her bed when it became too much, suffering from migraine and shivering fits, bouts of weeping and a general feeling of malaise, as well as a need to hide away from the public eye. This was turning into a compulsion, her shyness increasing by the day. She was fast becoming one of those sickly heroines of the romances she favoured as reading matter – wan, consumptive and, most of all, bereft of love.

'I'm most displeased with you,' Mervin said coldly.

He moved and she flinched. She shivered in anticipation, for he had assumed the right to punish her as he saw fit, and though she cringed under his blows she was also aware of strange, heated sensations in her loins, the same as those that possessed her when she looked at herself in the mirror. This horrified her. They were siblings, sired by the same father and born of the same mother, and she struggled to repress the wicked, incestuous thoughts that sprang up when in his presence. Even though she didn't know why she felt like this and what she wanted to take place, she feared it was sinful.

'I'm sorry,' she murmured again.

'Sorry isn't good enough. Stand up.'

Millicent swung her legs over the side of the mattress and got to her feet, and her white cambric nightgown fell from an embroidered yoke to the floor. It was buttoned high at the neck and had long, billowing sleeves fastened at the wrists. Her rich brown hair tumbled over her shoulders and down her back, her face a heart-shaped triangle between the tangled ringlets. She stood there with her head bowed, staring at her feet, her pose one of abject submission.

Aware of his scrutiny, her cheeks flamed and her head pounded. She could hear Dulcie's quickened breathing and knew the maid did not approve of the way Mervin

7

treated her. But there was nothing she could do – nothing anyone could do. Women had few, if any rights, though Millicent had read in the newspapers that there were valiant souls in the political field fighting to get the vote and fairer divorce laws, but these ladies were looked upon askance. This was the last quarter of Queen Victoria's reign and the man was all-powerful in every strata of society; at home, abroad, in pulpit and Parliament.

'Leave us, Dulcie,' Mervin commanded. 'Wait in the dressing room.'

When the maid had scurried off, he came closer to Millicent. She could smell him – horse sweat, his own sweat, the great outdoors, the sunshine of a fine April, leather and the personal odour of his hair. Her pulse raced and she was wet between the thighs. He lifted one of her curls, and of its own volition it coiled round his finger. He raised it to his nostrils and inhaled. Millicent quivered. She swayed and almost fell against him. One of his sinewy hands caught and held her. He sat on the bed and drew her down, a fist in the small of her back, forcing her to bend over his muscular thighs.

Biting her lip, her blood rushing wildly through her veins, she complied, sinking across his lap. The room looked strange from that angle, every feature of it florid and ostentatious – chinoiserie wallpaper with pagodas and quaint little figures, heavy furniture, a massive marble fireplace with its mantle upheld on either side by two figures representing Titans. There were knick-knacks all over – on the tops of cupboards, in glass cases, on the escritoire. The drapes were lush and made of heavy piled velvet, the carpets thick and luxurious, and the view from the curved bay windows was magnificent – fine, well maintained grounds with fountains and statues, arbours and mock Greek temples. But Millicent felt as if it was all closing round her. She had to get away from there – from *him*. She was being stifled!

'Bad girl,' he muttered, a harsh note in his voice, and

she let her head hang over his knee, her hair streaming down to brush the floor, breasts crushed, bottom raised, and that baton-like object distending the front of his breeches and pressing into her side. 'Naughty sister.'

He seized the hem of her nightgown and lifted it to her waist. She felt the cool air on her bare skin and his hands pinching her rounded hinds, moving over each and dipping into the crease between. She moaned and ground her pubis against his thigh, waves of pleasurable and frightening sensations rippling through her. She wanted – she *wanted*! She didn't know what she wanted. Then, with such speed that she was not aware, his hand swept up and came down on her left buttock with a resounding smack. Millicent yelped, writhed and gyrated, the hot feeling in her clit increasing.

Now his hand was soothing, and the few playful slaps he administered next confused and aroused her more. They fell like steady rain, harder and harder until she could feel them burning her skin and imagined the pink blush that would be spreading over each tingling buttock. Then he stopped and massaged the imprints of his fingers, diving a little deeper into the private territory of her sex.

'That's enough, Mervin, please!' she begged, tears running from her eyes and dripping on the carpet. 'I've apologised, and will even try to be at dinner. If I can sleep for a while, maybe I shall feel better.'

'Oh, you will, my dear,' he stated, 'I'll make certain of that,' and he continued to chastise her, his blows snapping and stinging and, which confused her totally, he frequently paused in the punishment to caress her fiery rump.

Then, as quickly as he had begun he let her go, tumbling her from his knee. She fell to the floor in an undignified heap and Mervin graciously offered his hand to help her up. 'May I go back to bed now?' she faltered, her eyes red with weeping.

'Of course. Rest a while and then have Dulcie dress you in your best. That new gown, I think, the blue taffeta.

It becomes you,' he said with a look of pride. 'You have inherited our dear mama's beauty. Sleep now, and grace our table tonight. I've been thinking about a means of making you better.'

'Have you, Mervin?' she replied, gulping back the tears. 'How noble and generous of you.'

'Yes,' he said, tapping his whip thoughtfully on the quilt. 'A companion, maybe? Some young lady of pious upbringing who would help you pass the time – shopping, working on your embroidery – whatever it is women enjoy doing. Would you like that?'

'But I have Dulcie,' she pointed out.

'Ah, yes, I know. But she is a servant. It would not be seemly for you to fraternise with her. And if I do find you a suitable companion, then you must keep her at a distance, too. We Bessboroughs must never forget our position in life. Way above the common herd, don'cher know.'

'Whatever you think best, Mervin,' Millicent answered meekly, knowing that once he had made up his mind it was impossible to shift him. Her thoughts raced. A companion? A young woman who might become her friend, though not too intimate. It must never be forgotten that Millicent was of superior rank, and that a companion was neither fish nor fowl in the household – not exactly a servant nor yet one of the gentry. She would never be permitted to sit at table with them, for example, and would eat alone, not welcome in the servants' quarters either, in the same insidious position as a tutor.

But oh the joy of having someone to help pass the tedious hours! What would she be like? Plain or pretty, modest and shy or bold and confident? She guessed that Mervin would not choose a girl who was too independent, but her spirits rose as she contemplated this turn of events. Was it possible that the companion would be experienced? A virgin, of course. Mervin would insist that Millicent should not be corrupted – but even so, she might be able to enlighten her on those unknown and exciting aspects of the physical differences between men and woman of which Millicent was so curious.

When Mervin left his sister he immediately turned the knob of the door leading from the landing to the dressing room, which in turn was connected to the bedchamber. Dulcie was waiting for him, a wary look on her snub-nosed, freckled face. This excited him and his cock surged, rising almost to his navel under the jodhpurs. This is how servant girls should be – willing and obedient, prepared to service their masters at a moment's notice. No airs and graces about them and he believed, along with his peers, that lower class women were made differently to genteel ladies and actually enjoyed intercourse and craved to have a stiff tool thrust up them.

He grabbed Dulcie by the arm and steered her onto the landing. 'Follow me,' he grated harshly.

Striding ahead of her he took the staircase that led to his private apartment. His ancestors smiled sardonically down on him from heavily carved and gilded frames. There were row upon row of them – swashbuckling privateers who had been made gentlemen, given titles and land by a grateful Virgin Queen when they whopped the Spaniards and filled her coffers with Castilian booty. They became feudal lords and landowners of Royalist persuasion and poured wealth into the ventures of their Sovereigns; also bankers who had been generous to the reigning monarch, and wily procurers who provided venues for dalliance and downright fornication among the aristocracy. They were all there, captured on canvas for posterity. Mervin was proud to be descended from them, and their foxy lady wives who, if rumour was to be believed, never hesitated to oblige blue-blooded members of the Crown Imperial and satisfy noblemen's lusts, motivated purely by greed and advancement.

What a family, Mervin thought smugly as he opened the door of his suite and thrust Dulcie in. Manipulative and devious, possessed of pronounced good looks and perverse desires, and a determination to wring every iota of pleasure from life and behave outrageously into the bargain.

He had Dulcie wait in the middle of the drawing room while he addressed his valet, Humphrey, who was standing to attention and apparently unruffled by his master's sudden appearance with Lady Millicent's maid.

'Get out, man! I'll ring for you later.'

Humphrey gave him a supercilious stare. He was blond, spare of build and immaculately attired, a typical gentleman's gentleman, but so attractive that he caused emotional havoc among members of staff, male and female alike.

'Yes, my lord. Certainly, my lord.' He bowed himself out, after subjecting Dulcie to disdainful scrutiny.

'Pompous prick,' Mervin remarked, and then guided Dulcie into the bedroom.

This was his sanctum, the place where he was most at home, where he plotted his deepest schemes and brewed the strongest mischief. This was but the antechamber leading to the place where he practiced his vices. From there, via a secret passage, a hidden staircase led down to the bowels of the house where once the dungeons had lain. He had returned them to their former use, though not for the punishment of miscreants, but rather as a backdrop to the scenes of delectation and delight enjoyed by the members of his secret society. Like him, they were hell-bent on experiencing all aspects of pain and pleasure, domination and slavery.

The bedroom was panelled in dark oak and sumptuously furnished in the Gothic style so popular in Victorian England, but this was the genuine article, not reproduction. Tapestries depicting hunting scenes covered some of the walls, executed by Bessborough womenfolk two centuries before. Mervin, much travelled in his misspent youth, had added various items of exotica obtained from as far away as India. Carved figurines of the flute playing Krishna, the elephant-headed god Ganesh, and the fearsome female deity, Kali, stood on ebony plinths with blue-grey smoke from incense wafting up in their honour.

The Indian temples he'd visited, with their boldly carved and sexually explicit friezes, had inspired him to collect similar statuary, and several shelves were lined with representations of couples in the throes of ecstasy, limbs entwined, joined at the genitals. Mervin cast a glance at Dulcie, satisfied to see her open-mouthed and goggling at these highly prized and rare examples of Eastern art. It was not the first time the girl had visited his den, but her shocked expression never failed to amuse him. It was all too much for a simple country wench and he loved, above all things, to shock and alarm, to be in control, especially of those whom he regarded as peasants.

He closed his hands over Dulcie's well-developed breasts and squeezed. 'Oh, sir… my lord, I mean… you shouldn't be doing that,' she protested, but in a half-hearted way, already seduced by the skilful manner in which he revolved his thumbs over her nipples.

He could smell her excitement, and breathed deeply of that scent he associated with the nursery maids who had looked after him from infancy. They, too, had been working class, redolent of sweat and carbolic soap, thick woollen stockings and sensible underwear. He rarely passed a young female servant without experiencing the same arousal that had marked his passage into manhood when one of the nurses, a bold-eyed, loud-mouthed trollop had taken him into her bed, whipped up her skirts and placed his hand on her hairy mound. She had displayed her pink slit and shown him how to rub her nubbin until she came, bedewing his fingers with her pungent juice. Then she massaged his budding cock till it stood firm, and slowly lowered herself onto it. He would never forget the sensation of slipping into her musky depths, his dick caressed as if by a velvet glove as she bounced up and down until he spent, shooting his load into her, once, twice, thrice. He had been masturbating for years, but she took his virginity, and he had never looked back.

The memory sent a surge of lust into his balls and made his prick rigid as a spear. With a low growl he ordered Dulcie to raise her skirts and take off her drawers, then lie facedown over a side-table. 'My God,' Mervin breathed, consumed with that driving urge that filled him as he stared at her firm haunches. 'I've never seen a lass so well designed for whip, cane or strap.'

She stretched over the table, clinging to its far side, her legs taut and wide apart. Her buttocks, though fleshy, were open and her plump purse, framed in crisp ginger curls, was exposed between the tops of her thighs. These were sturdy and bare, her black stockings reaching to just above the knee where they were kept in place with garters. Her feet in scuffed shoes were planted firmly on the floor. Mervin took his fill of the sight, then opened his breeches and freed the rampant serpent within. He moved into the harbour of her bottom crease and taking his tool in hand, rubbing the swollen helm along her cleft, dampening it with her dew, then easing it into her vagina.

'Oh, sir… you won't get me with child, will you?' she begged, face turned to one side, cheek resting on the unrelenting wood. 'I shall lose my job. My parents will kick me out. I shall be homeless, with nothing for me and my bairn.'

'Shut up, you silly tart!' he exclaimed, and dragged his cock from her, lubricated her anal opening with the moisture at its tip and then pushed forcefully so that it disappeared within her dark and forbidden place, inch by painful inch. 'Have I not always been careful? Though why I bother, I don't know.'

'Oh… ow… ooh,' Dulcie moaned, but spread her legs wider and arched her pelvis towards this invasion.

Mervin withdrew abruptly, his cock ramrod stiff. If he shot his load into Dulcie now he would only obtain half the pleasure. There were things he intended to do to her first, stoking his fire so that when he did finally obtain release it would be as explosive as the top blowing off a volcano.

But what an arse the girl had! He resolved to have her perform at one of his orgies. And as for her opulent breasts! He almost changed his mind as to his method of taking her that day, visualising forming those enormous tits into a channel wherein he might plunge his cock, pushing it in and out, her fleshy bosom encompassing it, till he poured his libation all over her in milky jets.

Resisting temptation, he unhooked a broad leather strap from the bedpost, wound it round his fist and brought it down with a whistling sound, printing a crimson stripe on her quivering hindquarters. Dulcie yelped and wriggled, then jerked as the strap fell again an inch or so above the first welt. Six more times it left its mark on those vast white globes that were now adorned with a crisscross pattern of scarlet embroidery that wrapped themselves round those generous curves.

Mervin made no attempt to pleasure the girl, though the wetness glimmering at the hairy lips bulging between her thighs betrayed her eagerness to be brought to climax. It might have amused him to do so, but not today. His mood was one of utter selfishness and no one would be considered, not even his sister, leave alone a servant.

'Mercy, master,' Dulcie sobbed as the leather bit home again.

It was the plea in her voice that finally roused him to a pitch where he could no longer restrain himself. He flung the strap aside, positioned himself, and propelled his cock into her nether hole. She screeched as he pushed in deeper, till his pubic hair pressed against her crack. This was bliss; she was tight there for he had only arse-fucked her once before and she had a virgin orifice then. Mervin closed his eyes as the extreme pleasure mounted. He rocked against Dulcie, his cock buried in her deepest, darkest, most private place, and she expanded to take him. He was coming, the feeling rushing through him with the force of a tidal wave. He was *there*! Coming in spurts, the heat, the wonderful sensation lifting him to the heights.

It lasted a second, no more, and when it was over Mervin withdrew from the girl's anus, already sated and disgusted and disillusioned, as he always was after fucking. His palate was jaded. There was nothing new under the sun. He'd enjoyed servants and whores and unfaithful wives of his social set who sought a diversion.

The companion for Millicent. As he wiped his cock and buttoned up his breeches, he thought about this. Perhaps she would prove to be not only good for his sister, but for him also – a new member of his harem whom he could control, bully and use to satisfy his ungovernable lust.

Chapter Two

Sunday, Sunday. The most tedious day of the week, thought Amelie Aston as she walked the short distance between the vicarage and St Stephen's church. The bells were ringing, summoning the faithful to prayer. Even were she not the Reverend Thacker's goddaughter, as a member of the Kemble community she would have been duty-bound to attend. Respectable and conventional folk, the villagers looked askance at anyone who avoided going to church.

So, like every other Sunday morning and evening for nigh on ten years, Amelie had dragged unwillingly to the services. She worried about her reluctance, for Joseph Thacker preached hellfire and damnation and she was sure there was a sinful force within her that prevented her from worshipping with the devotion she should have experienced. And yet, closeted at the vicarage, for he and his wife, Harriet, kept a strict watch on their four children and her, this was really the only time in which she could mingle with Kemble's inhabitants.

She shopped sometimes with Harriet in the store that sold everything from cheese to paraffin, but could hardly call this socialising, though a great deal of gossip and tittle-tattle was exchanged over the counter. Not by her, of course, she had to stand there meekly, doing precisely as she was told while Harriet and the two maiden ladies who ran the shop performed a thorough character assassination on any unfortunate who met with their disapproval.

Amelie, now eighteen, chafed under the restraints put

upon her. Too young to remember her parents who had died tragically abroad, she had yet never accepted Joseph and Harriet as her father and mother. She recognised that it had been kind and generous of them to honour the promise made at her christening, but she always felt the odd one out. Their own daughters, Agnes and Charity, a little older than her, concealed their resentment and jealousy in their parent's presence, but never ceased to tease and torment her when they were alone, often making her the scapegoat for their misdemeanours.

And as for the boys – Obediah and Caleb? They were older again, in their early twenties, and had at first ignored her. But as the years passed and she developed into a curvaceous young woman with a mass of chestnut hair and green eyes, so she became increasingly uncomfortable when they were around, avoiding being alone with either of them. Fortunately this coincided with them living away from home for most of the year, furthering their education at university.

She could see the graveyard ahead, reached by a lychgate. Beyond it was the solid grey stone church that had stood there foursquare for centuries, with its spire pointing heavenwards like an accusative finger and its beautiful stained glass windows that had somehow managed to survive religious upheavals and civil war. But its beauty was lost on Amelie. To her it represented a prison and she never entered it without a drop in her spirits.

The young people with whom she lived were not blind to this either, attending service as a chore but also taking the chance to show off. Their father was an important man in the community.

Now Obediah, the younger of the brothers, closed the distance between them for she had been forging ahead, grabbed her arm and whispered, 'I'll sit next to you, shall I?'

'There's no need,' she hissed back, trying to free herself, but it was impossible without making a scene and the farmers and their wives, the estate workers, anyone who was anyone in Kemble, all dressed in their sober best, were crowding through the gate and making their way towards the main door.

'Yes, there is,' he answered and squeezed her hand. 'I want to show you something.'

'And what is that?' she asked suspiciously.

There was no end to his practical jokes, and some were unkind, as when he produced a matchbox which, when she opened it, contained a large black spider and she abhorred these creatures above all others. This put him in a beaming good humour, always hilariously happy whenever he had frightened anybody.

He was a stoop-shouldered young man, tending towards the portly, his mother's favourite which meant that the tastiest titbits were saved for him. He was short and heavy-featured, unlike his brother, Caleb, and it seemed he favoured his grandfather on Harriet's side, who had owned a brewery. He had straight, light brown hair already receding from his brow, large ears, full red lips and roving, watery blue eyes. Amelie was very aware of them resting on her ever more frequently lately. If he insisted on occupying the pew next to her, there was nothing she could do about it, for these were special seats reserved for the vicar's family, set a little apart from the rest. She stiffened her spine, bracing herself for a stressful hour.

The strains of organ music reached her as she entered the porch, greeted by the verger and several members of the congregation. The vicar was popular, especially among the more well-to-do ladies who organised the flower arrangements adorning the naïve and officiated at the bazaars and church fêtes held in order to raise money for charity or the upkeep of St Stephen's.

Amelie, though absolutely naïve, wondered what emotions swelled the tightly corseted bosoms of these women, mostly middle-aged and lacking real purpose. Was it possible that they might entertain admiration, even feelings of romantic love for her stern godfather? They were dressed in rustling black, adopting the fashion that had gradually taken over from the crinoline, the skirts looped back into frills and flounces, upheld by the cane and whalebone cage worn beneath and fastened round the waist with tapes. Each lady present was tightly corseted, too, this restrictive undergarment reminding the wearers to have a well-regulated mind and well-regulated feelings. Their hair was piled high under feather-crowned hats with large brims.

Even Harriet was wearing a dress of similar style. Amelie had been with her when the pony-trap took them to the nearest station and from there by train to the town, where she was almost overwhelmed by the milliners, florists, dress shops, cafés, markets and public houses. A treat indeed, and one rarely repeated.

Agnes, Charity and herself were much more plainly attired, as became young ladies, though their hems had been allowed to drop to floor level and their hair pinned up, when they reached eighteen. Colours for churchgoing were sober, black, grey, dark blue or brown. Amelie's heart ached for something really pretty to wear, but this was frowned upon as vanity – so was the smallest hint of perfume, apart from lavender water. And as for cosmetics! Well, condemned as being 'no better than you should be', your fate would be that of 'ending up on the stage'. And why would that be so bad? Amelie wondered, rather admiring the gaudily dressed and painted actresses she had seen on the rare occasions when, as part of their education, the vicar had booked up for them to see performances of plays at The Theatre Royal in Bath.

It was cool under the high arched roof upheld by stone pillars surmounted by grinning, impish faces, or the strange, leafy bearded Green Man. The congregation walked across the brown and white hexagonal tiled floor to their chosen pews. The organ music continued. Amelie and the Thackers occupied two pews at the back of the aisle. She found herself sandwiched between Obediah and Caleb. The congregation shuffled and coughed and waited for the service to begin. There was a tension about Obediah too, as if he couldn't wait, though his excitement would have little to do with his father's oratory. She could feel his burly thigh pressing against hers, and she glanced sideways at Caleb, almost wishing it were he showing so much interest in her, not his plump brother.

Both men had only just finished at Oxford University, but whereas Obediah clowned his way through it, coming out with few grades, Caleb was set to become a teacher, probably rising to the post of headmaster at a prestigious school. He was darker than Obediah, austere and cultured, something of a Radical in his views, and unafraid to answer his father back during discussions on social problems and politics. He was handsome, too, with narrow features and thick hair swept back from a fine brow. His eyes were deep-set, dark blue and unfathomable. He smiled but rarely, and then in a slightly mocking manner.

Amelie infinitely preferred him to his uncouth brother, but he ignored her most of the time, though she had caught him looking at her speculatively more than once. Did he have marriage in mind? It would be in order, as far as she knew, for him to marry his parents' godchild. This didn't mean they were related in any way. And would she want to marry him? Amelie wasn't at all sure, uncertain if she wanted to marry anyone. She had seen how much of a chattel Harriet was, despite the fact that her husband was a churchman. And the village wives? Always bearing, always burying. Was this the fate she wanted for herself? The answer was a definite no!

Harriet and her daughters were in the pew in front. All eyes were fixed on the altar, waiting for Joseph to put in an appearance. He entered with all the aplomb of a thespian, wearing a dazzling surplice and surrounded by his acolytes. The service began with the first hymn. Amelie stood with the rest of them, but was prepared to yawn her way through the whole thing.

She didn't, however. No sooner were they re-seated and the vicar started to address his flock, than she felt a hand on her knee under cover of her hymnbook. It belonged to Obediah. She shot him a slanting glance but he was looking straight ahead at his father in the pulpit. Caleb, on her other side, was doing likewise. The pressure on her knee vanished. She heaved a sigh of relief, yet somehow missed the warmth and promise of that touch.

Innocent or rather ignorant, she had watched the domesticated animals mating time and again, the bull taken to the heifer, the stallion to the mare, the boar to the sow, but had somehow never associated this act with human reproduction. It just didn't come within her sphere of reckoning. She knew where babies came from, though a hugely embarrassed Harriet had only imparted this knowledge to her recently, on the birth of a friend's infant, but as for how it got in the belly or out of it remained a mystery. The bull mounting the cow, the cow producing a calf a few months later? Humans acting the same? It seemed impossible.

The vicar droned on and everyone watched and listened, and Amelie was aware of a touch on her knee, the insidious creeping of a palm. It paused, testing her reaction. She sat there frozen. The hand reached the welt of her stocking, stopped, tickled the inside of her bare thigh, then slid upwards till it encountered the legs of her drawers. It found the slit that divided them, a long slit especially designed for the relief of nature. Amelie's breath caught in her throat but she sat as still as a statue, gazing at her godfather, though deaf to his impassioned sermon.

She parted her legs slightly, and a hidden finger combed through the reddish floss that furred her mound. It was a tiny touch, like the brush of a butterfly's wing, but the spasms that shot through her loins were electric. She didn't move, controlling her desire to bear down on the finger, rub herself on it, continue doing so till those feelings rose

22

and rose, leading to – she knew not where. Would it be the same as when, greatly daring and hugely guilty, she sank her own finger between her wet lips and manipulated that little button she had discovered there? Oh, the sheer bliss of it! A hidden game, shared with no one. A shameful secret, yet she could not resist it. Was she the only one in the world to experience this? If so, then why was Obediah playing with her like that?

In a way it made her feel better, lifting the burden of sin she had harboured ever since discovering the wonderful world of sensation associated with her nubbin. So, it wasn't a sign of the devil, a stigmata imprinted on her private parts by Satan himself? It was a temptation she could not resist, yet after she yielded to it she suffered the torments of the damned, certain that when she died she would go straight to hell.

She could hear Obediah breathing jerkily and, looking down saw his knees in the black trousers that matched his suit waistcoat and jacket. His other hand was resting on his fly, massaging it slyly. Though his coat was buttoned it curved away there and she could observe the large lump that lay beneath the worsted and how he passed his hand over it again and again, but stealthily.

Why was he doing this? But then she lost interest in his concerns, only aware that the finger at her crotch had increased its search, parting her lower lips and homing in on the sliver of flesh between them that culminated in that tiny, sensitive head. The finger found it, hooked under it and caressed it briskly. Amelie recognised the feeling that any touch on her bud created. If the finger kept on rubbing, then she would explode into that aching, marvellous, sublime pleasure which she herself could induce.

Obediah was very skilful. His hand movements were so controlled that her skirt was hardly disturbed. Where had he learned to play this lustful game? She no longer cared, only wanting him to go on and on. His finger was wet, coated with the juice seeping from her virgin hole. It was so deliciously slippery, moving faster and faster, bringing her ever closer to her goal. Her nipples peaked, chafed by her tight bodice and she wanted to pinch and tease them, having already discovered there was a direct contact between them and that plump little pearl that was the seat of sensation. She moved one hand, concealed by the hymnbook, and managed to tweak one nipple as she pretended to read, causing mayhem in her clitoris.

She longed to cry out, 'Yes! Yes!' but had to remain silent as she was swept to the top of the rainbow where her climax broke in a shower of stars.

'That's what I wanted to show you,' Obediah whispered in her ear. 'How I could diddle your button till you came.'

She was speechless and red-faced and aware of Caleb's eyes on her, fire burning in his pupils, and in that moment she knew he knew exactly what they had been doing.

As well as the ritual of church attendance, there was the huge and heavy Sunday dinner, served at one o'clock sharp. On reaching the vicarage, Harriet dispatched the girls to take off their outdoor clothes and wash their hands. The young men were permitted to enter the smoking room and indulge in a cigarette, whilst their father, glowing with the triumph of a sermon well delivered and enthusiastically received, retired to his study, there to read over the homily he intended to preach that evening.

Amelie's nose twitched as she inhaled the succulent smell of roast beef wafting from the direction of the kitchen. This was a large area given over to the preparation of meals for the family, and also the staff needed to keep such an establishment going. There was the cook, Mrs Banbury, an ample-hipped, deep-bosomed, tyrannical woman who ruled her army of helpers with a rod of iron. The vicarage had been designed to house the current man-of-the-cloth and, nine times out of ten, his wife and numerous offspring. Joseph Thacker's progeny were few,

24

in comparison to some, yet the vicarage, old, draughty and inconvenient, provided work for an army of servants, both inside and out.

There was a laundry woman, a gardener, a woodsman, cleaners, a footman, two parlour maids and a butler. Joseph could never have afforded the upkeep on a churchman's stipend, but he came from wealthy stock, the second son of a baronet, and as such had followed the traditional role of someone in his position and become a priest. Even so, he did not employ a housekeeper and Harriet took on the job.

Amelie had always found the vicarage cold and creepy, failing to warm to it and regard it as home. The Thackers did what they could for her, but they had been trained not to show emotion, blind to the needs of the headstrong, beautiful girl. There was little laughter ringing down the lengthy passages, and not a great deal of fun to be had. Meek and demure, the girls were expected to comport themselves with humility, and the boys to restrain any impulse to rampage around.

Amelie, overflowing with feelings that threatened to make her rash, had difficulty in restraining the crazy urge to kick over the traces and simply rush about the place, or tear into the grounds, fling herself on a horse and gallop for miles. It was even worse this dinnertime, for she had recently come against Obediah's finger.

She did not know how she got through the remainder of the service, her clit throbbing, her knickers wet. She prayed the washerwoman did not notice the stains that were bound to be left on the linen. She blushed as she remembered how much she had enjoyed his frottage of her tender parts, which was awful because she didn't like him. And after surreptitiously removing his hand from her skirts, he had kept sneaking glances at her and smirking. She walked home in a daze, deaf to Charity's idle chatter and Agnes's catty remarks. If only they knew, she thought, panic-stricken, imagining what they would say, how they would act and the speed with which they would peach on her to their father.

Obediah was seated opposite her now at the rectangular dining table, Caleb next to his father at the head, and Charity and Agnes on either side of their mother at the far end. Joseph said grace and then set to work carving the side of beef that steamed on a massive china meat dish placed before him by the footman. Down the length of the table marched vegetable dishes of matching white with flower garlands, trimmed with gold scrolls. Beneath their ornate lids lay roast potatoes, cabbage and carrots. There were also two gravy boats with pottery ladles. The footman solemnly passed plates that were part of this Crown Derby dinner service down the ranks, starting with Caleb, as the eldest offspring. Amelie was served last, and this always happened, a constant reminder of her place in the Thacker pecking order. It was discouraging to say the least, and caused her never-ending pain.

The vicar chose to be affable. He was in an expansive mood, a dignified man with a profile that might have adorned a Roman coin. When he was feeling genial and expansive, as now, no one could have been better company, but his family and servants saw the other side of his personality – the bigot – the controller – a man who could poison the atmosphere with his evil temper.

Amelie, with her healthy young appetite, tucked in, only half listening to Thacker droning on, pompous, full of self-satisfaction, with Harriet chipping in dutifully and his daughters twittering and making big adoring eyes, with their 'Papa this, and Papa that'. Amelie despised them. She knew they harboured a dislike of their father amounting to detestation, but were too scared to admit it.

The first course progressed to its conclusion, the plates were removed, and then the footman bore in a large apple tart, dessert dishes and bowls of clotted cream. The tart was divided, and portions passed round.

'I'll have dry biscuits and cheese, Jennings,' the vicar

pronounced. 'Too heavy a meal will make me sleep all the afternoon, and I want to keep my mind fresh. Why, only this morning Lord Bessborough came up to me after the service and congratulated me on the succinct way in which I had made my points. He's a very fine gentleman, and shrewd. Don't you agree, my love?' he asked, including Harriet in the conversation.

'Indeed yes, Joseph,' she replied promptly, ever so well trained. 'But his sister doesn't look at all well. I glimpsed her before she disappeared behind the screen of their private pew. Very pale indeed, poor Lady Millicent.'

'I gather he is concerned about her,' he continued, tackling the cheese board. 'It seems she is subject to bouts of melancholy. In fact, he asked me if I knew of anyone who might take the position of companion. I said I would bear it in mind.'

The Bessboroughs were the landowners who sometimes honoured St Stephen's with their attendance. To Amelie they were remote figures and she had hardly noticed them that day, too preoccupied with Obediah. Bessborough was a tall man, if she recalled right and yes, she had noticed the sickly appearance of his sister. Apart from that, they could have been creatures from the moon for all the heed she had taken of them.

The conversation ebbed and flowed, with Joseph holding forth and Caleb adding his word here and there, making comments that were not well received by his father. Since Caleb had graduated and was living at the vicarage while seeking a position that would suit him, the differences of opinion between him and his father started to stretch like an abyss between them. Amelie found it incredibly boring, though was pleased to see that someone had the guts to stand up to that sanctimonious bully. Obediah was gutless, opting for a quiet life, pandering to his mother and following her example of kow-towing to him.

Amelie cast her eye round the pleasant, though darkly furnished dining room. A paper fan replaced the fire that usually burned between cast-iron dogs on the black marble hearth. Today the weather was considered too spring-like to warrant the expense of keeping coals and logs alight, to say nothing of the extra work caused by ash and smoke.

Caleb also glanced around his mother's dining room, remarking in that drawling voice he sometimes assumed, 'Mama has followed fashions set by Queen Victoria, be it in clothing or décor.'

'And morals, too, I hope,' put in Joseph. 'The queen has done this Nation a power of good, determined, when she came to the throne, not to follow the example of her forebears, the Hanoverian Georges, with their lack of morals and their predilection for fat mistresses.'

'Sir!' Harriet chided, but gently. 'Not in front of the girls.'

'Beg pardon, my dear. I was carried away. Our dear queen has laid emphasis on family values, correctness of behaviour, religious education and prosperity,' Joseph returned, smugly.

'Among those who have,' argued Caleb, having spent time at debating societies where liberal views were freely expressed. 'But the have nots are as hard-done-by as ever. As for morals? The English have become hypocrites of the worst sort. Even furniture legs are covered so as not to offend sensitive eyes, yet there have never been so many prostitutes plying their trade in London.'

'Caleb! Really!' Harriet expressed extreme shock, her hazel eyes sparking, her thin face flushed around the cheekbones.

'Yes, that's quite enough,' snapped Joseph. 'Keep such uncouth remarks for your student colleagues. Shame on you!'

But Amelie wanted to shout hurrah. It had broken the tedium of the dinner table. Charity and Agnes sat there goggling, longing to hear more. What on earth were prostitutes? Amelie didn't know either but guessed them to be something reprehensible.

Caleb pushed back his chair abruptly, rose to his feet, flung his napkin down and bowed stiffly to Harriet. 'Excuse me, Mama. With your permission, Father, I'll remove my odious presence from you, as you find my comments so offensive.'

'I'm prepared to discuss whatever you want, my boy,' Joseph conceded. 'But not in the presence of ladies. You may leave.'

This was the cue for the table to be cleared and the diners to remove themselves to areas where they could gainfully pass the hours till tea and another trek to church. Little in the way of recreation was allowed on Sunday. One could not read (only the Bible) or sew or knit or play cards, croquet or tennis. Walking was favoured, for then one could admire the view and God's handiwork.

Agnes and Charity, armed with the Good Book, opted for their rooms, though Amelie knew they would dive into one another's and there lie on the bed and talk about clothes and men and giggle about their real or imaginary swain. Both knew their father had already selected candidates for their hands in marriage, and that there was to be a musical soirée soon, where they would be introduced to their prospective bridegrooms. The thought of this sent them into paroxysms of excitement, though mostly to do with the gowns they would wear on this important occasion.

Obediah kept ogling Amelie, his head twitching on his thick shoulders as he tried to indicate, without rousing his mother's suspicions, that he wanted her to take a stroll with him and, presumably, find a secluded spot where he could repeat his actions of that morning. Amelie tried to take no notice, but to her annoyance and self-hatred found her wayward nodule thrummed when she remembered the extreme pleasure she had experienced.

She was saved by Harriet who, treating him as if he were five years old and none too bright, said briskly, 'Now come along, Obediah, there's a good boy. Give me your arm and we'll take a walk down to the lake. It's a lovely day and the daffodils will be out. Remember dear Mr Wordsworth's poem about these? "I wandered lonely as a cloud, that floats on high o'er dale and hill, when all at once I saw a crowd, a host of golden daffodils".'

'Charming, my love,' Joseph said patronisingly. 'That's right, son, escort your mother. I'm retiring to my study.'

So, despite Obediah's long face and scarcely hidden resentment, he was forced to obey, his mother dispatching him to fetch her shawl. Amelie, undecided what to do, set off in the opposite direction. She directed her feet towards the summerhouse, set apart behind a screen of bushes. It had always been a favourite retreat. Many a time she had taken her dolls there for a tea party, and sometimes she and the girls idled away hot summer days in its shade, though she much preferred her own company. It was a quaint wooden structure with a veranda in front reached by wide shallow steps. The odd-job man had already given it a fresh coat of white paint, picked out in green. The windows shone and lace curtains were hung across them. It resembled an informal room, an annex to the vicarage. Occasionally, on hot nights, Caleb and Obediah had been allowed to sleep there, but never the girls. Now Amelie gathered up her skirt and mounted the steps silently. There was a magical ambience about the place, and she did not want to disturb it.

It was then, when she had almost reached the door, that she heard a sound from within. She stopped, heart in her mouth. Could it be a robber? Or a tramp seeking shelter? Or maybe a gypsy child who'd decided to trespass? She heard it again, and this time it sounded like a stifled groan.

Amelie crossed to one of the windows and peeped between a crack in the curtains. It took a moment for her eyes to become adjusted to the gloom within, and then her sight cleared and she saw him. Caleb was there, lying on the wickerwork couch, with all the usual paraphernalia stacked up against the wall behind him – striped canvas deckchairs, tennis rackets, mallets, cushions and blankets for picnics on the grass outside.

Her gaze became riveted on him. Her mouth dropped open. Her pupils widened and her sex yielded fresh juice. He sprawled there, head back against a tapestry pillow. His legs were spread wide, his trousers down about his hips. His right hand was wrapped about the huge, fleshy object that sprang from the dark thicket of hair below his belly. It was hard as a rock, shining wetly, the shaft passing through his palm, the bulbous head with its single weeping eye appearing at the top as he stroked up and down.

Amelie was entranced. Her fingers twitched to touch that impressive tool, and she had the almost uncontrollable urge to lick it, close her lips around it, suck it. How disgusting! How amazing! And why did this idea make her button tingle and her virgin hole wet and her inside ache? How would it be if Caleb placed that mighty thing at her fork and, with a push, sent it into her untried maiden passage, rupturing her hymen?

Because none of these options were open, she lifted her skirt and frilly petticoat and found that oh-so convenient opening in her knickers. She started to rub herself. She couldn't help it; the sight of Caleb's erect cock was too much for her. It was the first time ever that she'd viewed a man's appendage. Of course, she had been paraded round the art galleries as part of her schooling and seen marble statues of male athletes from Ancient Greece, but their penises were always discreetly covered by the obligatory fig leaf, or cut off or so small that they were practically non-existent. Never, ever, had she seen anything as fascinating, shocking, alarming and downright rude and desirable as Caleb's.

Witnessing him pleasuring himself was a sacred, secret privilege. She knew instinctively that what he was experiencing was the same feelings she could produce by massaging her bud. And she did just that in sympathy with him, eyeing his movements eagerly, copying them as she slid her wetness up and down her own crack, then concentrated on the head, just as he did the tip of his cock.

He stroked it. He lubricated it with jism. He lifted his hips from the couch, bucking upwards towards the hand that had become his paramour. His face was contorted, transfixed, eyes half-closed as he dragged his fingers away, teasing his cock, making it jerk as if it had a life of its own. He squeezed it, gave it a few hard pulls, making it swell even more, starting then stopping, the foreskin strained back from the mushroom-like head while he groaned and pressed down at the base, delaying his conclusion.

Amelie's middle digit flew over the slick line of her clitoris. She was dying for completion. Soon, she promised her eager nub, pumping harder, dulling the sensation by her own brutality. Oh, she must bring this to its finish, but couldn't while Caleb hovered on the brink. She needed to see what happened when he reached his apogee. Would it be like the stallion's emission, fountains of creamy liquid? Perhaps he wouldn't shoot out liquid at all. She didn't know, and in her haste and eagerness she bumped against the window.

Caleb stopped, his hand cupping his cock. He looked straight at her through the glass. 'Amelie, is that you?' he asked, his voice low and husky. 'Come in.'

She reached for the doorknob, turned it and stood framed in the doorway. Her hand was still gripping her mound, those tumultuous floods of feeling held back by a miracle. 'I'm here, Caleb,' she whispered. 'What do you want me to do?'

'Look at this,' he gasped, exposing himself fully. 'Touch it. Rub it for me. Let me put it in you.'

She crept closer, skirts lifted high so he could see her lace-edged drawers and the fuzz poking between the slit.

She wanted to show him all her most private parts and have him poke and stroke and explore. She was utterly shameless, never ceasing in playing with herself. He grabbed her hand, pulled it away from her cleft and held it to his nose.

'Jesus, you smell wonderful!' he cried, licking her fingers where her moisture clung. 'And taste even better.'

Greatly daring, Amelie took his hugeness into her small palm, delighting in the heat and silkiness of it, moving up and down with the skill of a born courtesan. 'Is that what you want?' she enquired with a catch in her throat.

'Oh, yes – yes – yes!' he grunted, and watched his penis. His skin darkened. His facial muscles tightened. Something was going to happen at any moment and she wasn't sure what. His helm became even larger, red and shining and full to bursting. He moved his cock faster in her hand. He gave a sharp bark, held his breath, and Amelie was astonished when he suddenly jetted explosive bursts of milky fluid, wet against her face as it sprayed upwards, wet in her hand that held him. He pulled back then propelled his hips forward again and she milked him of every last drop.

In a second it was over. He slumped back against the cushions and she stared down at his wilting tool and her hand, creamy with his libation. She wanted more – much more. Her clit was throbbing with need. She had the urge to tear off her clothing and go down on her hands and knees, having him thrust that great prick into her till she juddered and his pubic hair ground against her opening.

It was then, while she was lifting her skirts high and reaching for him, that a voice cracked through the air from the door. 'Slut! Trollop! My God, what are you doing, Amelie Aston? Seducing my son! Viper in my bosom! Is this how you repay me for years of care?'

She was seized by the scruff of the neck and flung to the floor, Joseph Thacker looming over her like an avenging angel.

Chapter Three

Embarrassment. Shame. An urgent desire for the floor to open and swallow her. All these emotions chased through Amelie's mind in quick succession.

Joseph aimed a kick at her, which landed on her backside. 'Get up! Jezebel! Whore of Babylon!'

Amelie dragged to her feet. Her eyes cut to Caleb, but he was concentrating on stuffing his erection out of sight and buttoning his trousers, avoiding looking at her or his father. It was obvious that he had no intention of defending her. This was too much.

'Traitor!' she shouted. 'Say something! Tell him that you asked me to touch you. Go on. I dare you! And I'll involve Obediah. You know what he was doing to me in church this morning. You saw us and guessed.'

'Obediah? I don't believe it,' gasped Joseph, breathing fire.

'Oh, yes,' she said firmly, thinking; I may as well be hung for a sheep as a lamb. 'While you were boring everyone to death with your stupid sermon he had his hand up my skirts and was playing with my private parts.'

Joseph's face turned beet-red, a vein throbbing in the centre of his forehead and his eyes were manic. If looks could have killed she would be stretched out dead at his feet. 'If this is true then you led him on and encouraged him to perform lewd acts,' he bellowed. Then he rounded on Caleb and barked, 'I shall speak to you later. It's time we had a heart-to-heart talk concerning the facts of life. My sons need to be protected from forward hussies. Be in my study at four o'clock. As for you, Amelie, you will come with me. Now!'

Giving her no chance to protest further he frogmarched her to the door, out across the veranda and along a pathway towards the rear of the vicarage. She struggled rebelliously, but his hand was like a vice on her arm and she could do nothing but go with him. The house was very quiet, sunk in the somnolence of a Sabbath afternoon. She knew where they were heading; towards the paved terrace beyond which was situated the vicar's sanctum, reached by French doors.

A library-come-study, where visitors were not welcome unless especially invited.

Amelie had entered its sacred portals on very few occasions – maybe during the Christmas celebrations – but even then Joseph was extra busy preparing for the Yuletide services. She shivered, for once she was alone with him there would be little chance of interruption – and none at all of rescue.

He opened one of the glass doors and propelled her inside. She wondered if she might run for it, but realised that any means of escape would be blocked. It was a large room, lined with glass-fronted shelves filled with books. There were other things too; a fine desk from early in the century, leather-topped and brass-trimmed. Here Joseph sat when in the throes of inspiration, striving to bring enlightenment to those who attended St Stephen's. An oil-lamp with a frosted glass shade stood on the surface. There were others placed in wrought-iron girandoles and two large chandeliers with crystal drops dangled from ornate plasterwork roses on the equally elaborate ceiling, with its cornices and picture rails.

It was a masculine den where women were rarely admitted, and only when it was to amuse the owner – as now. There was something about him, an undercurrent as dark and swirling as that in the depths of a timeless sea. She had sensed it before, even when she was a child, but ever more strongly since she'd matured. Had he been an ordinary individual she might have thought he fancied her, but he was one of God's servants, and as such elevated above the lusts of mere mortals.

But now that sense of danger, of things that could not be mentioned, breathed out from him like a miasma. He was sweating, his skin glowing, his hair damp where it swept back from that patrician brow.

'Now then, Amelie, I want you to confess to me,' he said gruffly, all pretence of the beneficent tone he habitually adopted quite gone. 'Tell me what you think of when you're in your bed at night. Do you finger yourself in your intimate places? Are your actions as dirty as that of a whore?'

'Please, sir,' she answered, shaking like a leaf, fearful that the sins she'd committed had indeed come back to haunt her – her vanity, her boredom with the church, the pleasure she obtained from her little bud, 'don't be angry. I don't know what you mean by calling me a whore. What is that?'

'A prostitute,' he answered, mouthing the word with relish. 'A harlot. A woman who sells her body to men for money.'

'I've never done that,' she protested. 'I don't understand.'

'Stop playing the innocent with me!' he bellowed, and seizing her by the shoulders, shook her till her teeth rattled. 'Money may not have changed hands in your case, but you will have behaved as loosely as the lowest drab. Didn't you accuse Obediah of gross behaviour? And in church, too?'

'It's true, and it was his suggestion,' she cried, twisting in his grasp.

'Not only a whore but a liar into the bargain,' he ranted, then a fanatical light blazed in the darkness of his irises and he started to declaim, 'But it is not too late. It is never too late to repent. Look at this,' and he dragged her over to where a large painting was positioned above the fireplace.

It depicted a rock battered by stormy seas, and a young woman in a white dress with red draperies that, soaking wet, outlined her breasts, hips and legs, in a manner calculated to draw the eye. She was kneeling at the foot of a stone cross, her bare arms clinging to it. Her expression was that of supplication, her face raised to heaven, bathed in a shining ray that pierced the dark clouds.

Amelie had seen it before and wondered what the young woman was doing there and why. 'So, she's getting wet and that seems senseless,' she said boldly. 'It's not even very well drawn.'

'It's a fine picture and says it all. The artist entitled it *Saved*. There you have the Scarlet Woman who has seen the redeeming Light and begs Our Saviour to forgive her.'

'If what you say is right, and I didn't understand that bit in the New Testament before, then Mary Magdalene was a whore, and Jesus treated her like all the others of His followers,' Amelie replied, saddened because her godfather showed no compassion, even though professing to follow Christ's teachings. 'He didn't scorn, abuse and revile her.'

'It's true that she was a Fallen Woman and He showed her the error of her ways, saying, "Go ye and sin no more",' Joseph agreed, but even as he talked he seemed preoccupied, leading Amelie to where a ladder stood, giving him access to the higher library shelves. It had hooks at the top which linked it by rings to whatever shelf was required, making the steps strong and immovable. 'That's what I'd like to say to you, Amelie,' he went on, 'but I think you're already too far along the road to perdition. I saw you with Caleb's manhood in your hand. It was disgraceful.'

'And what he wanted,' she reminded, an awareness shooting through her as she saw the disturbance at the front of his black trousers. His phallus had risen. It must

37

resemble Caleb's. He was excited, despite his holier-than-thou attitude.

'Do you enjoy having a man penetrate you carnally?' he asked, and his breathing was ragged.

'I don't know, I'm a virgin,' she said levelly.

'Are you indeed? It is my duty to examine you.'

'How dare you? You have no right?'

'I have every right. As your vicar and guardian I need to know if you are virtuous. It will be my task to find you a husband in the near future, and I can't offer him soiled goods.'

He backed her against the ladder and she felt its hard rungs chafing her calves and shoulder blades. He pressed his body to hers and she was helpless to resist, his face close and out of focus, his breath tainted with brandy as it fanned her, and that hard object rooted at the base of his belly swelling upwards, warm and demanding.

'Let me go,' she pleaded, turning her head from side to side to avoid his thin lips that seemed about to possess hers.

'Not yet, you have to be chastised,' he whispered, each syllable carrying dreadful emphasis.

Much of it meant nothing to her. However, she did pick up on part of his intention – that of humiliating her and making her confess to playing with her slit, but she was not prepared for his next move. He wrapped ropes around her wrists and raised her arms above her head, tethering them to the ladder. She caught a glimpse of herself in a large mirror fixed on the wall opposite. Her body, delicately curving, formed a contrast with the harsh lines of the wood that supported her. Joseph pushed a hand into her hair, bringing it tumbling down, scattering pins and combs. He tugged hard and she shrieked. He let it run through his fingers, caressing the silken mass, and his expression softened, eyes closed, chest heaving, cock pulsing, as if he could not get enough of her youth and beauty.

The vision in the mirror was unnerving – the middle-aged man in clerical black feeding on the feel and sight of the young woman bound to the steps. There was something abandoned in her pose, a helpless victim of a man's greedy need to control and use. He released her hair and sank down, roping her ankles to either side of the struts. It was uncomfortable, legs forced open when she wanted to close them. She was so vulnerable, entirely at his mercy, and she quaked with anticipation.

Joseph reached out and unfastened the tiny ball-buttons that ran down the front of her bodice. It opened and though she wore a chemise beneath and her waist was encased in a tight corset, it gave him a view of the swell of her breasts and made them accessible to him. He did not hesitate, pinching and tweaking her nipples that rose into sharp peaks at his touch.

'See how your teats respond,' he grunted. 'They are so wicked,' and he bent his head and sucked first one through her chemise, then the other. Amelie could not repress a moan. The pleasure was exquisite. 'Do you pet these perfect little play-fellows?' he murmured, and she could feel the thin lawn of her undergarment cooling wetly around the hardened nipples as he removed his lips.

'Yes,' she confessed, wanting more.

'Ah, I thought as much,' he said, and lifted the hem of her skirt, higher and higher till it lay like a band across her belly, revealing the white cotton, lace-edged drawers. His hand cruised up her thigh and found the opening. She whimpered as his fingers stroked her bush. He touched her labia, holding the plump wings aside and massaging her clit. 'This is it, Amelie. You have enjoyed your nubbin often and often, haven't you?'

'Yes sir,' she confessed, cheeks flaming, pussy aching with need.

'And you deserve to be punished for it, don't you?'

'I think not,' she faltered.

He slapped her hard across the tops of her thighs. It stung, even though her knickers covered them decently.

'You have no say in the matter,' he snarled, and yanked at the drawstring that kept her drawers in place. The garment wrinkled down, and he did the same with her frilly petticoat. It was as if she stood in a foaming white puddle that clung to her lower legs, unable to go further because of her bonds.

Without further preamble he thrust a hand between her fork and stabbed his middle finger into her vagina, meeting the obstruction of her hymen. Amelie yelped with pain and he withdrew, seeming surprised as he said, wonderingly, 'So you *are* a virgin...'

'I told you so,' she sobbed. 'You hurt me.'

He sank down and parted her russet floss, then extended his tongue and licked the divide, landing unerringly on her bud. She jumped, straining at her restraints, but she was trapped. There was no way she could escape his determined sucking. Her clit rose against her will, hard as a pea, flooding her with pleasure. She didn't want to feel like this, every decent emotion within her in revolt, but it seemed that her body was controlled by fierce desires that outweighed any other consideration.

Apart from anything else he was Harriet's husband, and she had learned to respect, if not exactly like, that hardworking, conscientious woman. Whatever would she think if she were to walk in now and see him eagerly slurping at another woman's parts?

'You're lovely down here,' he declared, looking up at her, his mouth bedewed with her juices. 'You have a perfect minge... a delightful cunny... and the sweetest little bum-hole. Would that I were the man to deflower you.' Then he suddenly leapt up, a look of anguish contorting his face. 'Ah, God forgive me!' he exclaimed. 'You have tempted me, as Eve tempted Adam. Wretched creature that you are! Lust, lust, lust! Your taste and aroma would drive a saint to sin! Get thee behind me, Satan!'

He snatched up a short crop and started to belabour her. He did not spare her, deaf to her cries, cutting into the tender flesh of her thighs and belly, slash upon slash. He whipped her expertly, as if he knew what each blow would do, what agony it would cause – or what strange, dark pleasure. And it was true, spasms running up her legs into her loins, up her spine and down her shoulders to tingle from the ends of her fingers. He punished her with finesse, as if this was not the first time he had used the whip on tender female flesh. He was sweating and muttering under his breath. Amelie wailed as another blow cut across those marks already swelling and reddening.

Joseph suddenly dropped the whip and clutched his groin, doubled over as if in pain. His eyes rolled up and he grimaced, then cried out, 'Oh, God forgive me! You have caused me to spend, you evil girl! Oh… oh… it's sweet, so sweet… ah, my manhood has given up its seed.'

Amelie stared at him aghast. The sombre material of his trousers was rendered darker, wet patches spreading out across the fly area. He seemed to be in pain, yet his voice held a keening note of pleasure, too. What on earth was the matter with him?

'I'm sorry,' she mumbled, riven with guilt, although sure she was not at fault. 'What can I do to ease you?'

Joseph cast her an angry glance, unable to cope with his own strong feelings and blaming her for it. 'Nothing, girl,' he growled, gaining control and then releasing her from her bonds. 'You'll only make matters worse. You must go away.'

'But where?' she faltered, thoroughly alarmed, an insecure future stretching in front of her. She moved her stiff legs and bent down to retrieve her undergarments. 'You can't turn me out. You promised my parents to care for me.'

He rearranged his trousers, his long coat hiding the worst of the dampness, and passed a hand over his greying hair. 'And so I shall,' he vowed. 'Lord Bessborough seeks a companion for his sister. I shall suggest you. Let him take on the responsibility. I can no longer have you under my roof, you are too potent, too tempting. If you remain I fear for my immortal soul, and those of my sons.'

Millicent wanted to be there at the interview, but Mervin had forbidden it. She knew he was in the study, deep in discussion with the vicar and the girl who had accompanied him. When they were safely ensconced inside she crept down and hung around outside the solid, arched, tightly closed door; but all she could hear was the rumble of male voices. The girl said nothing.

That morning she had quite forgotten that she was ill. Curiosity and a wave of hope made her have Dulcie lay out one of her newest dresses and use her skilful hands on her hair, winding the back into a coronet and teasing little fronds down on either side of her face.

She despised herself for a fool, even as she sat still under Dulcie's ministrations. What was she hoping for? Something that would inject a modicum of interest into her life, to relieve the boredom and make her come alive? Now, lurking in the hall, she prayed and kept her fingers crossed. A companion! Someone with whom she could share confidences. She knew Mervin had already grilled two prospective candidates and pronounced them unsuitable. Maybe, just maybe, this one would meet with his approval.

Similar thoughts were running through Amelie's mind as she sat on the edge of a gilt-framed chair, unable to take her eyes off Lord Bessborough. For days she had been on pins as the time for this meeting drew ever closer.

Her godfather had acted swiftly, telling the other members of the family that he'd seen his lordship and put forward Amelie as a candidate for the position of companion. Harriet had expressed no surprise; perhaps he'd discussed the need for Amelie to find employment, but one thing was for sure: he wouldn't have told his wife about his own lustful inclinations. Charity and Agnes subjected Amelie to spiteful remarks, envious of her for even being considered to live in Kelston Towers among the gentry.

'It's not fair, Papa,' Charity had declared, pouting pettishly. 'Why should she be given the opportunity?'

'Because, my child, you are soon to be meeting your future husband. And you too, Agnes. I'm sure you wouldn't want to take Amelie's place under those circumstances, would you?'

'No, Papa,' they chorused, and Amelie was thoroughly fed up with them both – Caleb and Obediah, too. They could stay there and rot, for all she cared.

Yet she had been fearful inside, and never more so then when, early that morning, she rose, put on a full dark green skirt drawn back over a bustle, and a tight Scottish plaid bodice, with long sleeves and a high, demure neckline fastened with a lacy jabot. A short, matching cape and a pillbox hat perched towards the front of her high dressed hair, topped this. Gloves and a reticule completed the businesslike outfit, and Harriet pronounced herself well pleased with her appearance.

'Make us proud of you, dear,' she had said, kissing Amelie's cheek before the groom handed her into the pony trap Joseph intended to drive himself.

'I'll do my best,' she promised.

She had never been to the manor house before, though some of the tenants' children were invited there yearly for a Christmas party. The vicar's brood did not exactly fit the requirement of serfdom, thus missing out on such treats.

It was a fine spring day, the sky pale azure, with clouds like woolly white sheep and a hint of nature awakening in the air, sticky buds on the boughs, and male birds disporting themselves, finding mates before engaging in a frantic flurry of nest building. Amelie sat at the back of the gig and tried to control the butterflies fluttering in her stomach. She was not at all sure whether she wanted to be successful. She had never lived anywhere but the vicarage for as long as she could remember.

They left the village and the main road, turning into a lane, the patient sorrel pony plodding along obediently. On either side woods surrounded them, and a small stream meandered on the left, its banks cushioned with moss.

'This is not the main entrance, you understand,' said Joseph, his eyes fixed ahead. 'It would hardly be appropriate for us to use that.'

Amelie made no response. Her dislike of him had intensified since the episode on that fateful day when he chastised her. Once her feelings for him had been tempered with respect, but no more. He was a hypocrite and a liar, masquerading as a godly man. She felt quite sick when she remembered what he'd done and how he laid the blame on her. She fervently hoped she would not have to endure his odious company for much longer. It was as if her skin remembered too, the bruises left by his beating burning like fire and filling her with a deep resentment, mingled with another emotion as yet unnamed.

There was no one else within sight and she fidgeted uneasily in that cramped space. He was too close for comfort. The lane ran straight for half a mile, then turned sharply. The trap came out into open space and there, a little way off, stood the house. Amelie could not restrain a gasp.

'Is this Kelston Towers?' she whispered.

'Indeed, your future residence,' he returned sardonically. 'Comport yourself in a ladylike fashion, speak only when spoken to, and I hope you'll make a good impression on his lordship. You're bonny enough, God knows.'

He flicked the whip impatiently and the pony broke into a trot. The great bulk of the house came ever closer, and Amelie stared at it enchanted. It was a simple but elegant building with a central block and a curving flight of steps up to the first floor entrance. On either side wings were connected to the house by colonnades.

'It's immense,' Amelie gasped.

'Indeed,' he replied, and pointed with his whip to where the crenellated tops of ruins could be discerned. 'Do you see those towers at the back? They are all that is left of the original thirteenth century fortress. The earlier Tudor house was later altered to the Palladian design, then an extra wing was added, containing a library and a chapel.'

Amelie's heart was pounding with anticipation as she mounted the steps. A stately butler ushered them in and she walked through the marble-floored hall, flanked on either side by statues in alcoves and urns spilling over with flowers and greenery, the walls hung with splendid landscapes. It was flooded with light from a giant cupola, whose stained glass threw down brilliant patterns that dappled the scene with colour.

The butler bore himself like the major-domo he most certainly was, straight-backed and haughty. Joseph and Amelie followed him across the hall and paused outside a door. He tapped discreetly and a voice called to enter. The room into which she stepped outshone in magnificence anything she had yet seen, but even this was rivalled by the overwhelming presence of the man who stepped forward to greet them.

'My lord, allow me to present my goddaughter, Miss Amelie Ashton,' Joseph said, with a slight bow. 'Amelie, this is Lord Mervin Bessborough.'

She came under the scrutiny of a pair of grey eyes, his stare penetrating, as if he could read the secrets of her soul. She could feel herself blushing. His face was expressionless, yet she read volumes there as he said, lifting her hand to his lips, 'Charmed, I'm sure, Miss Aston.'

The brush of his mouth across the back of her gloved hand was enough to send fire through her and dampen the crotch of her knickers. 'Sir,' she answered, bobbing a curtsey though unsure if this was the right thing to do.

'Please sit,' he said, with an expansive gesture of his

aristocratic hands.

She was hardly aware of the conversation that then took place between Joseph and Lord Bessborough. Their words echoed round the room and in her head. She could take in nothing, except her prospective employer's saturnine face, his beautifully tailored jacket and trousers that fitted closely, drawing her attention to the finger-like shape that lay along the inside of his left thigh. She knew what it was. Concealed beneath the material was an organ like Caleb's – and Joseph's. Would his be different because he was an aristocrat?

She was so absorbed in this notion that she did not realise he was addressing her, finally coming to herself when he repeated the question somewhat sharply. 'I asked if you would like to meet my sister, Lady Millicent?' he said, with a trace of mockery in his voice.

'Oh… yes sir,' she stammered, sure she was as red as a beetroot. 'I'm sorry, sir. I was d-daydreaming.'

'And of what were you dreaming?' he questioned seriously, with that intent gaze that paralysed her.

'I don't know, sir,' she faltered.

He smiled faintly and asked, 'Do you like adventures, Miss Amelie?'

'I can't tell, sir. I've never had any.'

'Never?' he queried, with a sardonic lift of an eyebrow. 'I think you have, and that you enjoyed them, and would like to experience more.'

'Whatever you say, sir,' she whispered, and dragged her eyes from him and kept them fixed steadfastly on the Oriental rugs that bestrewed the highly polished boards of the floor.

His smile deepened. 'I have decided to take you on a trial period,' he continued graciously. 'But first you two must meet. I'll summon Lady Millicent.'

Acutely nervous, Amelie waited while he rang for the butler who entered, then departed, and returned in a short while accompanied by a dark-haired girl, who peeked at her shyly, her pale hands twisting together in a washing motion. Amelie's heart stirred with compassion. Finely reared though Millicent might be she seemed desperately unhappy, and in complete awe of her brother. Amelie could not even envy her flounced dress of floral-printed silk, her rings, necklace and pendant eardrops. She sensed there was something wrong beneath the apparent calm and magnificence of Kelston Towers. Just for a moment she did not want to become embroiled, then Millicent smiled at her and everything changed.

'My love,' said Mervin, going across and taking his sister firmly by the elbow, leading her forward. 'This is Miss Amelie Aston, and I am of the opinion that she will make an admirable companion for you.'

'I'm pleased to meet you, Miss Aston,' his sister said shyly.

'Honoured, I'm sure, your ladyship,' she answered, then their eyes met and something flashed between them, the instant recognition of two lonely people who have suddenly found a soul mate.

'Isn't she sweet?' Mervin said, his arm resting lightly round Millicent's tightly corseted waist, his patronising air making Amelie's hackles rise.

'She seems very pleasant,' Millicent replied in her soft, mellifluent voice.

'And you agree that we should try her out?' he asked, but everyone knew he was stating a fact, not asking her opinion.

'Whatever you say, sir,' she murmured, and Amelie could see she was used to obeying him in all matters.

He left her side and gave a self-satisfied smile. 'That's settled then,' he said. 'You will take her back to the vicarage, Reverend, and she shall pack her things and I'll send a carriage for her in the morning. It is agreed? And as for her wages, I think that four pounds a year and her keep will be more than adequate.'

'Very generous, my lord.' Joseph nodded in agreement,

and prepared to leave. 'Come, Amelie,' he added, 'let us not hold up his lordship further. Good day, Lady Millicent, and to you, Lord Mervin.'

Amelie wished she could stay there, wanting to get to know Millicent. And as for the brother? He fascinated, challenged and frightened her. She was on the threshold of a new and entirely different existence, where things beyond her ken, things normally unspoken of, could take place. What they might be she could only vaguely imagine, her limited knowledge unable to provide answers.

She went back to the vicarage in a daze. Harriet and the girls were bubbling over with curiosity, but Amelie went to her room and there sorted through her belongings. She put what she needed in a carpetbag and a wicker pilgrim basket, and stuffed the rest in a sack ready to go to the next charity collection for the poor and needy. This was one of Harriet's projects in which she was aided by the higher echelon of Kemble good-wives. They only helped 'deserving' causes, however, cold as the Arctic Sea when it came to unmarried mothers or adulteress who had strayed from the straight and narrow, or servant girls who had got themselves pregnant, never mind that it was their masters who had probably seduced them.

Amelie, though sadly accepting that this was the last night she would spend in the room that had been hers for years, felt an exhilarating sense of freedom as she thought of Kelston Towers, Lady Millicent and, last but not least, Mervin Bessborough with his eyes that held a depth of knowledge that was somehow enchanting and wicked, all at the same time.

Lying in her narrow bed, where the linen smelt faintly of lavender, she caressed her breasts under her cotton nightgown and let her hand stray down to her pubis, parting the hair-fringed lips and finding the seat of sensation, her little bud that started to swell. She rubbed it on each side, the engorged tissue culminating in that ultra-sensitive head, and though she feared it was sinful, it was also a glorious thing. She wanted to reach her climax, but also wanted to make it last.

She took her finger away, letting it hover over her bud, not quite touching, simply stirring it by the faint passage of air over its tip. She could not suppress a groan, telling herself recklessly that she could come now, and then enjoy another build up to orgasm a short while after. She had done this before, sometimes enjoying a dozen journeys into bliss during an hour's manipulation of her sexual organs. Her bruises prickled; her flesh recalled the pain/pleasure of Joseph's chastisement; she saw Lord Mervin's eyes as bright as any predators; she saw the long baton pressing against his trousers. Unable to wait she rubbed her clit furiously, swept up on a great wave of ecstasy that took her to the stars and made her cry out with the sharp sweetness of it.

Chapter Four

Mervin leaned against the battlement of one of the towers. He'd had repairs carried out on both, liking to stand there with the wind blowing through his hair as he surveyed his kingdom. He stared down at the stables and mews, the kitchen garden where the sun glinted on greenhouse glass, and the formal areas given over to lawns and flowerbeds. Beyond that lay a dark mass of trees, punctuated by the church spire in the distance, marking out Kemble. It was a patchwork of varying colours and shapes, and he indulged his satisfaction and pleasure in ownership.

This deepened and spread and the promise of things to come excited him, rousing his ever ready cock, as he thought about Amelie Aston.

His sister's companion? Ah yes, but he had other plans, not the least of which was his seduction of her. He was certain she was still a virgin; he had a sixth sense when it came to an unbroken hymen. He was king of all he surveyed, and this included deflowering the innocent. He regretted that the law of *droit du seigneur* no longer existed, where the feudal lord had the right to mount the peasant bride, taking her husband's place on the wedding night.

There were other delights available to him, however, and his love of whips and straps gave him endless pleasure. He would teach Amelie these games – turn her into a submissive, willing and eager to experiment.

Smiling to himself he slipped a hand down to his fly, almost idly stroking the protuberance that raised the material. Sensation passed from that hard baton, tightening his balls and making his groin ache. He undid the buttons and released his weapon from trousers and silk underpants. He caressed it, his eyes narrowed as he continued to admire the view. To do so added to the feeling of power concentrated in his shaft. It was all connected, a part of his personal myth; a man of wealth, influence and substance. Sometimes he wished he could walk around with his engorged dick exposed, showing the world its hugeness, making everyone envy him.

The breeze played around the bulging helm. He drew in a sharp breath and circled the ridge of foreskin, then pushed it firmly down, exposing the mushroom-shaped head even more. With his left hand cupping his balls he used his right to grasp his shaft, thumb rubbing over the slit that oozed pre-come, and fingers tight round the band of rolled down flesh. He pulled it upwards, part concealing the pulsating helm. His arousal was threatening his control, and even at such a moment Mervin hated to relinquish it. It was imperative that he was in charge – always. He pressed firmly on a spot between his scrotum and anus, thus halting ejaculation. Even so, the thought of Amelie's mouth encompassing him made it hard to keep his hand still, so eager was his cock to spill over. He pinched it, waiting for the feeling to die back.

He was not managing too well, visions of the young companion firing his lust. He imagined her fingers circling his nipples, her marvellous russet hair brushing across his prick as she mouthed it, her cries of ecstasy as he brought her to climax, the sight of her bound to the crosspiece. He succeeded in making it last, masturbating, then holding off, repeating this several times, but it became more and more difficult. His fingers acted on their own volition, rubbing the throbbing organ, his balls crimping in readiness. He knew he should stop, but could not resist another pump. This proved to be his undoing. His orgasm was upon him, relentless and divine.

A volley of milky spunk shot from him, spattering his hand, hitting the battlement below waist-level, trickling down the grey stone. Then another, and another, his hips jerking with the force of such delayed and manipulated release.

He gritted his teeth, muttering, 'Dear God!' as the contractions continued and his knees weakened and he leaned on the wall for support.

His pulse slowed to near normal. His loins calmed. His cock drooped, freed from the burden of desire. Mervin came to himself slowly, drawing a monogrammed handkerchief from his jacket pocket and carefully wiping his sensitive organ. Then he returned it to his trousers and buttoned up. He was peaceful now, having basked in a flood of pleasure. Amelie would be arriving soon and once in his lair, he was convinced his sensual dreams would come true.

Amelie!

Even to whisper her name caused a stirring in his recently satisfied dick, and he strode from the tower, intent on not overindulging himself. He was saving his strength for her.

Amelie had ridden in the vicar's carriage often enough, but the one sent to collect her far surpassed it in elegance, slung on giant springs, lacquered in bottle-green picked out in gold, with an escutcheon on each door. The coachman sat on his box out front like the captain of some proud galleon, clad in the Bessborough uniform and controlling his four-horse team with rein and whip. A postillion, similarly attired, leapt down when it drew up outside the manse, and took Amelie's luggage, fastened it to the roof then opened the nearside door, let down the folding iron step, and helped her in.

She had already said her goodbyes, surprised because there were tears in Harriet's eyes, and her final embrace was a warm and motherly one. I shall miss her, Amelie thought, and wanted to cry.

This soon passed once she was seated on the plush

green velvet, deeply buttoned upholstery. She clasped her bag on her lap, feeling the rolling motion beneath her as the coach moved off. These fine trappings seemed perfectly natural to her. She knew little about her parents, but wondered if it was possible that they had been well bred, and that she had inherited this love of luxury from them.

On arrival at Kelston Towers she was greeted at the front door by a stern-faced woman dressed in rustling black taffeta, with a lace-trimmed apron around her lean waist and a cap with purple lappets perched atop her greying hair. She wore a belt from which dangled the symbols of her office – keys, a purse, scissors and a penknife.

'I'm Mrs Tanner, the housekeeper,' she announced, nodding to a footman and adding, 'Take Miss Aston's luggage to her room via the backstairs.'

The man whom Amelie had seen on her first visit materialised beside Mrs Tanner. 'Let me introduce myself, miss,' he said, tall and thin, his hair receding from a domed forehead. 'My name is Mr Brock, and I'm in charge.'

'Indeed you are, sir… in charge of the male servants, that is,' Mrs Tanner simpered.

'And the wine cellar,' he reminded, 'and the pantry and ensuring that his lordships wants for nothing when in residence.'

'Of course, Mr Brock,' Mrs Tanner agreed, giving him an arch glance. Then her eyes fastened like gimlets on Amelie's face. 'You, young lady, are in a different category. I shall do what I can for you, but you'll not fraternise with the rest of the staff. It wouldn't be right or proper, though there may be occasions when Mr Brock or myself will invite you to take part in our entertainments. Do you understand?'

'I think so, Mrs Tanner,' Amelie said clearly, holding her head high, aware of undertones in the conversation but unsure of what they portended.

She started when Mrs Tanner reached out and placed a hand on her arm, smiling in a sickly fashion. 'You are a very fine young person,' she remarked, and there was something in her eyes that was truly unpleasant. 'Play your cards right, keep Brock and me sweet and you'll have nothing to complain about.'

Amelie shook her arm free, and spine straight, manner dignified, she answered crisply, 'I expect Lady Millicent is waiting. Will you conduct me to her, please?'

'Hoity-toity!' Mrs Tanner commented, her expression a mixture of envy and malice. 'Don't go giving yourself airs, miss. That won't do… won't do at all. You're not beyond the reach of my tongue, or my cane, even though you're not a servant. You'll treat me and Mr Brock with respect.'

'Of course, I was taught to be respectful to most people,' Amelie responded. 'Now, could we please get on?'

Mrs Tanner hesitated, but only for a moment, something in Amelie's mien halting any further attempts at familiarity. Even so, Amelie was uncomfortable in her presence, and that of Mr Brock. It was as if they were peering through her clothes, rendering them transparent so that her naked body was on display for their perusal.

The housekeeper led the way up the grand central staircase, pausing when they reached the top and then taking a right hand passage. Amelie's feet sank into the rose-patterned fitted carpet, and she tried to look straight ahead and not stare at the paintings on the walls or the shaded wall-lamps, or the several doors they passed. They arrived at one near the end of the corridor.

'This is Lady Millicent's room, and yours will be along to the left,' Mrs Tanner informed her. 'In not quite such a grand area, you understand, but fitting for someone in your position.'

Amelie ignored her disparaging tone, the early optimism fading in the light of the reception received from both her and Mr Brock. It seemed they were in charge, and it boded ill.

A comely maid with wisps of toffee-coloured hair escaping her white cap opened the door. She had a tip-tilted nose dusted with a sprinkling of freckles, bold hazel eyes and a generous figure. She wore a sprigged cotton dress and a frilled apron. She eyed Amelie closely, as if gauging her suitability.

'Let me pass, Higgins,' Mrs Tanner said rudely, thrusting her way into the room.

'Are you the new companion?' the maid asked, winking at Amelie. 'My name's Dulcie… Dulcie Higgins, but we're mostly known by our surnames here. Not you, of course, we'll have to call you miss. I'm Lady Millicent's maid.'

'Stop chattering, girl,' Mrs Tanner snapped. 'Where is her ladyship?'

'In the bath,' Dulcie retorted with admirable spirit. 'D'you want me to get her out? Or would you rather clump in and disturb her ablutions?'

'No, no, just tell her the companion has arrived. I'll leave you to it. Good luck, Miss Aston. You're going to need it,' the housekeeper said dourly, and left the room with a disapproving rustle of skirts.

'She's a bitch,' Dulcie commented, folding a fluffy white bath towel over one arm. 'You want to watch out for her, and that old goat of a butler. No girl's safe when he's around, and she's not much better.'

'What do you mean?' Amelie ventured, impressed by the décor, drapes and furnishings that were entirely to her taste.

'You don't know?' Dulcie rolled her eyes skyward.

'Know what?' Amelie was utterly bewildered.

'That there are women who don't like fucking men, preferring to make love to those of their own sex. Then there's the other type, like Tanner, who'll eat pussy or cock with equal enjoyment.'

Amelie was embarrassed by such outspokenness, much of which she did not understand. Dulcie talked in a lively, confident way, as easy as if they were discussing the weather.

'I've lived in a vicarage for years,' Amelie explained, feeling like a green and stupid schoolgirl. 'Such matters weren't discussed there.'

'Don't worry, petal,' Dulcie said cheerfully. 'Sit down, put your feet up and make yourself at home. I'll go and fetch Lady Millicent.'

She disappeared through a door, leaving Amelie alone. She sat gingerly on a delicately fashioned bedroom chair, gazing around. The chamber was large; her own room at the manse would have fitted into it several times over, and the vicar's house was not small by any means. She admired the flower-patterned wallpaper and eggshell-blue paintwork, the dimity curtains at the large bay windows and the matching ones that hung from the tester over the bed. It was a frothy, feminine room, and she wondered if the one allotted to her would be half as pretty. And would Lady Millicent be kind? On their brief meeting she'd had the impression that she would.

She did not have long to wait. Millicent appeared, swathed in the bath towel with a smaller one wound, turban-wise, round her head. Her cheeks were pink and her eyes bright. 'Miss Aston,' she said. 'Welcome, welcome. I'm delighted you're here. Please excuse me while I dress.'

She disappeared behind a screen covered in black silk embroidered with Chinese motifs – pagodas, little bridges, birds and quaint figures. It was only shoulder high, and Amelie could see her as Dulcie freed her dark hair and rubbed it dry. Dainty underwear hung over the top of the screen – petticoats, a chemise, drawers and corsets. Amelie could hear her speaking with the maid who was obviously towelling that dainty body, and the urge to look grew in her and she visualised future scenes where they might have become such close friends that intimacies could be exchanged, even going as far as viewing each other naked. Her cheeks grew hot at the thought.

'I shan't be long, Miss Aston,' Millicent carolled. 'What shall I call you? I've never before had a companion, but miss seems frightfully formal, though Mervin, that's my brother, says I'm not to become over familiar.'

'My name is Amelie, and I'd have no objection if you wanted to address me as such,' she answered, and then swung round in her chair as, without a by-your-leave, Lord Bessborough strode into the bedroom, went straight to where his sister was concealed and peered over the edge of the screen.

'You're still a mite too thin, my dear,' he observed. 'It's as well that Lord Nigel has no objection, though he does prefer his women to be well-fleshed... ordinary women, that is... it will be different in your case as he is about to propose to you.'

'I'll never accept him, never!' Millicent shot back, and Amelie was astonished at her vehemence.

Mervin clicked his tongue reprovingly, and glanced slyly at Amelie as if gauging her reaction. 'That's not a very nice way for a lady to address the head of the family,' he mocked, reaching over and fondling his sister.

'You know what I feel about him,' Millicent retorted and shrank away. Dulcie snatched the undergarments from the top of the screen and hastily helped her lady into them.

Mervin's expression became darker and more sinister. 'You are foolish,' he commented. 'In fact, I sometimes wonder if you're a simpleton, not quite right in the head. If you insist on defying me I might call in a doctor and have you committed to a lunatic asylum.'

Millicent turned ashen, eyes huge in her heart-shaped face. 'You wouldn't dare,' she breathed.

His smile was even more mocking as he replied, '*Dare*? You say that to me, Millicent? You should know better than to dare me to do anything.'

'But why? Why force Nigel on to me?'

'Because I want to; it's as plain as that, my dear sister,'

he replied, and suddenly yanked the screen aside, exposing Millicent in her drawers, chemise and waist-clinching stays. Her small breasts popped out over the edge, the nipples concealed only by a scrap of lace edging.

'Mervin! My lord! Don't!' Millicent begged and folded her arms over her breasts in an attempt to hide them.

'You're too shy. I'm your brother, remember? I've seen more of you than this. Have I not?'

Millicent seemed to shrink into herself, head bowed, shoulders slumped. 'Let me get dressed,' she begged humbly.

Dulcie brought her gown, but Mervin held up a hand. 'Not yet. First you must agree to attend a soirée I'm holding this evening. I fancy putting on a show for my guests.'

'What sort of show?' Millicent asked suspiciously.

'I propose Living Pictures,' he said triumphantly.

'And what is that?' Millicent was still in her underwear, rubbing her hands up and down her bare arms as if to warm them, though the room was not cold.

'I'll use the stage at the end of the ballroom. There I shall erect a large gilded frame. Behind this, looking as if painted, you and Dulcie and some of the other maids will pose, clad in fragile Greek costume, as nymphs, or goddesses... perhaps naked. And you will hold the pose, quite motionless, giving my friends the opportunity to enjoy such a delightful spectacle.' He caressed his sister as he spoke, gentling her like a frightened filly, and she acquiesced, putty in his hands.

'You won't permit Nigel to make free with me?' she whispered.

'Nothing shall be done without your consent,' he promised, and turned to Amelie. 'It would please me greatly if you were to join in our thespian effort. Would you do it, Miss Aston? I said I thought you liked danger.'

'What? Take my clothes off in front of an audience? I think not, sir,' she answered staunchly.

'It won't be like that. Nothing vulgar. You won't even move. It's against the rules of Living Pictures. One of my friends is a judge and he will pronounce the winner of the best tableau. This is a serious study of art, each pose taken from an existing, respected painting executed by one of the Old Masters. My friends are connoisseurs, dedicated to the arts. Did you really believe that I would allow anything improper to take place in my house?'

Dulcie looked sceptical, Millicent downright upset and Amelie was finding it hard to concentrate on anything with him standing so close and breathing out sensuality through his very pores. Strange visions passed across her mind, of herself kneeling before him and taking his penis into her mouth, of his libation pouring over her face and dripping down to her breasts, forming a glistening pearl necklace round her throat.

'Will there be ladies present?' she asked, while her loins melted and her voice was hard to control.

'Oh, no,' he replied, with a little frown. 'We gentlemen are in agreement that whereas we can study nudity dispassionately, purely from the point of view of artistic appreciation, should it be made available to women, children or the lower classes, then this would merely encourage the lustful tendencies they may already have.'

Amelie was rendered speechless by such a contrived male oriented statement that he, presumably, believed to be true. Even so, she guessed him to be throwing down the gauntlet, challenging her to pick it up. And she did so.

'Very well, my lord, if you're sure it is proper, then I have no further objection to joining in your Living Pictures,' she said, with a lift of her chin.

He clapped his hands, applauding her. 'Capital! Capital!' he shouted, then cut to his sister, adding, 'You see, my love, what a difference having a companion makes? Already she is encouraging you to come out of your shell. I want you both to present yourselves backstage this afternoon and Mrs Tanner will show you what to do.'

He bent and kissed Millicent's cheek, gave Amelie a searching stare, then left.

'My goodness, he's like a whirlwind, if you'll forgive the expression,' Amelie burst out.

'That's my brother, ever full of schemes and ideas and never letting the grass grow under his feet,' Millicent replied, holding out her arms so that Dulcie could slip the dress on. The bodice fitted closely over the tight corset, the bustle cage fastened by tapes to her waist, the skirt supported over it at the back. Dulcie fastened the domed buttons all the way down.

'I see,' Amelie murmured, though she couldn't understand him at all. 'Does he have parties often?'

'Oh yes. More so when he's at the London residence near Hyde Park.' Millicent sat on the dressing table stool in front of an oval mirror on a carved stand and Dulcie arranged her hair.

'And this man whom he wants you to marry?' Amelie felt she could talk to her frankly, unaware of the social barriers between them. It was as if they were of the same class.

'Lord Nigel Balfour. His father is a duke and rich as can be. Mervin has decided that with all that money and those titles Nigel would make me an ideal husband.'

'And you don't like him?'

'He's a repulsive toad!' Millicent said with a shudder. Then she swivelled round and reached for Amelie, clasping her by the hand, saying on a sob, 'Oh, I'm so glad you're here. You make me feel strong. The two of us together can combat this dreadful male dominance. Mervin thinks he can do what he likes with me and threatens to have me shut up in an asylum for the mad if I don't comply with his wishes.'

'Don't worry, my lady, I'll protect you,' Amelie promised stoutly.

'I believe you will,' Millicent answered, her grip tightening. 'May I call you Amelie?'

'Yes.'

'But not in Mervin's hearing perhaps, or that of Mrs Tanner and Mr Brock. And to you I'll be Milly, in secret.'

Amelie nodded, her palm warmed by Millicent's, and devotion blooming in her heart for this girl who had everything she could want – except love and freedom.

Amelie's suspicions regarding the housekeeper and butler were confirmed that afternoon. She feared them to be corrupt but had not realised that, beside their own predilections, they were obeying their master's orders.

She arrived at the area at the back of the stage, finding it equipped with a dressing room containing mirrors, costumes on racks and greasepaint for enhancing the appearance. Half a dozen women drawn from the staff were already there in various stages of undress. Millicent, Dulcie and herself had been instructed to wear loose robes with nothing underneath. They were barefoot, and Amelie was thankful it was a warm day. But none of these possible discomforts to the performers seemed to matter one iota to Mrs Tanner and Mr Brock.

'Have you done this before?' she asked Millicent.

'No, I have succeeded in avoiding his parties by being ill,' she said, and drew her robe more closely about her.

'Then why now?'

'I fear what he can do to me. Besides, you give me courage.'

'My lady,' Mrs Tanner began, fawning on her. 'What an honour! Please do as I say. I'm simply following Lord Bessborough's instructions.'

They were conducted to the dressing room, asked to disrobe and then draped in billowing white gowns of such transparency that their limbs, breasts and furry triangles showed quite clearly. Amelie was so intrigued to glimpse Millicent's treasures that she scarcely heeded her own exposure as Mr Brock raked over her with hot eyes and Mrs Tanner lost no opportunity to paw and pinch her thighs and buttocks.

Some of the other women were already attired as bacchantes in tunics so short they showed their forks, and leopard skins that slipped from their shoulders and left their breasts bare. The small space seemed filled with pussies and nipples and the oceanic odour of female arousal. There was no denying that they were enjoying this opportunity to flaunt their asserts. It was a better option than being a skivvy, any day. Maybe some rich man might take a shine to one of them and set her up in a decent little house where she would be her own mistress as well as his, beholden to none.

Amelie had no such ambitions. She was content to climb the ladder slowly, courting success by taking one step at a time. She could not deny that Mervin interested her more than anyone she had ever met. Instinct told her that he was bad, but then, wasn't this the element that aroused her? Didn't she long to tame him and make him hers alone? An impossible dream, but one worth striving to attain.

She started, wanting to sink through the floor as she caught a glimpse of herself in the pier-glass. Such flagrant nudity! Well, almost entirely naked. White silk chiffon was all that stood between her and complete exposure. What would the villagers have thought of her? And Joseph Thacker and his sons? She was wise enough to know that such a sight would have stiffened their cocks and the thought made her throw an arm across her breasts and cup her mound with the other hand.

'Don't hide your wares, deary,' crooned Mrs Tanner, pulling Amelie's hands away none too gently. 'What tits, eh, Mr Brock? What a silky little bush!'

'Yes, indeed,' he said throatily, cradling Amelie's triangle in one hand, his middle digit seeking her clit-head and brushing across it briskly.

'Enough, Brock,' Millicent said sternly, and he dropped his hand and stepped back deferentially. 'Dear me,' she went on, addressing Amelie. 'He needs putting in his place sometimes... seems to forget that he's a butler and therefore not on equal terms with us. Not that he should be so free with his caresses, even were he titled. Nigel is, and I hate the touch of his flabby hands.'

Amelie had never been so embarrassed. Wherever she looked there were women flaunting themselves in skimpy costumes, the air redolent with female desire. Regardless of who observed them they were intent on solitary pleasure. A buxom blonde lay on a couch, legs relaxed, showing a full view of her fair fleece and the dark line of her divide. She was pinching her nipples into brown-red points with one hand, while fingering her slit with the other. Another was spread-legged over a chair, knees wide open, grinding her sex into the velvet-covered seat. A third stood before a long mirror, pelvis thrust forward, eyes fixed on her black-furred crotch as she rubbed herself vigorously. She was grunting, near the point of no return and then her eyes rolled back and her mouth dropped open and she shivered in a spasm of ecstasy.

A plump brunette knelt with her thighs apart, using both hands until she too was swept away by pleasure. Several males had been roped into the tableaux, representing shepherds, or minor gods or armoured soldiers. As the women cavorted before them so they could not keep their hands from their pricks, lifting their short tunics and finding the bulging tackle beneath. Their cocks came erect and they applied pressure to them, rubbing and caressing, holding off momentarily so that they did not spend prematurely.

Brock paced around, intently gauging each performance. 'Dirty bitches!' he growled at the women, plunging a finger into each wet hole and rotating it, bringing it out creamy with their juices. 'My lovely little gardens! What would I do without them, eh?'

'Sleep better at night, snore less and get rid of your backache,' snapped Mrs Tanner, though she was following his example and familiarising herself with their private parts. She clapped him on the shoulder, declaiming loudly, 'Pull yourself together, man! I know there's pussy galore, but you're under orders. Let's get on with the rehearsal.'

The time sped by as each tableau was arranged within the frame, props added – a Grecian column or a pyramid here, a woodland backdrop there, the half a dozen participants in each put through their paces until they were perfect. By the end of the afternoon Amelie had lost her initial stage fright, nerves and bashfulness, posing like a seasoned trouper. She was glad she'd been given the central role in her particular Living Picture, that of Cleopatra and her handmaidens attending the arrival of Mark Anthony, played by a dashing young footman who was continually giving her the gladdest of glad eyes.

Millicent was Venus, resting in a grove, surrounded by her nymphs and swain. Amelie thought she suited the role superbly, though not perhaps as voluptuous as one might have expected of the Goddess of Love.

'Mervin's put me last so that Nigel will be so excited by what he's already seen he won't be able to resist pawing me,' she said crossly.

'Don't worry, my lady,' Amelie assured her. 'I'm sure your brother means you no harm.'

'You don't know him,' Millicent answered despondently.

They were allowed to take time off for afternoon tea and a nap, but it seemed that dinner would be out of the question, the guests arriving around eight. Mrs Tanner had prepared snacks to be served with drinks. Acutely nervous, Amelie accepted Millicent's invitation to share her bedroom, though she rather wanted to go to her own charming chamber that was a scaled down version of her employer's. She had taken to it at first sight – the tester bed, the tallboy and wardrobe, the marble fireplace, the floral wallpaper and curtains, the light and airy atmosphere.

But, uncomplaining, she drank tea and ate cake curled up under Millicent's counterpane. Despite this new turn of events that had transformed her into Cleopatra, she counted herself fortunate to have landed such a congenial post. The lovely Millicent, snuggled in bed beside her, was an added delightful bonus, and though the longing to touch her quivered through Amelie's fingertips, she did no more than chatter brightly and hand her the plate of tiny, triangular sandwiches.

She dozed, roused by Dulcie with a bright, 'Wake up, your ladyship, and you too, miss. It's seven o'clock and Mrs Tanner's on the warpath.'

'Have the guests arrived?' Millicent asked sleepily.

'Oh yes, my lady. They've been at it on and off all day. Some local squires, a couple of bigwigs from Bath and others by train from London.'

'So they'll be staying?'

'Yes, it'll be in the nature of a house party, but without ladies. The usual thing, with the gents trying it on with the servants. We need to keep our drawers well and truly padlocked or we'll be in trouble, and I'm not only talking about the women.'

'Is Lord Nigel here?'

'Oh yes, he's been incarcerated in the study with your brother for hours. I've got wind of the fact that he's brought over a batch of dirty photographs from Paris. I expect they'll inspire his lordship to have us pose like that next time. Art is one thing – smut another entirely. The women who bare their all for the photographers are nothing more than common prostitutes.'

'Selling themselves for money?' Amelie put in, curiosity aroused.

'That's it, miss. Sixpence for a knee-trembler up against a wall in some dark alley.'

Amelie had so much to learn, but her knowledge was growing by leaps and bounds. And the evening should push it on a stage further. She wanted to know all there was to know, tired of being an ignoramus. The prospect was exciting but terrifying too.

The whole atmosphere of Kelston Towers was different.

Amelie picked up on it as soon as they stepped from the bedroom. It was charged, as if fired by an electric current. In the distance she could hear male voices – loud, jolly, excited. The servants were bustling about downstairs and the Great Hall, glimpsed from the corridor above, seemed filled with figures in evening suits – Mervin's cronies who were there in anticipation of witnessing the 'artistic' performance.

Mrs Tanner and Brock were in the dressing room. The other actors were already in costume and the stage had been prepared, hidden from the spectators by a blood-red curtain. A pianist sat at a concert grand close by, playing dreamy music, though this changed as the curtains parted on the first tableau. Amelie peeped through a side drape at the audience. They had taken their seats, some were drinking and others had opera glasses to hand, eager to view the performers at close range. They all had a well-heeled look about them. Some were young, but the majority were middle-aged roués of profligate habits, seeking something new to titillate their jaded appetites.

'Yes, those are my brother's friends of the bosom,' murmured Millicent in Amelie's ear. 'Gentlemen of leisure who never soil their hands with honest work, living on the proceeds of generations of inheritance.'

'And which one is Lord Nigel?' Amelie asked.

'The fat one in the middle of the front row. He has the best seat so he'll miss nothing, subjecting us all to his lustful gaze.'

Amelie stared at him. He was a tubby little man with sandy hair liberally larded with Macassar oil, swept back and parted at the centre. He had sideburns and a full moustache, bulging fishy eyes, red cheeks and a pouting mouth. He seemed boyish, blatantly eager for the show to begin, nudging his companions on either side and making snide remarks, blowing cigar smoke in their faces. Altogether a not very prepossessing suitor, and pity for Millicent welled up in Amelie.

He leaned forward eagerly as tableau after tableau was revealed. At last it was Amelie's turn, wearing an Egyptian headdress and a wide jewelled collar that did not cover her breasts. These were bare, exposed between the collar's edge and the high waist of her wrap-around skirt. Her nipples peaked, two luscious cherries excited by the draught. Mrs Tanner had painted her eyes, elongating the outer corners with kohl, adding rouge to accentuate her cheekbones, and carmine to her lips so that they looked wet and oh-so kissable. Her eyes were huge, almost emerald with the addition of green-gold powder on the lids.

The curtains were drawn across the proscenium, and Amelie and the others hurriedly took up their poses. The handsome Mark Anthony bent over Cleopatra who was reclining wantonly on a couch, full of allure and Eastern promise. 'Blimey,' he gasped, sotto voce. 'You've got a fine pair on you.'

'Don't be so rude,' she chided, but couldn't help but be interested in the erection that lifted his white kilt. 'That's no way to speak to the Siren of the Nile.'

'I reckon old Cleo would have loved it,' he replied cheekily, totally unrepentant. 'And what I've got here,' and he grabbed her hand and laid it briefly on his bulge.

Her fingers responded to the heat between his thighs, but at that moment the curtains parted and there was an audible gasp as the gentlemen caught their first glimpse of the exotic scene. The pianist obliged with psuedo Eastern music; the slave girls were suitably submissive; their guard impressive, all blacked up to look negroid and hefting a long bullwhip. The spectators murmured their appreciation. Amelie could not see them clearly through the dazzle of candles floating in a trough of water and providing the footlights. However, she was aware that some of the women who had appeared in earlier scenes were now servicing those men who demanded satisfaction, on their knees between black-trousered thighs, taking large, small or indifferent penises in their mouths, while their own assets were fingered.

But it was herself who was causing a stir and she could hardly believe the men who were so conversant with the female form should find her desirable. Mervin was there. She could see him leaning over the back of Nigel's chair and making comments, his eyes never leaving her. Then the curtains closed and she was relieved to return to the dressing room. Now it was Millicent's turn to be put on show like a prize heifer.

She wanted to resume her robe but Mrs Tanner would have none of it. 'Oh no, deary. Lord Bessborough has given his orders. You're to remain in costume. The night's not yet over, not by a long chalk.'

Amelie watched from the wings as Millicent pretended to be Venus. Glancing across at Nigel, she could see him staring fixedly at the blushing and embarrassed lady. Poor Millicent, as much a slave as the girls who had pretended to be Cleopatra's attendants. At last the ordeal was over, or so she thought, but Mervin jumped onto the stage and made an announcement.

'My friends,' he declaimed, like the wicked ringmaster of some debased circus. 'I'm about to introduce you to something unique… not Living Pictures… but Motion Pictures, inspired by the wonderful new invention of cinematography.'

He jumped down, clapped his hands and at once half a dozen semi-nude girls were chased across the stage by burly men still attired as Greek gods or Roman soldiers. The women were seized, then bound and forced to submit to intercourse. Not that their protests seemed in the least genuine; far from it. Their shrieks quickly changed to moans of pleasure as they were thrown on their backs or made to bend over while their attackers plunged eager weapons into widely stretched cunts or arseholes.

The spectacle drove the audience into a fury of lust. No one was safe from their desperate need for orgasm. The elegant ballroom had been transformed into the setting for an orgy. Everywhere Amelie looked it was to see couples engaged in copulation, men with women and sometimes men with men. Mrs Tanner had her legs clamped round Mr Brock's waist while he held her to him, arms under her bottom, pushing his massive tool in and out of her hairy crack.

Amelie felt someone behind her. Hands closed like talons round her naked breasts. A male body was pressing close, the hard bar of his exposed sex pushing between her buttocks. His breath played round her neck, raising the fine down on her limbs, and when he spoke it was the most seductive sound she had ever heard.

'Ah, Amelie, sweet innocent girl, doesn't this make you want to indulge, too?' whispered Mervin Bessborough, his tongue caressing the rim of her ear and making darts of desire shoot down to her bud. 'Don't you long to have me make love to you, show you all the delights of the flesh and bring you to undreamed of heights?'

Chapter Five

'Lady Millicent, don't run away!' pleaded Nigel, making a grab for her in the dressing room. 'Ah, my dearest girl, you know how much I love you. I've asked Mervin for your hand in marriage and he has consented. Say you'll agree, and make me the happiest man in the world.'

Millicent stood stock still in his arms. To struggle would be undignified, and she was certain do nothing but spur his ardour. There was no one else about, all either engaged in or watching the enactment of *The Rape of the Sabine Women*. Even Amelie seemed to have deserted her.

She could smell Nigel's excitement and feel the pressure of that engorged thing behind his fly buttons, while his sweaty hands were mauling her, rapturously claiming the moist area between her thighs. 'Let me go, sir,' she hissed, anger rising at his cavalier treatment. 'I won't marry you. I don't love you and never could.'

'I don't expect love,' he said with a leer, and his finger wormed its way between her labial wings, pressing the fragile silk chiffon against them. 'Who needs it anyway? As my wife you'll want for nothing. I shall be your master and plant my heirs in your belly. Come on, Millicent. I'll wager you won't get a better offer.'

His conceit appalled her. How could Mervin have given his blessing to this match? Now Nigel was becoming too bold, his finger brushing aside the silk and encountering that little nodule crowning her cleft, giving her weird sensations that alarmed her with their intensity. She had been aware of them before when touching herself down there accidentally. She put up her hands and shoved at his chest, surprising them both with her strength. He stepped back and she broke free.

She grabbed up her negligee, shrugged her shoulders into it and wrapped it around her shrinking flesh, covering the revealing Venus costume. She was trembling from head to toe, and could feel hysteria sweeping her, wanting to scream and weep and run away.

'But, Millicent…' Nigel started to protest, as if unable to credit that any woman would refuse his offer. 'You don't know what you're missing,' and he unbuttoned and displayed his swollen prick, wagging it at her archly.

Millicent gasped in revulsion and turned tail and fled, her cries drowned out by the uproar taking place all around. Reaching her chamber she rushed inside, locked the door behind her and hid in the bathroom. There she slid down the wall and collapsed in a heap on the floor, sobbing piteously. Her head was throbbing, her heart pounding and that dreaded malaise was on her again, robbing her of energy and comprehensive thought.

'My lord, this isn't right, let me go,' Amelie protested while Mervin sought to press home his advantage, fingers between her bottom cheeks, seeking even closer intimacy.

From side stage she could not avoid seeing couples in the throes of copulation, and here was Lord Bessborough wanting to try the same thing with her. Under other circumstances it might have been flattering, even romantic, but not like this.

He chuckled, laughter reverberating through his chest pressed so close to her back. 'Silly goose. What is right and what is wrong? You want me, don't you?' And one of his hands slid under her arm and closed around her breast, thumb rotating across the nipple. Amelie could not suppress a moan.

'Not now, sir,' she panted, but could not help arching her spine, seeking more and more pleasure from this caress.

71

He bent her slightly from the waist, raised her skirt and inserted his penis into that vulnerable gap at the top of her thighs, the helm rubbing against her slit, wet with the juices that, despite her protestations, she could not hold back. Her body had taken over, a wanton creature completely out of her control.

'Amelie, I'm your master,' he continued, taking his cock in hand and rubbing it up and down her avenue, lingering at vulva and anus alike. 'I'm going to take you to my punishment room, and there teach you what every disobedient slave ought to know. In the end you'll be begging me to fuck you.'

'Never!' she whimpered, but her mental promises to herself were weakening. Mervin was so strong, powerful and handsome and she longed to yield to him, body and soul. She grabbed his hand, holding it closer to her breast and wriggled her bottom against the driving force of his tool that was intent on penetrating her.

'Miss Amelie... oh, miss... you've got to come quickly... it's Lady Millicent,' shouted Dulcie, expressing no surprise at finding them in such a compromising position.

'What's the matter with her now?' Mervin demanded, his eyes blazing with rage.

'I think it has something to do with Lord Nigel,' Dulcie went on, and grabbed Amelie by the hand. 'She needs you, miss.'

'Amelie, stay with me,' Mervin commanded.

'I must go to her,' Amelie replied, thanking heaven for this reprieve, as she had been just about to throw caution to the winds and give in to her basic instincts.

Without a backward glance at him she followed Dulcie to the bedroom. The maid had a key and they were soon inside and bending over the sobbing form of Millicent lying on the floor. Dulcie rolled her eyes skywards at the sight, and arms round her, coaxed her into a sitting position.

'That's right, my lady,' she encouraged, speaking as if to a child. 'Ups-a-daisy. We'll soon have you tucked in bed with a hot water bottle.'

Millicent's eyes were huge in that wan face and her fingernails dug into Amelie's hand with the force of her emotion. 'It was Nigel… he asked to marry me and I can't bear him! And now I feel so ill again and Mervin will be furious with me.'

'To hell with Mervin!' Amelie pronounced loudly, surprised by her own boldness.

'He'll have me committed,' Millicent wept, as Dulcie got her to her feet and supported her to the four-poster.

'He'll do no such thing,' Amelie said, with more conviction than she was feeling. 'Is there no one else in the family who can protect you?'

'Our brother, Ralph, younger than Mervin but older than me. Alas, he is away a great deal… an artist, studying in London and Paris. He's kind and never forces me to do anything I don't want.'

'Can I get in touch with him?' Amelie hovered anxiously by the small form dwarfed by the bed.

'You could try writing to him at his studio. The address is in my notebook on the desk over there.' Millicent pointed weakly.

'I'll do that,' Amelie said resolutely and pulled the quilt around her, then went through the address book and found one for Lord Ralph Bessborough, 8 The Mews, Chelsea, London.

'Don't let Mervin know,' Millicent warned, while Dulcie laid a cold compress on her forehead and fed her sips of herb tea. 'He and Ralph don't see eye to eye on most issues.'

'I won't,' Amelie promised. 'But how am I to post this?'

'Don't worry, miss, I'll pop it in the box myself,' Dulcie promised. 'No need to get Mrs Tanner or Mr Brock involved. They usually handle the mail, minding everyone else's business. I don't trust 'em.'

Amelie sat at the desk, dipped a pen into the squat brass inkwell, and scribbled a note on Bessborough headed notepaper. It was odd to be penning a missive to a man she had not even met, and all she could think to write was: *Dear Sir, I feel you should contact your sister, Lady Millicent, on a matter of some urgency. She is unwell and I am writing on her behalf. I am her new companion, Yours truly, Amelie Aston.*

She found an envelope and a stamp and wrote the address, then handed it to Dulcie who slipped it into her pocket. The maid was once more dressed in normal clothing, discarding the trappings of Living Pictures. Then the moment Amelie had dreaded was upon them.

Mervin strode in with the blackest scowl she had ever seen on a man's face.

'Millicent,' he thundered, looming over the bed like an avenging angel. 'Why have you left the party?'

'I'm ill,' she answered in a faint voice.

'Nonsense!' he said scornfully. 'Nigel tells me you were rude to him and refused his offer of marriage.'

'I've already told you. I can't accept him. He is abhorrent to me.' Millicent was sobbing, tears flowing down her cheeks and dripping on to the ecru lace of her negligee.

This was too much for Amelie. She rounded on him, well aware that she was still attired as Cleopatra, though she had succeeded in adding a shawl to protect her modesty. Maybe some of that famous queen's authority would brush off on her. 'Stop harassing your sister. How could you expose her to that disgusting spectacle in the ballroom? You promised nothing improper would take place.'

His eyes slashed down her body, sharp as swords, and his upper lip curled contemptuously as he said, 'Do you dare criticise me, a lowly thing like you? It is time that both you and my sister learned what life is all about. Sex… my dear Miss Aston. It is sex, not love, that makes the world go round.'

'What a sad philosophy,' she retorted. 'I'm sorry for you, Lord Bessborough. You don't have a human heart. Yours is made of granite. You'll never know the blessing of true love.

'And will you, Miss Prim-and-Proper Aston?' he mocked, quickly whipping the shawl from her upper body and gloating on her breasts. 'You liked it when I touched these beauties earlier. You were wet between the legs... couldn't wait for me to roger you.'

'You lie,' she cried, and lashed out with her hand, catching him across the cheek.

His head jerked back, then he straightened and his smile was tigerish. 'That was a foolish move, my dear,' he said silkily. 'Very foolish indeed.'

Before she knew what he was doing he picked her up, flung her across his shoulder and stalked towards the door. She hung there, headfirst; hair streaming as she beat his back with her clenched fists. 'Put me down!' she shrieked.

He did not reply, one arm clamped around her thighs, holding her firmly.

'Mervin, she's my companion, what are you going to do with her?' shouted Millicent.

'That's my business,' he growled as he walked out, then he added the rider, 'Be very careful what you say or do, sister. Never forget that I am head of this house and you and everything in it are at my disposal.'

Amelie could see nothing but the dizzying expanse of carpet as he bore her along. Her struggles had become weaker as she accepted that she was wasting precious energy. She would never break free from his vicelike grip. She must keep a reserve of strength to face whatever he had in store for her.

The journey through the house seemed interminable, along corridors, down steep stairways, the final one a twisting spiral that led into the cellars. Flares stuck into the grey stone walls lighted the way and Amelie's fears grew. Mervin opened a door at the foot of the stairs and carried her into a vault with an arched ceiling. A slim blond young man looked up from arranging ropes on a wooden couch.

'Humphrey, fetch Lord Nigel, Lord Crombermere and Sir Jollian,' Mervin commanded, and dumped Amelie down on the bench. She made to rise, but his hand came to rest on her shoulder.

'Who is that?' she demanded as the man bowed and left.

'My valet. Don't get any ideas of trying to use your wiles on him. He is only interested in cock, loving to have it shoved up his arse.'

Amelie shuddered, glancing in terror around the gloomy place. It resembled a medieval torture chamber, with hooks from which hung implements the use of which she could only hazard a guess. There were whips, chains, gags and blindfolds, along with switches, taws, handcuffs, legs irons and other manacles.

'Where have you brought me?' she said, her voice low.

He smiled grimly and his fingers dug into her like claws. 'This is my special chamber where people come to punish or be punished, according to their particular fancies. Have you never heard of pleasure through pain?'

'No, I have not. I was reared in a vicarage, remember. I didn't choose to be brought down here.'

'I know, but you defied me and that deserves chastisement. I can't have you leading my sister into ways of thought unsuitable for a lady. You're not one of those females who demand rights for women, are you?'

'No sir, but neither am I willing to become any man's slave,' she replied spiritedly, making to rise again, only to be pushed back.

'We shall see,' he answered confidently.

Humphrey returned, accompanied by three men, one of whom Amelie recognised as Nigel Balfour. The other two were middle-aged, one lean, the other corpulent. All were somewhat the worse for drink, but still game for whatever was on offer.

'Mervin, old boy, where's your delightful sister?' Nigel shouted, walking with a definite stagger.

'Taken to her bed, quite overcome with emotion at your proposal,' Mervin lied with a smoothness that Amelie found sickening, yet impressive. Nothing seemed to disturb him. 'But I've brought her companion, Miss Amelie Aston, along to receive a little punishment. She has been displaying an unseemly amount of defiance.'

'Oh, naughty, naughty,' scolded Nigel, waving a finger in her face. 'You'll have to do better than that, girl, if you want to keep your job.'

He hung around while Humphrey and Mervin lifted Amelie and then positioned her across the bench, bottom up, arms spread and hands padlocked into place. Her transparent skirt was then pushed waist-high, her thighs prised apart, a spreader placed between them and her ankles manacled to ringbolts in the floor.

'Good, good,' Mervin muttered, pacing round her. 'Not so proud now, are you, my beauty?'

Amelie wanted to spit at him but her head was in a collar so positioned that she could not move. She tugged at her restraints to no avail, fully aware of the other gentlemen enjoying to the full the sight of her naked pudenda with its inviting opening and soft, fleecy hair. It encouraged exploration. Someone touched her there, but Merlin saw and hurled a mouthful of abuse at the unfortunate man.

'Not yet, Nigel! She is to be introduced to every nuance of sexual encounter by me, and only me. Do you understand? Later you may join in, but I want her vagina un-violated. It pleases me to have her remain a virgin for a while longer. Not in the fundament, you understand. This may be invaded, but then again, only by me. I don't trust that one or other of you hasn't a dose of Cupid's Measles, and I've no desire to catch it.'

'That's unfair, Bessborough,' humped Lord Crombermere, his rheumy eyes wandering over Amelie's rounded buttocks. 'Keeping it for yourself, eh, man? I call than damn unsporting.'

'I'm sure we can find an alternative,' Mervin replied, and jerked a thumb to where Humphrey posed, leaning one elbow against a pillar and twiddling with his curls.

'A bum-boy, to boot,' Crombermere said, and sidled closer to the valet. 'I've never found it matters much who or what gender when my old fellow needs a hole to burrow in.'

Amelie listened and wondered and was disturbed by the tenor of the conversation. She strained her ears to hear what might be taking place around her, nerves stretched like bowstrings as she thought of Mervin selecting the instrument he would choose to chastise her. She heard rustlings and his footsteps and the sound of something swishing through the air. A whip? A cat-o-nine-tails? Her skin was stippled with goose bumps and her pussy ached, her nipples rising against the hard surface of the bench.

There followed a hush, the air loaded with anticipation. Waiting was a gruelling enough punishment on its own. Butterflies fluttered in her stomach and she panicked and struggled against those impossible bonds. Then there was a whoosh behind her, followed by a thwack.

'Ow!' he screamed as leather connected with her bottom and fire lanced her. 'Oh, ow!' She almost wet herself with the shock of it, so harsh, so brutal, so inescapable. Worse than when Thacker had whipped her – far, far worse.

It must be a short whip Mervin was using, for it didn't hit her wildly, but in controlled swipes to the left cheek, then the right. The pain glowed brightly, worsening with each stroke. She imagined her skin flushed with stripes and turning crimson. Mervin went on and on in a long, fluid motion, then paused to take a breather.

'Enough,' Amelie pleaded, eyes running, devoid of all

dignity now.

'Not yet,' he said calmly, and started again.

The agony went on, over and over, and something in Amelie snapped. She drifted on high, somewhere she couldn't explain. Pictures formed in her brain, colours, faces known and unknown – and she was losing consciousness. Then she came to herself sharply, realising that Mervin had stopped whipping her and was now positioned between her spread legs and creaming her anal hole with a thick, pungent-smelling substance. She felt it sting as it penetrated her, and this was followed by his fingers, going in deeply till she seemed to be on fire from inside. They went in deeper, two, then three, and then they were withdrawn, leaving her void.

'Oh no, please,' she begged.

He laughed and something else was inserted into her now willing fundament. But it was too large; pain blanked out pleasure and she screamed and tried to avoid it. He swore savagely and pulled out his cock, then slapped her hard on her sore hindquarters.

'She's too tight, my lord,' observed Humphrey. 'I suggest that we insert butt plugs to stretch her. What do you say?'

'Do it, but not until she's brought me off,' Mervin snapped, and moved round till he stood in front of her. 'Open up, girl,' he ordered, his rampant weapon in his hand, guiding it towards her lips.

She gasped at the size of it, gagged at the thought of it, then did has he commanded, feeling the tip slip into her mouth, the fat helm and rolled down foreskin, the long thick shaft all pressing in till the end butted against her throat. She managed not to choke and quickly learned how to move her head even given her restrictions, wrapping her tongue around his tool, sucking it, relishing the strong, meaty taste of it. He wound strands of her hair round his fingers, holding her in exactly the position he required for the greatest sensation. She smelt the odour of his dark thatch, the freshness of expensive linen, the tail of his shirt poking through the gap in his trousers, forming a frill round his monstrous appendage.

His movements became frenzied. 'Do it, girl,' he muttered, eyes glittering as he watched his penis forge in and out of her mouth. 'Make me come! That's it!' and with a final thrust he released his emission. Amelie's mouth filled with warm spunk. She swallowed it, but there was more as he withdrew a little, spattering her face, her chin and her curls.

He removed his cock, wiped it dry on her hair, and then buttoned up. 'She'll do,' he remarked to Humphrey. 'See that she's plugged. Start right away... give her an hour or so before you release her, then send her to her room.'

'Can't we have a feel of her?' whined Nigel. 'You did promise.'

'Oh, very well, but only fingers.'

'Or tongues?'

'Maybe tongues. Try rimming her anus.'

Amelie was left in bondage, unable to see who was licking and touching her, but feeling them everywhere, finding her nipples, stroking her clitoris, then tongues lapping at her most private places. She sensed Mervin was watching, then heard him say, 'Enough. Get to work, Humphrey.'

Amelie tensed, but could not escape the object the valet started to slide into her anus. It was a similar sensation to when Mervin stuck his fingers in, but it felt icy cold. Humphrey left it there for a moment, then worked it in deeper. It was just short of painful. He withdrew it and replaced it with a larger one. Then several others, each bigger than the last, were worked in till she became used to the penetration.

'Not yet as big as a man's cock,' the valet said cheerfully. 'You'll like that, deary, especially his lordship's. He has a fine weapon, as you already know.'

'And do you?' she retorted.

'Of course, pet. What do you think he does on wintry nights when there's no cunt available?'

'He uses you,' she hissed, unbelieving yet having to accept it.

'That's right. Now then, here's the last and largest. If you can take it and keep it in, then we're getting somewhere,' he said, and plunged another rubber dildo into her darkness. Amelie gasped, resisted, then surrendered. It was easier that way.

'I want to go to the lavatory,' she said, the pressure on her bladder becoming unbearable.

'Sorry. Can't untie you yet.'

'Do it there,' Mervin ordered. 'I want to see you pass water.'

'I can't... I've never... not in front of someone else,' she protested, but the urge to relax her sphincter was becoming uncontrollable.

'Do it,' Mervin insisted and pressed a hand into the small of her back, adding to the pressure existing in her full bladder.

She could do nothing but let go, feeling his hand on her and the dildo in her rectum and hearing her urine trickle to the floor and feeling no shame, only enormous relief.

The studio was vast and cluttered and had a huge north-facing skylight. There were various props that might be used for backgrounds – curtains, pitchers and throne-like chairs, animal skins and cupboards overflowing with stage costumes. Mirrors hung on the whitewashed walls between framed and unframed paintings. There were Indian vases and chalices set with polished gemstones, along with necklaces, bangles, headdresses and exotic items from all over the world.

This artists' den was situated on the top floor of a rambling house near the Chelsea Embankment bought with the Bessborough money. Ralph always occupied it when in England, seldom returning to the family seat.

Much as he loved Kelston Towers, his brother's lifestyle was anathema to him. They had always disagreed on most issues and time did nothing to promote concord between them. In spite of their father's will, Mervin kept him short of money, another proof of his power. But Ralph was becoming a successful artist. Many were the rich and famous who now entered the studio, wanting to sit for their portraits. A recent exhibition in a top London gallery had given him valuable press coverage, and well-known hostesses were beginning to lionise him at their parties.

Ralph revelled in work, an almost endless stream of ideas flooding his brain. He was at the moment engaged on a Biblical epic, commissioned by a wealthy industrialist who wanted it to grace his Manchester boardroom. It featured Salome with the head of John the Baptist on a silver platter. The stepdaughter of King Herod was, in reality, a local whore who had not yet lost her looks due to the ravages of her profession. She was eighteen, with creamy olive skin, raven hair and black eyes and she moved divinely. Her name was Maggie.

Such a waste, Ralph mourned. He dipped his brush into a puddle of oil paint daubed on the palette held on his thumb, and added a touch to Maggie's sensual lips. She really did pose awfully well, and with her mouth tight shut, for she had a most pronounced Cockney accent, her language strident and foul, straight from the gutter, she could look positively aristocratic. A natural, she took up graceful positions whenever and wherever. She was seated on a divan with the plaster head between her thighs, gazing down at the holy man's face with almost drooling sexuality.

'The industrialist is going to love this,' Ralph remarked, concentrating on the inky bush that could be glimpsed at Maggie's fork. 'He'll pass it off as art.'

'Dirty old bugger!' Maggie vouchsafed, though continuing to hold the pose. 'I'll bet 'ee'll stand in front of it in 'is posh office and bring 'imself off. And I'm supplyin' him with wank material for the pittance you're payin' me! It'd cost 'im a mint to 'ave me do it for 'im.'

Her crude words uttered in that guttural voice sent the blood coursing hotly through Ralph. He'd had her before, and never met a harlot so able to feign passion as she did, almost convincing him she was enjoying having his cock in her cunt. He knew she wasn't. Like the majority of prostitutes she did it for money, not lust. He didn't care. The more he looked at her, the more difficult it became to concentrate on Princess Salome. He was distinctly uncomfortable in the groin area. His testicles were tight and his cock hard. He wore a loose, paint smeared smock and baggy trousers, but even so he kept himself concealed behind the easel supporting the huge canvas on which he was featuring his model life-sized. There was no way he wanted Maggie to see and take advantage of his need to ejaculate.

That's all it was, he knew. He had never yet been in love and wondered if the poets were mistaken when they praised that state of being. All he had ever known was the satisfaction of the senses that began at puberty, first with masturbation, and then through a succession of maids, shop-girls, whores and artists' models, all willing to have him penetrate them if he paid enough for the privilege.

Maggie switched her gaze from John's severed head to Ralph, amusement in her eyes. 'Ain't it time for a rest, yet? I'm bloody stiff sitting like this, and I've got a draught up me minge.'

'I should have thought you'd be used to that,'· he commented acidly, but could not keep from staring at the dark mystery of her crotch, longing to touch it. Instead, he dabbed a smear of ebony black on the exact spot belonging to Salome.

But this brought no relief. He wanted to stroke Maggie there, to open her and expose the deep pink flesh within, stroke the swollen stem of her nubbin, bare its head and make her lose control. He wanted her to writhe against his finger, rub herself up and down, sob her climax into his mouth, lose herself in his caresses, and then impale her body on his rampant prick.

He flung down his brush and laid aside the palette. It was no use. He'd not be able to continue work until he'd poured his libation into her, dirty little scrubber that she was!

'All right, Maggie,' he said, and approached the divan, unbuttoning as he went. 'You shall have your rest and a cup of tea, but see to this for me first.' And he thrust his cock into her hand.

She held him off for a moment, saying, 'I'll want an extra quid.'

'All right, anything you say, just get on with it,' he groaned, and nearly came as Maggie seized his swollen penis and started to massage it.

He touched her between the thighs and felt her yield a little to allow his finger in. She was wet there and smelled strong, a potpourri of female essences – sweat, pussy-juice and cheap perfume. Such odours roused him to fever pitch. He tumbled her onto her back and she opened her legs wide, dark-fringed snatch like a fissure eager to swallow him whole. He knew fear, but was overwhelmed by desire, the need in his throbbing cock blinding him to all else – the danger of disease, of blackmail and scandal – none of it mattered except this driving urge to rid himself of his seed.

'Come on then, 'andsome,' Maggie urged. 'Put in yer plonker and get it over with.'

Ralph knelt over her, positioned between her legs, then guided his rock-hard cock, pushing the head into the slit that parted for him. The feeling was exquisite. He forgot everything except the compulsion to get in as far as he could, till his pubic hair brushed hers and the frantic drive towards completion made him blind and deaf to reason, control, decency or commonsense.

'Lovely, lovely,' he sighed, the feeling building up in his

loins. 'Oh, Maggie, you little beauty!'

He meant it, fired by animal lust that would make him swear any vow, promise her the moon, forget she was a streetwalker. Just for those moments she embodied womanhood. She was deified, and he worshipped her. He closed his eyes and thought of nothing but his dick in the tight grip of her body, the warmth, the wetness, the pre-orgasmic spasms. His glans rubbed against the hot lining of her sheath. She was still tight there, not yet stretched by birthing and supplying a channel for dozens of punters. Perhaps he should make her his mistress, take her into keeping, spurn other women and cleave to her alone?

'Hurry up, darlin', I'm dying of thirst 'ere,' she said, breaking the spell as she wriggled impatiently.

The pressure in his testicles increased, heralding the approaching crisis. His hips pumped automatically. Nothing would stop him now, hell-bent on reaching that rapturous release. His thigh muscles tightened and it came like a tidal wave, his fluid shooting from him in a series of spurts, the sensation acutely pleasurable. Contractions made his cock jerk, and then it was over. He wanted to slump down on her and sleep, but Maggie would have none of it. She squirmed out from under him, grabbed up a paint-smeared rag and jammed it between her thighs.

'Messy sod,' she grumbled. 'That's the trouble with you men... all that spunk. Ugh! Where's me cuppa!'

Ralph sat up, completely recovered from the madness of a few seconds ago. His cock was flaccid and sticky. Not a pretty sight. Neither was Maggie, once more the trollop not the beloved. Like most men, once he'd had it he could have thrown his hat at it.

Maggie sashayed across to the pot-bellied stove that warmed the studio. A kettle was almost permanently positioned on its cast iron lid. She topped up the enamelled teapot, gave it a swirl and poured herself a cupful, then added milk and several heaped teaspoons of sugar. She fished about among the pile of clothing she'd left on a chair and strolled back to the divan.

'I found this in the 'all when I come in,' she said, handing him an envelope. 'The postman must 'ave delivered it.'

Ralph, back to normal and angry because she had not served him tea, snatched it from her. It was addressed to him and he ripped it open and drew out a single sheet of paper, his eyes narrowing as he recognised the crest. The words seemed to leap from the paper. Millicent was in trouble. He was certain it was something to do with Mervin. And who was this mysterious Amelie Aston?

He replaced the letter and put it in his pocket. 'Let's get as much done as we can while the light lasts,' he said to Maggie. 'No work for you tomorrow. I'm going home for a few days.'

Amelie's world had turned upside down. The night of the show was dreamlike, a strange affair, during which she made a rapid excursion into adulthood. She would never be the same again, and this was not entirely due to the treatment she'd received in Mervin's hands. She also discovered a great deal about herself.

Humphrey had conducted her to her room, once the butt plugs had been removed after an hour's endurance. There she fell into bed, exhausted, aware that the valet had made sure she was comfortable. Since then there had been no reference to the incident. She remained with Millicent who gradually recovered, and after the weekend was over and the guests departed, they had gone shopping, driven to Bath in the coach and there forgetting their problems in the milliners, dress and shoe shops. Generous to a fault, Millicent insisted on Amelie being kitted out as a young lady, not a companion. It seemed that she looked upon Amelie as the sister she had longed for but never had. It was touching, and Amelie did not take advantage, reluctant to accept her offer, though no money changed hands. The Bessboroughs had an account in the majority of major shops.

Mervin had gone to ground, or so it appeared, busying himself with the Kemble Hunt, out chasing foxes all day and drinking far into the night with other equestrian sportsmen. It was a blessed relief and, though the soreness in her anus and from the stripes he had laid on her tender flesh were a constant reminder, she was happy to hide away with Millicent. They talked girlish talk and read poetry aloud, sat in the sunshine, occupying a secluded nook near the terrace, and exchanged intimate confessions. Neither had much to relate, though Amelie began to understand Millicent's fear of her brother. Apparently she, too, had been subjected to his domination, but knowing no difference, submitted to what she considered to be a brother's right.

'I know nothing of what happens when a couple marries, do you?' Millicent said one morning a few days later, looking up from her embroidery. She was blushing, the sunlight playing over her flawless skin and curling brunette hair.

'When they are alone, you mean?' Amelie sat on a stone bench, admiring her surroundings of flowerbeds and stone pots where daffodils where appearing, heralding the spring. 'I know little, being reared in a vicarage. Anyway, it's not the kind of thing ladies think about, let alone put into words.'

'So we are expected to go to the marriage bed in complete ignorance? That's not fair,' Millicent grumbled, jabbing the needle through the canvas stretched over a small round frame. The light flashed on it, as if it were a tiny dagger.

Amelie did not answer straight away. She was feeling guilty, remembering her own games played by herself, when she teased the little tyrant that nestled between her lower lips, rousing it till she attained bliss. She was certain this had something to do with mating, and was hot to find out. Every man she had encountered so far, intent on wooing her, had demonstrated that he possessed a large, stiff organ, which it seemed he was intent on sinking inside her, or have her rub it for him, or take it into her mouth. But she could not say this to Millicent, not yet.

However, curiosity getting the better of her, she whispered, 'Don't you caress yourself?'

Millicent raised her eyes from the flower she was creating from silk thread. 'How do you mean?' she said.

Oh dear, Amelie thought, wishing she had never raised the subject. 'Well, I mean... don't you sometimes touch yourself down there, between the legs? It's nice to run one's fingers through one's bush, then part the crack and find that which is within.'

Millicent frowned slightly. 'Oh no, I don't do that; Nanny told me that nice girls never touch themselves there,' she said primly.

'It's all right, I'm sure. There is such pleasure in it that I can't believe it to be wrong.' Then Amelie took a deep breath and added, 'Would you like me to show you?'

'I'm not sure, it sounds rude,' Millicent countered, but she laid aside her sewing and was leaning forward, staring at Amelie intently.

As if possessed by something other than herself, Amelie raised her skirt and petticoats and leaned against the back of the bench, her hips thrust forward, her legs parted. One of her hands crept down and found the wide hem of her drawers, seeking a point where her fork divided. She found the vital spot and pressed on it for a second, then unable to resist, pushed the knickers aside and exposed her foxy triangle. She was aware of Millicent seated opposite her but leaning closer, her lips parted, face flushed, eyes keen.

Amelie continued to play with her swollen nodule. Her labial wings were engorged, and moisture seeped from her virginal opening. She pressed down with her middle finger, wetting the tip and drawing it back and up, skimming over her crack and landing on her clitoris. Her heart was beating so hard she was sure it could be heard, and she tipped back her head, the warm sunshine on her face reflecting the heat in her pussy. Holding her knickers open with her left hand she drew a circle round her bud, hesitated, teased it, patted and vibrated it. A mewling sound came from Millicent's throat.

Amelie stopped, lifted her head and stared at her. It was hard to keep her finger still, or stop her hips from writhing, mad for contact with that seat of all delight – her nubbin. 'You want to see more?' she asked Millicent huskily.

'Oh yes, if you don't mind.'

Mind? There was nothing Amelie wanted so much as to have her friend watch her reach her climax. She started to massage her pink folds again, concentrating on the hard clit that resembled a shimmering pearl. 'Sometimes I make it last for ages,' she said, her breathing ragged. 'At others I do it quickly, and then go straight on to have another, and another. But today... ah, today, my dear friend, I can't hold back. I'm too excited by having you watch me.'

'I see,' Millicent said, moving ever closer till she was kneeling between Amelie's legs and staring intently at her crotch.

'I usually try not to touch the tip too much if I want it to take a long time,' Amelie murmured, while spasms began within her belly and it was impossible to hold back. She lifted her pelvis and moaned, 'Oh, I can't stop it... oh... ohh...'

The orgasm was violent, a plunge into almost agonising pleasure. Her anus ached in unison and the bruises left by Mervin throbbed. This added to the intensity. She jerked and rubbed herself frantically, then peace descended and she returned from that place which resembled an electrical storm.

'Oh, my goodness, are you all right?' Millicent said, rising and leaning over her solicitously. 'Are you ill? Is it convulsions?'

Amelie laughed, she felt cheerful now and in the mood for talking. 'I've just had the most amazing sensation, and it happens every time I do what I've just done. I rise to the stars. My whole body tingles, and as for my privates... well, it's like a miracle taking place down there. I'll teach you, if you like.'

Millicent shrank back. 'Oh no... I don't think I want to learn,' she stammered, but perspiration beaded her brow and she moved uncomfortably, as if unwillingly aroused by the sight of Amelie masturbating.

Then Dulcie appeared around a corner of the pergola and Amelie covered her legs with her skirt. The maid looked flushed and breathless, as if something unusual had happened.

'Oh, there you are, my lady,' she said. 'News, news. The post-boy has just cycled over with a telegram. The master read it and then sent the gig to the station to pick up your brother, Lord Ralph. Apparently he's arriving unexpectedly, and his lordship looked none too pleased.'

All three females exchanged worried glances, then, 'This is in answer to your letter, Amelie,' Millicent said, and despite the healthy colour she had acquired outdoors, her face went pale. 'Oh dear, I hope Ralph doesn't tell Mervin that you wrote to him.'

'So do I,' Amelie said fervently, visualising the punishment she would receive if her dominating master knew the truth.

Chapter Six

He was the most attractive man Amelie had ever met. She walked into the drawing room behind Millicent and saw him immediately, even before he leapt forward and embraced his sister. His similarity to Mervin told her who he was – Ralph Bessborough. He eclipsed his brother in looks and she momentarily forgot his lordship was present.

Ralph had a mane of nut-brown ringlets and a neatly clipped beard. His face was strong, mirroring the underlying currents of passion that fired his genius. He was broad-shouldered and tall, with chiselled features and deep-set blue eyes beneath arched brows.

'Ralph!' Millicent exclaimed, face lighting up with joy.

'I thought it was time I dropped down to see if you were all alive and kicking,' Ralph said, catching her in a bear hug, but eyeing Amelie the while.

'You left it long enough,' Mervin said sarcastically. 'To what do we now owe the singular honour of this visit? Run out of funds, have you?'

'Not at all,' Ralph answered, cool as ice. 'Actually, I'm doing rather well. Paintings selling like hot cakes.'

'Indeed, there's no accounting for taste,' Mervin responded nastily.

'Oh really, give him some credit for talent,' put in Millicent.

Ralph laughed and raised her hands to his lips, kissing them fondly. 'Don't worry, dearest. He's a grumpy old bear. Now, why don't you introduce me to your charming friend?' He nodded towards Amelie.

'She is no friend, merely our sister's companion… a paid post and she's the ward of the Reverend Joseph

Thacker,' Mervin interjected, making sure there was no mistaking Amelie's inferior station.

Ralph's eyes twinkled as he smiled at her. 'Charmed to meet you,' he said, and took her hand. He made her feel she was the only person of interest anywhere around, and she hoped his sincerity was without question. 'May I know your name?'

'Amelie Aston,' she replied, her voice strong and clear. She was not shy with him. It was as if they were already acquainted – sometime, somewhere, not necessarily on this planet.

'"Well met by moonlight, proud Titania,"' he quipped, misquoting Shakespeare.

'Oh, Ralph, how absurd!' Millicent cried, clapping her hands with glee. Amelie had never seen her so animated. 'It's daylight, not moonlight. Come, recount your adventures. Where have you been?'

'I'll tell you, but how about some refreshments?' Ralph said, addressing his brother. 'Ring for that old reprobate, Brock, and have him send in some tea and cake. I'm famished. The restaurant car from Paddington to Bath only served dried-up sandwiches, and Gifford was late arriving in the gig to pick me up, so I missed luncheon here.'

Mervin, though looking disgruntled, tugged at the bell-pull near the fireplace, saying, 'You'll have to amuse yourself. I'm out to dinner tonight and leading the Hunt early tomorrow morning.'

'No problem, I've my sister to keep me company,' Ralph said, smiling at her and slipping an arm about her waist. 'We've lots of catching up to do. Have I told you about my apartment in Montmartre on the Left Bank? That's in Paris and all we Bohemians live there.'

'What are Bohemians?' Millicent asked eagerly, as Brock appeared with catlike tread to receive his instructions, then equally silently take his departure.

Mervin answered for his brother. 'They are riffraff,' he

92

snarled. 'The word means gypsy, but it has come to include artists, writers, musicians, anyone who sets the social conventions aside. Not the kind of people I would want meeting my sister. I hope you feel the same, Ralph.'

Ralph threw him a shrewd glance, and said, 'Well, actually, I don't. Some of my best friends are Bohemians. So much less stuffy than the English upper classes. I wouldn't hesitate to introduce Millicent or Miss Aston to them.'

'Not if I have anything to do with it,' Mervin growled, and an uneasy silence prevailed, broken by a discreet knock and then the entrance of a footman carrying in the tea things. A maid followed with a silver cake basket loaded with some of the cook's finest confectionery.

'Ah, Dundee Cake, how splendid!' Ralph said, helping himself to a slice. 'I've sometimes dreamed of this when in my garret in France or my studio in Chelsea,' and he winked across at Amelie.

'Do you employ models?' Millicent asked shyly, balancing a delicate porcelain cup in one hand.

'We won't discuss that,' said Mervin flatly. 'I'm sure no one wants to hear about Ralph's exploits among the shady ladies of Soho or the Latin Quarter.'

'I do,' she said, all round-eyed innocence.

'Not now, Millicent,' he replied, his face set in stern lines.

He reminded Amelie of her godfather; beneath this front of respectability there lurked a prurient interest. There was little doubt that Mervin knew all there was to know about these women. Had been there, done that, and was merely taunting his brother and trying to make him feel unworthy. But he was not succeeding. Ralph was unmoved, relishing the rich fruitcake, holding out his cup for a refill, and smiling encouragingly at Millicent.

'How long are you staying?' she wanted to know.

'Not too long,' he said, and glanced at his scowling brother. 'I have a commission to complete. But I wanted to see if you were better, Millicent. Last time I was here you were very poorly.'

'She is subject to hysteria,' Mervin said, brushing aside her protests. 'I am considering sending her to a doctor in London who specialises in women's complaints of a similar nature. She is refusing a very tempting offer of marriage from Lord Nigel Balfour.'

Ralph frowned, then laughed. 'Old Piggy Balfour! Is he still trying to find a wife?'

Amelie wanted to giggle, and Millicent looked considerably relieved. Mervin, however, decided to take this as a personal insult. 'He's a fine man and comes from one of the very best families,' he declared, a thick vein appearing in the middle of his forehead, a sure sign that he was in a rage. 'I have given my consent, but our foolish sister declines.'

'Can't say I blame her,' Ralph interjected, keeping his tone light, but Amelie could see he was concerned.

'Oh?' Mervin replied. 'I rather hoped you'd back me up.'

'I think she is old enough to know her own mind.'

'You forget, and so it seems does she, that the authority invested in me allows that I make decisions of such an important nature. Our father would have done so, had he been alive today.'

Amelie sensed the ebb and flow of old disagreements, jealousy and resentment. Had these brothers ever liked one another? And there was poor Millicent caught in the crossfire. For her own part she was torn; her good side favoured Ralph, but the dark skein of sexuality that Mervin had unravelled within her cleaved to him.

'I beg to differ,' Ralph said, placing his cup on the low table. 'Papa would never have forced Nigel on her.'

This started an argument that rattled back and forth and seemed set to go on for ages, but Mervin suddenly pushed back his chair and rose, saying impatiently, 'I've business to attend to. This estate doesn't run itself, you know. We'll talk further tomorrow,' and with that he took himself off.

'Oh, Ralph, it's wonderful to see you, I feel better already,' Millicent cried. 'You'll help me, won't you? He has threatened to have me pronounced insane if I continue to be ill and refuse Nigel.'

She began to cry and Ralph pulled out his handkerchief and handed it over, saying, 'He can't do that, dearest. No doctor would agree.'

'But it is true that I do suffer from nervousness, insomnia, heaviness in the stomach, muscular spasms and wild dreams of a... dare I say it... bodily nature,' Millicent said, wringing her hands in her lap and blushing profusely.

Ralph smiled at her tenderly, disengaged her restless hands and held them in his own. 'You need to get away from Mervin and this house. Gay surroundings and light-hearted company are what is required. There's little wrong with you physically, but you are being stifled by Mervin.'

'Nigel offers me a means of escape.'

'You'd simply exchange one prison for another, and I can't imagine that he would know how to bring you to completion.'

Millicent raised her tearstained face to his and said, 'I don't know what you mean by that. No one has ever talked to me about marital intercourse, except perhaps Amelie... and then only a little. She is a virgin, too.'

Ralph cut to Amelie and the look in his eyes made her tingle. 'I suggest you go and rest, Millicent,' he said. 'I'd like to chat with Miss Aston and get her opinion about Mervin's treatment of you.'

To be invited to walk in the garden with this personable young man was an unexpected treat. Amelie refused a parasol, the brim of her straw hat enough. She envied the country women their sun-kissed complexions, even though it was the fashion for ladies of quality to remain pale, thus insuring that no one mistook them for members of the working class.

'You'll get freckles like me, miss,' Dulcie had warned as she helped Millicent out of her dress and corsets and settled her in bed for an afternoon nap. Amelie ignored the maid, who said this every time she set foot outdoors.

Strolling along in Ralph's company, she gave him a sidelong glance. His clothing was unconventional; a felt hat with a big brim set at a jaunty angle, a black velvet jacket and red plaid trousers, a canary yellow waistcoat, a shirt with a soft collar and a flowing silk cravat. He was quite lovely, she thought, and wanted to touch him, to trace over his sensual lips, stroke his chest, dip into the gap between the button holes, then down, down to where his trousers fastened over a very promising bulge. Would it get bigger if he kissed her?

Neither spoke as they took a path between lush rhododendron bushes, heavy with pink, white or pale blue blossoms that languished in the embrace of shiny dark green foliage. There was an exhilarating smell in the air; damp soil and newly mown grass, herbs and fertiliser, all combining to form a rich brew that was entirely untamed and earthy. It affected Amelie, filling her with the urge to fling herself down in some secluded glade and have Ralph show her all the things she knew she was missing out on – sex between a man and woman – sex with which Mervin had tantalised her without performing the act. Sex, without the addition of butt-plugs or anal penetration or pain – simple and straightforward, the sex that expressed the love between a couple and might, eventually, create another human being to enhance their lives.

'I never expected to find someone like you buried in the country,' Ralph said, holding back a branch so she might pass.

'And what is so extraordinary about me?' Amelie asked, her lips curving in a pleased smile.

'When I read your note and you said you were Millicent's companion, I visualised an old maid with spectacles and greying hair, not a beauty with emerald

96

eyes and curls the colour of burnished chestnuts. What, in the name of all that's holy are you doing here?'

'I'm just that… Lady Millicent's companion and the vicar's goddaughter. He found me this position.'

'How could he bear to lose such a treasure?' He cupped her elbow in one hand, helping her over a slippery bit.

'If you only knew,' she murmured mischievously. If this was flirting, then she was really enjoying it. 'I may be a virgin but I'm not entirely inexperienced. He feared for the virtue of his sons, Obediah and Caleb, but it was they who were trying to seduce me, not the other way round.'

'Tell me more,' Ralph urged, seating himself on a fallen tree trunk and patting the space beside him.

She took it, wondering how much of the tale to tell, unwilling to jeopardise her place with Millicent. Should she shock Ralph too much, then he might have her dismissed, and this would be so upsetting for that tender lady who now looked upon her as her best friend. However, he did not give the appearance of one who was easily shocked; a man of the world, no doubt, much travelled and knowledgeable.

'Well… I'd known for some time that they admired me… at least, I was sure Obediah did,' she said slowly, pleating her striped skirt over and over, cream crossing pink. 'They were away at college much of the time, but on the last occasion when they were home, having obtained their degrees and considering careers, Obediah sat by me in church on a Sunday and sneaked a hand up under my petticoats.'

Ralph was staring at her, half-smiling, and she felt the brush of his knee against hers on the log. Her bud quivered. 'Did he, by thunder? And what did you do?'

He was so encouraging that she longed to pour out the whole story. She went hot all over, from her toes to the roots of her hair, but it was just too tempting to put into words the things Obediah had done, and her response to it. She was alarmed to discover that she even wanted to tell Ralph that she frequently played with herself.

'I didn't stop him. It was impossible for the service had begun. His father was in the pulpit and I didn't want to make a fuss.'

'Is that the only reason?' Ralph asked, and rested an arm across her shoulders in what could have been a friendly gesture, but there was a sudden tension about him and her heart started to thump.

'I was stunned,' she returned swiftly.

'And that's all?'

She hung her head and replied, 'No, that isn't all. I felt his hand on my knee, then higher, stroking the inside of my thigh.'

'Like this?' Ralph enquired, and dipped under her skirt, smoothed her leg, found the silky skin just below her fork, passed the opening in her knickers and then toyed with her russet pubic hair.

Her clit pulsed and her nipples rose like stones, pressing against her constricting bodice. She wanted to be free of clothing, rolling naked on the grass with Ralph. 'Yes, yes... it was like that,' she squeaked.

'And you didn't want to stop him?' Ralph murmured, and continued his exploration, parting her rapidly moistening lower lips and rubbing the ripening bud between. 'You knew all about your nubbin and bringing yourself off. Isn't this so?'

'Oh, sir... I beg you to stop,' she gasped with little conviction.

Ralph paused, but did not take his hand away. 'Did you say this to Obediah?' he whispered.

'I couldn't speak... the sermon was in progress.'

'That's a lame excuse,' he murmured, his breath on her lobe making her shiver, and when he inserted his tongue-tip in her ear she almost came against his finger.

'It's true,' she protested, attempting to oust him and close her legs. He did not let go. 'You've no idea how straight-laced they are in Kemble.'

'Oh yes I have. Don't forget I was brought up here and couldn't wait to get away. You should come to London, Miss Aston... travel broadens the mind, so they say.'

It seemed absurd for him to address her by her surname when his hand was cupping her mound and his finger pressed to her bud, but then conventions had to be maintained and it would not be polite for her employer's brother to call her Amelie; even though he was handling her with utmost intimacy; even though she longed for his kisses and for him to penetrated her with his erect cock.

'I'd love to. B-Bath is the only city I have v-visited,' she managed to stammer.

Oh, were it not such a golden day he might have been easier to resist, but to be there with him in this green copse, with the birds singing and a gentle breeze blowing and a spread of daisy-starred meadow beyond was all conspiring to rob her of her virtue. It was too romantic, and her head was spinning.

'Perhaps I can organise a trip for Millicent, and then you would be able to accompany her,' Ralph suggested, trailing nibbling kisses down the side of her throat, leaving her weak in the knees.

'Will Lord Bessborough allow this?' she managed to ask, her breasts aching and her nipples twin points of fire. She could not help squirming against his finger, urging him to rub her.

'Maybe, if I can convince him that she will be staying in the town house, with servants spying on her every movement,' he replied, then removed his hand from her private place and stood up, drawing her with him. 'There's no way he'll allow her to reside with me.'

Disappointment flooded through her. Was this it, then? Had he, like all the rest of the so-called 'gentlemen' merely gratified his curiosity about her?

But Ralph hauled her against him, the pressure of his penis apparent, even through his trousers and her layers of clothing. He seized the back of her neck in steely fingers, bent his head and captured her lips. His tongue thrust between her teeth, fleshy and smooth, caressing the inside of her mouth, and his other hand toyed with each uplifted breast in turn.

Amelie went limp in his arms, her tongue mingling with his in a dance of desire. He tasted wonderful, his breath clean and wholesome with just the tiniest trace of Havana cigars. This proclaimed him to be a wealthy man, for they were expensive imports and only the chosen few could afford to buy them. It added to that feeling she had of him being someone special. His beard, too, was a novelty, silky smooth as it brushed her cheek. She wound her arms round his neck and buried her fingers in his long curls. Yet she could not succumb to him lest he get her with child, the worst of fates for any unmarried woman, disastrous for someone like her. She had feared this when with Mervin, grateful when he left her vagina unassailed.

Ralph leaned her back against the bole of a tree and his tongue darted in and out of her mouth, his hands cradling the roundness of her breasts, nipples chafed by her bodice. 'My dear girl, what are we to do about this?' he murmured. 'I want you beyond endurance.'

He opened the buttons of her dress, all the way down the front, pushing aside her chemise and baring one pebble-hard teat, sucking and biting it with a fierce need that numbed her mind. The dell was hot with the sun high above the trees, and her senses swam in that golden glow. She wanted to sink to the forest floor with him and abandon herself. What did considerations like pregnancy, decency and reputation matter? Ralph would look after her, wouldn't he? She refused to believe he was just another rake out to rob her of her virtue and then cast her aside.

He raised his head, staring into her eyes intently, and then slid his hands round to her bottom, gripping each buttock and squeezing. 'Ouch!' she exclaimed, pain shooting through her, the skin still bruised and sore.

He stopped, frowned and said, 'What's the matter?'

'It's nothing... nothing at all,' she replied, flustered.

'You had better tell me,' he insisted and spun her round, then before she could prevent him whipped up her skirts and pulled down her knickers, displaying the reddish stripes that had not yet faded. 'Who did this to you?' he demanded.

'It's all right... nothing, really?'

'Was it Mervin?' he interrupted, refusing to be put off.

She looked down, unable to meet his eyes, and her face was flushed. She did not know how to handle the situation, fearing to increase the bad blood between the brothers. Yet she could not lie to Ralph, sure he would see through any fabrication.

'Lord Bessborough is my master,' she said. 'He is within his rights to chastise me if I displease him.'

'What rot!' Ralph said crisply, and his hands came up to hold her round the waist with encouraging gentleness. 'You're in his employ, that's all, isn't it? *Isn't it*?' he repeated loudly.

'Yes, yes.' She wished she had never started the conversation.

'Don't lie to me. I know my brother and his peculiarities. Has he been forcing you to take part in some of his so-called entertainments put on for his disreputable cronies, including Piggy Balfour?'

'There was one occasion not long ago,' she confessed.

He let her go and took to pacing the glade, driving his right fist into his left palm 'I guessed as much,' he raged. 'Things haven't changed during my absence. He's as decadent as ever. Has he seduced you?'

'No, I'm still a virgin.'

Ralph stood stock-still before her. 'What else has he done?'

'He has had his valet place dildos in my most secret place, in order to stretch me.'

Now Ralph's eyes were like an Arctic sea and his face

was set in lines that made him look older, more formidable and masterful. His ancestry shone through and there was no mistaking him for other than a Bessborough.

'Humphrey, that pervert! So, he does Mervin's dirty work for him, does he? Tell me the truth, Amelie... have they hurt Millicent?'

She did not know what to say. She had not seen Mervin strike his sister, but guessed by her absolute terror of him that it had quite likely happened. 'Not in my sight,' she whispered. 'He threatens her, though, and Dulcie, that's her maid, has told me that he sometimes puts her across his knee and spanks her.'

Ralph's face sobered and he let her go, merely holding her hand. 'He wants her to marry Nigel, and has threatened her with an asylum,' he declared forcibly. 'She's not insane She needs to be loved by the right man, her body awakened to passion and those passions fulfilled. That's all that ails her, I'm sure of it.'

'I'll do all I can to help,' Amelie promised, wanting him to continue caressing her, but he now seemed absorbed in his sister's predicament.

His attention reverted to her and his eyes softened as they met hers. 'I know you will, Amelie, and, oh my dear, if you could only see your way clear to love me... just a very little. I'm no saint and have had women galore, but have never met anyone like you. Say you'll think about it.'

'Oh, Ralph, I have no need to give it thought,' she sighed, melting into his embrace once more.

Then they both froze. There was a rustling in the bushes. A bird? An animal? Ralph swore and leapt in the direction of the sound. He crashed through the undergrowth and disappeared from sight. She wanted to dash after him, but was undecided what to do. He returned very shortly, and his eyes were dangerous icy spears.

'It was that damned valet spying on us,' he shouted. 'I saw him, cycling down the path as if the hounds of hell were after him, as they assuredly would have been had I been able to lay hands on him. He must have followed us on his bicycle, obeying orders perhaps, or just seeing what he could see in order to ingratiate himself with Mervin. The man is a pest! My brother's toady, unprincipled and greedy!'

Amelie's desire died as surely as if someone had thrown a bucket of cold water over her. Fear took its place. Supposing Humphrey tittle-tattled to Mervin? She readjusted her clothing and replaced her hat.

'We had best return,' she said.

'I suppose so,' he answered reluctantly, then kissed her cheek. 'I meant what I said, Amelie. You are a lovely girl and I would be proud to call you mine. We'll speak of it later. Meanwhile, let us go back and try to find out what mischief Humphrey is concocting.'

Millicent had been too excited to sleep. Ralph's coming was like a breath of fresh air. He had always been her champion, a little older than she, standing between her and Mervin, protecting her. The sunshine slanted through a gap in the curtains and she propped herself up on one elbow in bed and scanned the newspaper he'd bought on Bath station. Amongst general news, it contained snippets of information about what was happening in that Queen City of the West – plays being performed at the theatre, concerts in the Pump Room, and lectures given in the Assembly Rooms.

One piece caught her attention. It was an article about a certain Professor Macbain, who was a student of the teachings of the late Friedrich Anton Mesmer. This Frenchman who, so the journalist wrote, had lived from 1733 to 1815, had been renowned for his work with agitated females whom he claimed to have cured of hysterics by the use of 'magnetised water' and his ability to put them in a trancelike state. Macbain was coming to Bath, it seemed, and demonstrating his powers in a private house near Pultney Bridge. He was only appearing for one evening, and those interested could apply for tickets for which a fee would be charged.

Could he cure me? Millicent wondered, hope springing up in her breast. Is there any way I can stop feeling so disturbed? Oh, if only Mervin would let me go and see this professor. I must try to convince him that if I am made better, then I may consider marrying Nigel.

By the time Ralph and Amelie returned, she had made up her mind that she simply must see Macbain, and Ralph, after reading the article, nodded in agreement. He would put in a word too, and persuade Mervin on this course of action. Millicent felt so much better, with Ralph there and Amelie, though she had the feeling that something had happened during their walk and that they were keeping it from her. But nothing could cloud her enjoyment of their company and they sat on the terrace and were served tea, with sandwiches filled with wafer thin ham and watercress, and iced fancies. It was most civilised and she wished it could always be so, with Mervin gainfully occupied elsewhere, not spoiling everything with his scowls and sarcasm and filthy moods. Why couldn't Ralph have been the eldest and heir, instead of him?

'I've heard of Mesmer, of course,' Ralph said, in his shirtsleeves as they were all being so casual and eating alfresco. 'His unconventional methods caused an uproar in his lifetime. Since he was not a qualified physician his enemies dubbed him a charlatan and accused him of stirring up unclean passions in his female patients.'

'I don't care, I want to see his disciple, this John Macbain,' Millicent said stubbornly. 'I'm so weary of being listless and unhappy and discontented. I shall never find a husband of my choice like this, but would rather stay single to the end of my days than marry Nigel.'

She could not find words to express her inner turmoil. Ever since Amelie demonstrated the way in which she toyed with her secret parts, Millicent had ached to do it

104

too, but her early indoctrination by nanny was too strong. She simply couldn't. Yet, somewhere deep down, she was aware that such frustration was the root cause of all her woes. It just wasn't fair!

'When will he be in Bath?' Ralph asked.

'Next week. Oh, Ralph, can't you take me… and Amelie, too?'

'I can't. Must get back to London. If Mervin, agrees, and I've a feeling he will if only to get you to accept Nigel, then I expect he'll escort you to Pultney Bridge and visit his club while you are at the lecture. I'll see what I can do.'

It was a shock to be sitting in one's room after stripping to stays, chemise and drawers and suddenly attacked from behind, a blanket thrown over one's head and then lifted bodily and transported to an unknown destination. Amelia had been quietly contemplating the pleasant evening spent with Millicent and her brother. There was no warning of storm clouds to come, but here she was being roughly manhandled.

'Who are you?' she shouted, her voice muffled by the scratchy blanket. 'I'll scream and scream if you don't put me down!'

No one answered, but within seconds she heard the squeak of an opening door and was set on her feet. Her covering was removed and she blinked in the lamplight that illumined the old schoolroom where once the young Bessboroughs had received education. And there was Mervin, seated at the teacher's desk on a low platform at the head of the room, wearing a black gown and a mortarboard. There were benches and tables once occupied by pupils trembling in fear of that figure of authority who ruled the classroom.

'Good evening, Miss Aston,' he said, holding a ruler in one hand and gently tapping it on the wooden surface before him.

'I thought you were at a dinner party,' she returned, refusing to be intimidated.

'I beg your pardon,' he replied, and rapped the desk with greater effort. 'Is that the way to address your teacher?'

'You're not my teacher and I'm not your pupil, so shall we stop this silly charade?' she snapped back. Ralph had injected her with a fresh dose of courage.

Mervin rose, a commanding figure in flowing gown and scholarly hat. 'Miss Aston, you are speaking out of turn,' he thundered. 'Humphrey, bring her forward.'

She was already aware that it was the valet who had taken her there, and she despised him from the bottom of her heart, yet remembered that he'd seen her and Ralph in the dell. It was obvious he had run to his master with the news. Now his hand was in the small of her back and she was pushed towards Mervin. He stepped down from the dais where he commanded a full view of the room, and the ruler had been replaced by a Malacca cane made of brown rattan. Amelie's heart dropped.

Mervin paced slowly towards her, his attitude very much that of a cat with a mouse. She did not give him the satisfaction of shrinking back, maintaining her poise. 'What do you want with me?' she hissed.

'Word has reached me that you've been engaged in lewd acts with my brother,' he began, and the tip of the cane moved upwards from her right foot to her outer thigh.

Humphrey, she thought. So Ralph was right about him. 'How so, sir?' she returned with spirit, unwilling to confess to anything. 'We walked together this afternoon. Is this a crime?'

'Don't bother to lie to me. You were seen. What have you to say for yourself?'

'It's nothing to do with you, sir. I'd be grateful if you were to mind your own business.'

His smile vanished and his eyes were hard. 'Do you forget that I am your master? You're getting above yourself, miss, and need taking down a peg or two. What did you hope to achieve with Ralph? He's a vagabond, you know, and will never marry and be a faithful husband. I'm grieved and angry at your behaviour. You did not ask my permission to canoodle with him.'

'Ha!' She gave a bark of laughter. 'So it has come to this, has it? I must ask you if I want to dally with a man?'

'I thought you understood that on the night of the tableaux. I am the only one who is to know the delights of your virgin body. Now, you need a little reminder that I expect obedience. Bend over and grip your ankles.'

'Certainly not,' she said defiantly, tossing back her hair.

He nodded to Humphrey who, grinning widely, pushed her down with a hand at the back of her neck. He was stronger than he looked and Amelie was soon bent double. Her drawers ripped as he pulled them away from the waistband. The cool air wafted over her bare flesh. Then agony possessed her as Mervin's cane performed a baptism of fire on her tender hinds.

She bucked and clasped her ankles. Her instinct was to lash out, but the cane landed again, snapping and stinging, reducing her to jelly. Tears ran unchecked down her cheeks and she yelled for mercy. 'Oh, sir... please stop! I won't disobey you again.'

'I hope not, my dear, though I must admit this adds a little piquancy to our relationship.'

He paused and she thought he was about to be merciful, hoping against all hope that he had not guessed it was she who had summoned Ralph. But her ordeal had only just begun. In a split second he had flung the cane aside and was sitting on a wooden chair, and she was over a pair of muscular thighs with her naked bottom raised in the air.

'This is going to hurt, isn't it?' she whimpered, her buttocks aching from the cane.

'Yes, but it will arouse you too, as you already know.' He stroked between her cheeks, finding her clitoris pulsing hotly. She had felt warmth and affection for Ralph, but

107

nothing like that for Mervin. Over his lap she was prey to strange thoughts and sensations, need and humiliation getting confused in her mind. His hand was soothing and her slippery wet kernel responded. She jerked her hips, fearful of disappointment, but Mervin carried on, teasing and stroking. She was rising on waves of sweetness, blind to everything except the compulsion to reach orgasm. Nothing would stop her, and she climaxed in a violent explosion of sensation and heat, collapsing across Mervin's knees.

'Ah, I misjudged it, I didn't know you were so near,' he complained, partly amused, partly annoyed. 'I was going to make you beg for it. I still may, when you want a second helping.'

A few playful slaps followed, soon increasing in intensity, her skin burning. He was right. She needed another orgasm and wriggled under his hand, pressing her pubis into the sturdy knee beneath her and feeling the solid bar of his cock boring into her side. He continued to spank her, bringing her to the edge of agony, then holding off, leaving her pleading for more.

'You're a randy little slut who needs to be treated like this so she can come off over and over,' he said grimly, and slapped her a little harder. 'Ralph wouldn't be enough for you. I'm your master and you love it. Don't you? Confess, slut. Say, "I love it when you hurt me, master".'

'No,' she moaned, clinging desperately to her own identity. She must not become Mervin's slave.

'No? Dear me, we are wilful today, aren't we?' he crooned, and she felt his fingers worming their way into her bottom crack, dipping and spreading her love-juice up and over it, even entering the rosebud of her anus.

He tumbled her from his lap and frogmarched her up the shallow steps to his desk. There he arranged her over the flat top. She lay there lifeless as a puppet, accepting it was not worthwhile struggling. The wood was hard against her cheek, the surface worn as if it had seen generations of use. There were vertical slots for pens and two sunken inkwells. It smelled faintly of beeswax and chalk. She could feel Mervin moving behind her, then started as a cold, creamy substance was spread between her buttocks and into her bottom-hole.

'I'm going to put this in you,' he said, appearing on front of her, his cock in his hand, covered with a generous dollop of grease that he was working in with evident pleasure. The cock swayed, growing larger, longer, thicker.

He vanished from sight and there followed an unpleasant interlude during which he managed to insert the tip of his hungering meat just inside her channel. He swore and thrust and she gasped. It seemed to be stuck; a monstrous serpent denied access to its nest.

'She's been stretched, just as you ordered, sir,' Humphrey said, in mitigation.

'I don't doubt it,' Mervin panted, sweat running from his brow and dripping onto Amelie's buttocks. 'Stuff a cushion under her belly.'

Amelie was raised as the valet slipped a chair pad beneath her. This raised her hips, giving Mervin greater access, and it was then that his rounded helm dilated her rectum forcibly. She felt she might split; it was far more painful than the largest of the dildos.

'Oh my!' she screeched, but he ignored her, grinding his way in pitilessly. His glans entered her to the rolled back rim of his foreskin. She could feel her rectum painfully distended. The grease made it easier, but the sensation was atrocious. She squealed again as, with another brutal thrust, the whole tip forged into her, followed by inches of shaft till she was sure he had penetrated her very bowels.

She clenched her inner muscles, making it hard for him, trying to dislodge the cruel invader of her most secret and private part. Mervin stopped moving, as if to accustom her to the sensation of his cock. Amelie panted and swore, using words she did not know she knew. He was violating her and she hated him. And yet, as he remained still and her delicate membranes became used to the object buried inside her, so she became aware of a warmth that, oddly, was echoed in her clit. She wanted to come again, but when he started to press home his advantage pain swamped all and she bore down, using every vestige of strength to expel him.

He exited her like a cork from a bottle and as she slumped, every delicate membrane within on fire, so he let go his libation. It spattered her bottom like stinging rain, warm, wet and sticky.

Chapter Seven

'Was it necessary for you to roger Miss Aston?' Mervin asked coldly, settling down to breakfast, a generous helping of bacon and eggs set before him, and a side plate of white bread and butter. The footman had just withdrawn, leaving the brothers to eat alone. Coffee steamed at their elbows.

'I didn't,' Ralph replied calmly, spreading marmalade on toast taken from the silver rack.

'But you would have done, had not Humphrey disturbed you,' Mervin reminded, as if speaking to a recalcitrant child.

'I thought it was him, the slimy spy,' Ralph retorted angrily, biting into the toast as if it were Humphrey's head. 'I respect Miss Aston, and would do nothing to harm her in any way. More to the point: what have *you* been doing to her?'

'Training her. She will be grateful one day. I'm grooming her, and later on she may find a gentleman willing to marry her, and possibly elevate her in society.'

'Bullshit!' Ralph grunted. 'You can't fool me, Mervin. No doubt you have some perverted agenda of your own worked out for her.'

'And what has this to do with you?' Mervin added cream to his coffee and stirred it reflectively.

'I like her. I really do, and can see that she is fond of Millicent who, by the way, is concerning me with her ill health and listlessness. What are you going to do about that? And don't mention marrying her off to Piggy Balfour. That's a bad idea.'

'I'm considering having a Harley Street specialist take a look at her.'

'That's fine, but why not start by letting her attend this demonstration?' and Ralph handed over the newspaper cutting.

Mervin scanned it, then passed it back. 'Sounds like bunkum to me. Never did think much of these hypnotist chappies. Do you think it might help her to become normal? I don't mind telling you that I find her attitude damned infuriating. She's behaving like one of those droopy damsels who admire the playwright, Oscar Wilde. All right, you take her along to the lecture.'

'I can't. I've already explained that I'm due back in London but, tell you what, I'll get a train to Bath first thing Monday morning, go to this address in Pultney Street and find out how the land lies. If it proves to be genuine, will you give me your word to escort her there?'

'Done,' said Mervin, and they shook hands on it, though neither trusted the other.

Millicent was agog. She was wearing a new outfit, very suitable for a serious, scholarly lecture. She was certain that sobriety would be the object of Professor Macbain's demonstration. Amelie was with her, both dressed as befitted young ladies out and about in the evening. Not to a ball, or concert or to the playhouse, or even dinner with friends. There was nothing frivolous in their clothing, made of plain material, with full skirts tucked back over bustles. The tailor-made jackets were in contrasting colours, and showed off their tiny waists and full breasts to perfection, with long straight sleeves, revers and lace jabots. Round, tip-tilted hats adorned with ribbon bows completed these ensembles, along with white gloves and kid shoes with spool heels and rhinestone buckles.

Both of them had been in a lather of excitement ever since Ralph returned from Bath and discussed the project with them and Mervin. Apparently a most respectable lady,

Mrs Cornhill, who was a friend of the professor, owned the house near Pultney Bridge. So convinced was she that he could do enormous good among the upper class female population in the provinces, that she offered him her drawing room so he might bring this blessing to the West Country.

'It's ladies only,' Ralph had said, standing spread-legged on the hearthrug before an empty grate, thumbs hooked in his waistcoat pockets. 'And is by arrangement and invitation, to keep the audience small and select. I have paid for two tickets, for which I expect reimbursement, Mervin, and Millicent and Miss Aston are on the guest list.'

'I shall accompany you to the door,' Mervin stated firmly. 'I hope our efforts bear fruit, Millicent.' He had stared at her in that stern way which never failed to give her pleasurable spasms in the loins and caused wetness to gather at the gusset of her knickers.

Ralph had left for London and Wednesday arrived, and here she was, in the beautiful eighteenth century house in a most sought after area of Bath. A butler had conducted her through a magnificent gas-lit hall to an equally impressive drawing room. A dozen well-dressed women were already present, and their hostess, too, who welcomed them in.

'Be seated, ladies,' she gushed. 'The professor will be with us shortly and, meanwhile, perhaps our gifted pianist will provide us with music.'

He could. He did. The grand piano reverberated to a Nocturne by Frederick Chopin, a romantic, thrilling piece that affected every female there. The pianist himself was worthy of attention, with a rather gaunt face, dark eyes, a mane of black hair and the most elegant hands, that looked fragile but attacked the keyboard with astonishing vigour and aggression.

'I knew we were doing the right thing coming here,' Millicent whispered. 'Oh, well done, Ralph, it was you

113

who made this possible.'

'This is a real treat, isn't it?' Amelie remarked, glancing around her, cheeks pink and eyes alert. 'So was taking tea in Fortes Restaurant, in Milsom Street.'

'I know,' Millicent agreed. 'And I feel so well today. I'm sure something wonderful is about to happened.'

Mrs Cornhill held up her hands for silence. She was a well-built lady, magnificently dressed. Of middle years her cheeks and lips were rouged, and her hair was of that brassy blonde that betrays the use of artificial colouring, but there was nothing vulgar about her. Mr Cornhill, apparently, was away on business, but it seemed they lived in style.

'Welcome, ladies, I am so pleased to see you here tonight,' she began, her voice vibrant with enthusiasm, the pianist tinkling away quietly so as not to override her. 'I can assure you that you're about to receive an enlightening and, dare I say it, an inspiring experience. I am proud to know Professor Macbain, and it is a singular honour to have him here.' She nodded across to the footman and he went out, closing the door firmly behind him. 'No one else shall enter during the demonstration, apart from the professor's helpers. I hope you will keep an open mind and not repeat what happens here. Yours will be a unique experience and one which I assure you, will never be forgotten.' She stood back, pointed dramatically to a curtained alcove behind her and announced in ringing tones, 'I give you… Professor Macbain!'

The hush that followed ended in a gasp from a dozen female throats when he appeared between the curtains. He was of upright bearing, wearing a formal dark suit as befitted a medical man, and his smile was beneficent. Middle-aged and craggily handsome, his snowy white hair swept back from a fine brow and his eyes were piercing. This is what struck Millicent most – the power and persuasiveness of his eyes. She was intrigued and hoped he would single her out for attention.

'I am so happy to see you, dear ladies,' he began, addressing them in a lilting Irish accent. 'Such a fair, distinguished company. But I sense that some of you are not as well as it is the right of every one of God's creatures to be. I hope to be able to assist you to gain full health and happiness. Do you trust me?' he added, with a positively winsome smile.

'Oh, yes,' they chorused, completely won over.

Millicent noticed that Amelie did not join in. She was sitting there with her hands in her lap, watching the professor keenly. 'Isn't he a fine man, Amelie?' Millicent whispered.

'Fine enough,' Amelie replied, but without much conviction. It seemed she had reservations about the beguiling Macbain.

Some of Millicent's joy in the event started to evaporate, but she was soon leaning forward and listening eagerly as he explained about his mentor, Franz Anton Mesmer, who had practiced in Paris prior to the French Revolution.

'He was very popular and many claimed he had cured them of their ailments, particularly the ladies,' Macbain went on. 'Of course, he met opposition and made enemies, but what great man doesn't? He is long dead but left a quantity of written material behind. Suffice to say many physicians since have worked upon his principles, treating the mind as well as the body. I myself have used his methods and found them wonderfully effective. Now, while my assistants are bringing in an important piece of equipment, I shall go to each of you in turn so you may recount your problems.'

Millicent was in a fever of indecision. Shyness reduced her to a blushing heap, but she so much wanted the professor to take her hand, look into her eyes and read the secrets of her heart. Maybe he would relieve her of the burden of guilt, shame and frustrated longings that made her life a misery. She was distracted by the appearance of six good-looking young men, wearing military uniforms, kalpaks at a rakish angle on dark, fair or sandy hair. They wore scarlet jackets with brass buttons, gold epaulettes and frogging. Figure-hugging buckskin breeches outlined their muscular legs and the thick cock-fingers that lay as if entrapped against the insides of their left thighs. Shiny black leather knee-high boots added to this impression of soldierly might.

Two of the men hefted in a large wooden tub with a lid. It was opened and the others poured in buckets of water. The lid was replaced and iron rods were inserted through holes, and bent at right angles. Macbain was still occupied with the ladies who could not wait to describe their symptoms.

'I want to cry all the time!' exclaimed one pale girl, looking about to faint.

'And I am so irritable and tired, and I worry about every tiny thing,' chimed another. 'And I worry, and have dreams of a violent… I'm ashamed to say… impure nature.'

'And I have peculiar feelings in my tummy whenever I see a manly person,' confessed a third, the feathers in her hat quivering. 'I want to touch him, kiss him, embrace him! I can hardly control myself and, when I do, I feel quite sick and develop an awful headache.'

So the list went on, with Millicent recognising many of the symptoms as her own. Macbain listened and nodded, sympathised and promised help, and transfixed them with his hypnotic gaze and irresistible voice. When he reached Millicent she was terrified to meet his eyes, but could not resist doing so. It was as she had imagined; she felt herself drowning in those lustrous black pupils, willing to put her life and even her immortal soul into his keeping.

'And you are…?' he said in husky undertones that made her tremble. 'Your given name will do. We don't use titles here.'

'I'm Millicent,' she gasped, thrilling as he took her gloved hands in his, looking down at them and adding, 'I want

116

you to remove these. For our experiment to work your hands should be uncovered. In my own private clinic, I ask that my patients undress. Now, my dear, do you suffer from dizziness, nausea, fear of people, nervous depression?'

'Oh, yes... yes I do.'

'And you feel bloated below, and your most private regions itch and are overheated. You have morbid fears and headaches, in fact, show all the symptoms of hysteria?'

Millicent had a strong desire to fling herself on the floor at his feet, bare her bosom and have him bend her to his will, even though she was unclear as to what this would entail. But he was so strong an individual, stronger even than Mervin, and she was already disoriented, disappointed when he passed on to Amelie.

She listened to what he was saying to her companion, who disclaimed any mental or physical disturbance, simply explaining that she had come along with Millicent. He seemed unaffected by her cool reply and, the tub now filled to a foot deep, he stood by it and said, 'Mesmer believed in the effects of magnets on the body. He called this "magnetism", and maintained that he could affect cures involving it. This tub or "baquet" contains bottles, some empty and pointing towards the centre, while others are filled with magnetised water and point towards the circumference. There are several rows of these. Iron filings and powdered glass have been added.'

'Isn't this thrilling?' piped Mrs Cornhill, all fluttering fingers and big eyes. She was obviously besotted by him. His attendants stood in a row by the alcove, upright, feet slightly apart, arms behind them as they stared straight ahead.

'Draw up your chairs, ladies,' Macbain went on, 'and form a circle round the tub. I want you to hold hands and touch knees, sometimes reaching out and making contact with the handles that transmit the magnetic power, then back to conduct that power to those sitting either side of you. Do you understand?'

Giggling and chattering, embarrassed yet aroused, the audience obeyed him. The pianist launched into a rendition of works by Liszt, more savage and sensual than that of Chopin. The atmosphere heightened, charged with female pheromones. The ladies were already affected. Several had taken off their hats and unpinned their hair, disarranging it so it flowed over their shoulders and down their backs. One, bolder than the rest, loosened her bodice, unfastening the buttons and exposing her throat. Millicent made no concessions to abandonment; too frightened of what might happen. She yearned to learn, to lose her silly virginity and become a woman in her own right, but the prospect was daunting.

The magnetees were concentrating hard, breathing deeply. Millicent, one hand clasped in Amelie's, and with a stranger's in the other, could feel heat radiating from somewhere; she imagined it to be from the tub. When she tentatively gripped one of the handles she was sure she experienced a surge of power that energised her.

'Can you feel it, Amelie?' she murmured eagerly, wanting her to share in the wonderful frisson.

'No,' Amelie answered stonily. 'All I can feel is your wet palm and that of the girl next-door, and all I can smell is your sweat and perfume and a whiff of myself from down below.'

'Oh, Amelie,' Millicent sighed. 'How disappointing. I do so want you to share in this. It's quite extraordinary.'

All around her women were reddening. They wriggled on the hard wooden seats, as if trying to bring pressure to bear on their crotches. Macbain signalled and his troop of assistants came forward. Millicent stared in amazement and envy as they embraced the women, pushing back their skirts and massaging them between the legs, or loosening lacing and fondling breasts and nipples as they gazed into their eyes. There was pandemonium. Some of the ladies burst into rapturous tears, while others seemed to have been taken by convulsive fits. Some sobbed and tore at the young men's uniforms, others shrieked and screamed till they became insensible, but most, as with those females involved in Mervin's disgraceful Living Pictures, appeared to reach violent spasms, collapsing in ecstasy. Mrs Cornhill did not join in, her eyes fixed on Macbain as if he were God. Perhaps he had promised her a session in private later on.

Millicent wanted one of the handsome men to come to her, but found herself facing Macbain. He stood before her and caressed her breasts, and spine erect she forced them against his expert fingers, her nipples hard and aching, her loins in turmoil. He fondled her spine, then her lower back till she almost threw herself at him, drawers abandoned and legs wide apart. He touched the division between her buttocks and then cruised round to explore her belly. And this was all outside her clothing! She dreaded to think what he might have done had she been nude! Dreaded, yet hungered for it.

She saw from the corner of her eye that Amelie was being thoroughly frigged by a brown-haired soldier. She was squirming and moving her hips against his fingers. Millicent recalled vividly her behaviour in the garden when she exposed herself and rubbed her slit as she rolled her head back and moaned, 'Oh yes... yes!'

Macbain smiled across at her and then stared into Millicent's love-drugged eyes and muttered, 'That's what you need. That's what all you frustrated bitches need! It's not green-sickness or chlorosis or hysteria. There's nothing wrong with you except sexual frustration. You need a good hard cock up your cunt and someone who knows how to work your love-button. A night with me or one of my lads would soon put you right. Shall I arrange it?'

'Oh no!' Millicent averred and tore away from him. 'I can't... I mean, I mustn't. Don't ask me again.'

She was shocked and horrified by what was taking place

all around her. There was no penetration, but the women were being satisfied by fingers and tongues, the young men giving them the benefit of vast experience gained through working alongside the professor. His demonstrations were lucrative, and no wonder. There were hundreds of unsatisfied females, married or unmarried, and the richer or higher up the social scale the greater the problem. Macbain was sitting on a goldmine.

But, in spite of this visual and audio scene that caused her to experience such agitation, she could not relax, pushing Macbain away and rushing to the door. It was locked, however, and she was forced to wait and watch until the ladies collapsed in the arms of the soldiers, sighing and happy, apparently relieved of any of their previous symptoms.

The bolts were sprung and the butler entered. Wine was served and decorum reinstated. The attendants took their leave and so did Macbain, only Mrs Cornhill remained to extol the professor's virtues and encourage the audience to purchase signed copies of the book he had written about Mesmer's methods. Millicent bought one, but all she wanted to do was escape the overheated room.

'Well, how was it?' Mervin demanded when he helped Millicent and Amelie into the hansom cab he'd hired to drive them to the station.

'Interesting,' she replied, glad it was dark so he could not see her colouring up. The cab's oil-burning headlamps hardly mitigated the gloom, while the gas flares outside each house were yellowish and uncertain.

'Is that all?' he barked, seated opposite her and banging on the cab roof with the silver head of his walking cane. 'No miracle of healing? No sudden transformation? No change of heart regarding marrying Nigel?'

'No,' she whispered, and Amelie hated to see her so crushed. She may not have had much faith in Macbain as a genuine healer, but had hoped Millicent's eyes and body would have been opened to the experiences she was missing out on. For her own part she had relished the way in which her soldier fondled her bud until she climaxed.

'What a waste of time, to say nothing of money! I've spent several guineas on this wild goose chase.' He complained bitterly, and then fell into a gloomy silence that lasted throughout the train journey and the drive back to Kelston Towers.

Millicent put herself to bed for several days after the visit to Bath. There was no improvement in her condition, if anything she seemed worse. Amelie, on the other hand, looked upon the whole thing as a clever stunt to make money and used her soldier as an adjunct to masturbation fantasies, when she wasn't daydreaming about Ralph.

Mervin was a foul mood. It spread like a malignant cloud over the whole house. Even the servants picked up on it and went about their tasks in a subdued manner. All heaved a sigh of relief when he was out butchering game. Amelie wondered why it had all gone quiet with regard to his unnatural demands on her. She suspected he had some other nasty little trick up his sleeve, liking to keep her dangling, unsure of his intentions.

In order to avoid contact with him Millicent did not leave her room, the fine and sunny weather shut out by heavy curtains at the windows. She cried a great deal and seemed woefully depressed.

A week after Macbain's demonstration, of which neither girl had breathed a word to Mervin, he stormed into Millicent's bedroom brandishing a letter. 'This is it,' he announced loudly, 'an answer from Mr Spollet, a specialist in women's disorders. This is my final shot, sister. If he doesn't cure you, then I'll be forced to take more drastic measures.'

'But Mervin, I'm too weak to undertake a journey to London,' she protested, pale hands moving like restless doves in the semi-darkness.

'No excuses, it is all arranged. I shan't open the townhouse for you, but you'll stay overnight in the Kingstone Hotel in Bloomsbury. Amelie will accompany you, and you can take Dulcie too, and Mrs Tanner shall act as chaperone. On your return I expect you to accept Nigel without more ado, or else.'

He stomped out, leaving Amelie to soothe an inconsolable Millicent. Dulcie tried to cheer her, promising that, 'It'll be a lark, my lady, us three let loose in the City, away from old misery guts... sorry, your ladyship... him being your brother and all. 'Cor, I'll be able to wear my new hat and get off with those Cockney blokes. Pity Tanner's coming with us, but she'll take the opportunity to drink and whore about, and that will leave us free.'

All Amelie could think of was: I may see Ralph.

London was exciting, with its crowded streets, its smoky atmosphere, the multitude of vehicles – carriages, brewer's drays, coal carts, cabs and, wonder of wonders, a few of those noisy, smelly, new-fangled motor cars. It was a miracle to Amelia and even Millicent sat up and took notice, though it was not her first trip to the capital.

A cab dropped them outside the impressive pillared portico of the Kingstone Hotel. It was protected by a striped awning. Crossing sweepers with brooms and buckets were insuring that the road was clear of horse manure. Mrs Tanner paid the cabby as grandly as if she was a lady, not a housekeeper. She was wearing her customary black; a severe costume made of bombazine, a fur tippet and a large picture hat. She told the waiting porter to bear their luggage into the foyer and then registered their arrival at the reception desk.

It was a spacious place, lofty and with a mosaic floor, rooms leading off, the sound of a string quartet playing somewhere and genteel voices murmuring as guests sipped tea or coffee at small round tables set in nooks. Amelie stared at the crystal chandeliers placed at regular intervals along a ceiling that was vaulted and decorated with plaster swags and roses and winged cherubs. She had not seen electric light before, and the hotel blazed with it, bulbs reflected in huge mirrors, in the sparkling cut glass and highly polished surfaces.

The manager appeared from his lair behind the desk, bowing and saying to Mrs Tanner, 'Can I help you, madam?'

'Have Lady Bessborough's cases taken to her suite,' the housekeeper said grandly, thoroughly enjoying lording it over a mere member of the hotel staff, albeit the manager. 'Number eighteen, on the second floor, I believe. And also those of her companion, Miss Aston, and her maid, Dulcie Higgins. I am her chaperone, Mrs Tanner, and part of her entourage.'

'Mr Ridley, at your service, ma'am,' he returned, a dapper individual in pinstripe trousers, pristine linen and a black morning coat.

Amelie realised with a jolt that he was looking at Mrs Tanner as if he wanted to kiss her. That old hag? A man was finding her desirable? Then she remembered the orgy and Mr Brock and that a woman did not necessarily have to be young and fair to fan a man's lust. All she needed was to be willing to open her legs and show him her pussy.

A pageboy in a red suit and pillbox hat took the luggage and Mr Ridley directed them to the lift. This was another miracle for Amelie, and she stepped into the mahogany-panelled elevator, with its carvings and operational knobs and fancy mirrors in which one might check one's appearance. The iron gates clanged and her stomach dropped as they began their ascent.

'Isn't this jolly?' Millicent commented, clinging to the brass rail.

'A pleasant way to avoid stairs, my lady,' Mrs Tanner replied, handbag clasped firmly to her bosom. 'It's all down to electricity, of course. Pity we can't have it at Kelston Towers.'

'We'd get fat as porkers if we did,' Dulcie put in. 'We needs the exercise.'

'You certainly look as if *you* could lose a few pounds,' the housekeeper said scathingly, patting her own sleek waist.

The suite proved to be luxurious. It had a saloon and two bathrooms, one for servants and a larger, more splendid one for their master or mistress. The main bedchamber looked out over Bloomsbury and was finely furnished, the smaller one consigned to Amelie and those remaining occupied by Dulcie and Mrs Tanner.

Amelie loved it, bouncing on the beds, spinning the taps, eager to try out the shower. This was real living, and she could get very used to it. Would she not jump at the chance if a man offered her all this in exchange for her virtue?

Millicent's appointment with Mr Spollet was at three o'clock. She rode there in a hackney carriage with the housekeeper and Amelie. Dulcie stayed behind, ordered to wash out stockings and make herself generally useful.

This part of London was a far cry from the slums and factories, meat and fish markets and seedy riverside lodging houses. It was elegant and gracious, the architecture mostly from the Regency period or before. There were palaces and stately mansions and, in Harley Street, consulting rooms for some of the most renowned doctors in the world. It was outside one of these that the driver halted. Millicent was acutely nervous. What would Mr Spollet expect of her? What would he say, or do?

A parlour maid in black opened the door and they were shown to a room on the ground floor of the grand house. It was occupied by a balding man who said, 'I am Mr Spollet's secretary. And this is Lady Bessborough's appointment, I believe? Come in, my lady, Mr Spollet will be with you directly.'

He was so unassuming and diffident that Millicent's fading courage returned. Also the surroundings were reassuring. It resembled a parlour more than an office. The malachite clock in the centre of the marble mantelpiece struck three times, and at the last chime a door opened and a man appeared. He swept in rather than walked, his impressive bearing making him seem taller than he actually was. Millicent compared him to Macbain, and found the professor wanting. Mr Spollet appeared to be a real gentleman, and kindly, too. He had a keen brown face with a strong nose and firm lips. His coppery hair was neatly styled and he had a full moustache. He wore a tailcoat that emphasised his broad shoulders and narrow hips.

'Ah, Lady Millicent Bessborough, I believe,' he said, raising her hand to his lips, his touch firm and sure. This was a person who knew his own skills and worth and never doubted either. 'Would you care to accompany me into my consulting room?'

'I want my companion, Miss Aston, to come with me,' Millicent declared, chin set stubbornly.

Mr Spollet's pale blue eyes cut to Amelie. 'Certainly, your ladyship,' he said, then looked at Mrs Tanner, 'and the other lady?'

'Is Lord Bessborough's housekeeper, acting in the capacity of chaperone,' Millicent replied, glad of the opportunity to put the objectionable woman in her place. 'She will wait here for us.'

Spollet led the way through the door from which he had emerged, across another room, this time a library with book-lined walls, and into a further sanctum. It was smaller and conveyed a feeling of intimacy. It had white walls and plush drapes at the tall sash windows, Persian rugs on the polished floor, a screen and several pieces of equipment whose purpose she could only guess.

She stared round her with scared eyes, almost deciding to call it off and flee to the Kingstone Hotel. Both she and

Amelie sat gingerly on the chairs Spollet indicated.

'Now, Lady Millicent, I want you to lie on the examination couch,' he said in a charming, avuncular way. 'Will you do that for me? You will? Well done.'

It was a high couch covered in horsehair and spread with a white sheet. Strongly structured, it had a wooden frame supported on four sturdy legs. It was reached by a set of shallow steps. Millicent took off her hat and handed it to Alison. Her gloves followed, and then her shoes. She pattered on stockinged feet to where Spollet waited. He helped her up and made her as comfortable as possible on so unyielding a surface, placing a pillow beneath her head.

Feeling rather giddy in her prone position, Millicent lay flat on her back with her legs pressed tightly together. There was an adjustable lamp above and Spollet turned it so that it shone on her lower regions. He stood close to her, lifted the hem of her skirt and petticoats and laid them back waist high. Next he untied the drawstring of her knickers and eased them down.

She raised her hips to make it easier for him, but all the time she had to keep reminding herself that this was perfectly in order, as he was a medical practitioner. Now she was devoid of underwear, naked between the tops of her black stockings and the bottom of her pink stays. Spollet stared at her hairy triangle, and she had never been more embarrassed as he patted the soft fur, then used his strong fingers to part her labial wings.

Millicent jumped. It was just too sudden a contact. She wanted more, and he continued to explore her, saying, 'Your brother tells me that you suffer from head pains, bad temper and… anything else?'

'I'm often wet down there,' she whispered, blushing profusely. 'At first I thought I was losing bladder control, but it seems to be a clear, slippery liquid.'

'Quite, quite,' the doctor said, and dabbled his finger in her moisture. 'We doctors find this with women who come to us for help.'

She lay back, enjoying the warmth and firmness of his hands. Her heart was racing and her breath caught in her throat. Her skin tingled, heat settling in that forbidden spot between her legs. No longer ashamed of her naked parts she yearned for him to go on stroking her, winding his fingers in her dark bush and seeking out that fiery nodule that was rising, hard as a sugar-sweet pea at the apex of her slit.

'Oh, that feels strange, but not unpleasant,' she gasped.

'This is how we treat hysterical symptoms,' he went on. 'It is beneficial to the woman if her genitals are stimulated. There is no penetration, of course, and this being so, it does not constitute a sexual act. It will be interesting to see if you react as my other patients have, hopefully reaching an hysterical paroxysm, after which you will feel much better.'

He pushed back his cuffs, and then concentrated on her delta. At his touch she opened her legs, for once assured that the strong emotions coursing through her were justified. He was seeking a cure for her malady. There could be no sin if a medical man performed this treatment.

He was breathing regularly, and massaging her at the same time. His fingers were magical, wands of power, rubbing each side of that sliver of tissue that lay between her labia, circling it, stretching it back so that the tip was even more exposed to his touch. He kept it wet, sliding over it but never ceasing in producing that wonderful, paralysing, extraordinary feeling.

It pervaded her whole being, so piercing and intense that she cried out, 'I'm going to die!'

'Is the paroxysm upon you?'

'I don't know what to expect… oh, oh, something is happening to me. Ah… ah…'

'Tell me what you are feeling, my dear,' he said tenderly, so kind and considerate that she could have fallen in love with him.

'I can't explain it,' she sighed. 'It's so nice… so good

when you rub me there. Stroke it. Coax it. Give me relief.'

It was as if waves were bearing her to the top of their crest. She could not help uttering cries as she entered that enchanted territory where completion was a heartbeat away. Up and up she went, breaking in sharp spasms, lifted to the stars in the most exquisite sensation she had ever known. Her body arched as she was bathed in bliss.

'Ah, yes,' commented Spollet, holding her mound in his hand, taking her down gently. 'You've achieved an hysterical paroxysm, and will feel much better now.'

'Oh, I do,' Millicent answered, feeling so relaxed it was as if every bone in her body had melted. She did not want to move, only to grab the hand that had brought her such joy and kiss it rapturously. 'Will it happen to me again?'

Spollet moved to the basin and washed his hands. 'If you have more treatment,' he said. 'Could you visit me again tomorrow? I have a machine I'd like to try on you. It is called a vibrator and is a new invention, powered by electricity.'

'I would indeed be prepared to have you use it,' Millicent replied, sitting up. Amelie helped her pull on her knickers and find her shoes. Millicent noticed her cheeks were flushed and suddenly wanted to share her experience with her. 'Would you like the good doctor to give you an hysterical paroxysm?' she asked.

'I am rather busy,' he demurred, but Millicent was insistent.

'I'll double your fee.'

Spollet looked at Amelie and she met his gaze boldly. Millicent was more than convinced that she already knew of this tremendous wonder, but she wanted to watch her undergoing the doctor's manipulation.

He shrugged. 'Very well, take off your undergarments and lie face down across the couch, Miss Aston.'

Millicent stood where she could get an uninterrupted view of the proceedings, surprised when, after he had lifted Amelie's skirts waist high, he seized a pliable paddle and whacked her bare buttocks with it. Amelie yelped and flinched, but did not try to break away. Millicent saw the crimson spreading across the firm white globes like sunlight over snow, and excitement burned in her lower belly and that tiny nodule sprang from its cowl and demanded more.

The paddle rose and fell and then Spollet rolled Amelie over and repeated the actions he had used with Millicent. He rubbed quickly and Millicent was spellbound, willing her companion to have one of those amazing paroxysms. Glancing down at Spollet's trousers, she could see a fullness there, absent when he was bringing her to full spasm.

Amelie was jerking and convulsing. 'Now... now!' she cried.

Spollet hung over her and seemed to be pressing his crotch against her side. Then he withdrew, washing his hands again while Amelie recovered. 'It appears that your companion achieved her relief quickly, Lady Millicent,' he remarked thoughtfully. 'It makes one wonder if this is her first time, or if it has happened before.'

'I shall accompany her ladyship tomorrow,' Amelie said, meeting his gaze without hesitation. She was fully dressed again and ready to escort Millicent to the emporiums, or a teashop or wherever she wanted to go. 'It will be interesting to sample these vibrators of which you speak. I confess, I've not heard of such a thing before, but anything that can assist we poor, suffering females must be of benefit, don't you agree, sir? Including your use of the paddle on my hinds. I'm sure this helped to rid me of my "hysteria", though I don't recall telling you that I was prone to this.'

Millicent saw the glance he gave her companion and could not understand its significance. All she knew was that somehow Amelie and he were on the same track, even though miles apart in lifestyle and status. They knew something that she, as yet, did not.

She bade him good afternoon as he bowed her out of his consulting rooms and, glowing warmly inside, her loins at peace yet eager for more, she could not wait till tomorrow afternoon. She had opened Pandora's Box and her life had changed dramatically.

Chapter Eight

The things that took place in Mr Spollet's Harley Street establishment astounded Amelie. At a time when, on the surface anyway, polite society was prudish in the extreme, even going so far as to attach frills to the legs of tables or grand pianos in the name of modesty, it was considered to be perfectly in order for a doctor to rub a lady's secret parts.

Hysterical paroxysm? Is that what she had been bringing herself to all this time? To say nothing of males doing it for her. She had the strong feeling that hysteria was all nonsense, something invented by men to excuse their abysmal neglect of women and their needs. She wanted to talk this over with Ralph, but when they went to his house in Chelsea it was to find he was out. Millicent left a note with his manservant.

They had dinner and went to a performance of the Gilbert and Sullivan operetta, *The Mikado*, at the Savoy Theatre. Amelie felt like a queen, seated in a stage box. If only Ralph had been there her happiness would have been complete. Millicent had sent a telegram to Mervin, informing him that they would be in London for a further day, and Amelie was pleased to see her taking control. Apparently the paroxysm, or whatever Spollet liked to call it, had worked wonders.

Her cheeks were flushed and her eyes sparkled. She no longer shrank into herself, but stood upright, shoulders back, bosom thrust forward. It was a miraculous transformation, and Amelie contemplated what other changes would take place tomorrow. For her own part she could not wait to try the instruments that Spollet had sworn would bring about amazing and healthful 'spasms'.

The cab dropped them off at the hotel and they giggled as they took the elevator upstairs. Mrs Tanner, pleading a migraine, had stayed at home. They should have remained there, too. It was unheard of for young unmarried women to go anywhere alone. But Millicent's new confidence brushed this aside, so determined was she to see the comic opera. She already knew some of the tunes, having purchased the sheet music, playing it on the piano and singing the witty lyrics.

There was no one in the suite. Apparently Dulcie had gone to bed and Mrs Tanner had retired also. 'Oh, good!' Millicent exclaimed, kicking off her shoes and tossing aside her evening cape.

'I'll help you disrobe,' Amelie said, and poured two glasses of red wine from the decanter on the sideboard.

'I wish I had a phonograph,' Millicent enthused. 'What a wonderful invention. We could listen to *The Mikado* all over again.'

She collapsed on the deeply buttoned chesterfield, forgetting to be genteel, legs asprawl, arms linked behind her head, hair tumbling down. Amelie picked up Millicent's cape and took it into the main bedchamber. There she opened the wardrobe door and was about to hang it inside when she heard a sound. A tiny ray of light gave her a clue as to its origin.

The rooms had been divided at some time, and the armoire constructed so that its back was part of the lathe and plaster wall behind. Unable to resist she ducked under the rail and applied her eye to the chink, and what she saw riveted her to the spot. She had a clear view of Mrs Tanner's bed. The lights were on, illuminating the housekeeper clearly. She was in her dressing gown, which was parted down the front showing her dangling breasts, her scrawny belly, and the thick mat of dung-coloured pubic hair that covered her triangle.

She was sitting with her legs wide open, a hand mirror angled so she could see her crevice and watch as she played with it. She was using a realistic rubber dildo, with veins and foreskin and a rounded helm. Her expression was softer and more relaxed than Amelie had ever seen it, and she moaned gently as she buried the mock penis inside her, and then pulled it out, shiny and wet, and applied it to her nubbin. Then, still moaning, she slipped it back into her depths, the greedy vaginal lips sucking at it eagerly till it almost vanished from sight.

'What are you doing?' Millicent said from behind Amelie, almost giving her a heart attack.

'Hush… don't make a noise,' she whispered and guided Millicent to the hole. 'Just look.'

Millicent stared without moving for some time. 'Goodness gracious,' she murmured.

'Let me look,' Amelie said, elbowing her aside. Being a voyeur excited her, and this was not the first time her bud had throbbed and her breasts tingled when she watched someone else playing with their genitals. She wanted to touch her own.

Millicent, too, was affected, lifting her hands to her breasts and toying with her nipples, eager to see more, but they had to take it in turns. Mrs Tanner was approaching her crisis, but just then someone tapped lightly at a door. The housekeeper dropped the dildo and jumped up to answer the summons, and the nocturnal visitor proved to be Mr Ridley, the hotel manager.

'Arthur,' she cried, and Amelie speculated on when they had become so intimate. Was it during their absence that evening? Had the manager and housekeeper spent the time rolling around on her bed?

'Mavis,' he returned fondly. His trousers were already undone and his hand was moving over his cock. Amelie could see it clearly as the helm appeared and retreated in his fist. When he took his hand away the swollen prick stayed upright as a lance, needing no support as he showed it off to Mrs Tanner. At that moment Amelie was forced to give way to Millicent, who was agog for more. Mrs Tanner fell back on the bed, her legs wide to receive him, her dressing gown slipping away from her nakedness.

'Come on, Arthur, don't bother to undress,' she urged. 'I'm dying for your old fellow. I wants to feel it going in me… right in as far as you can shove it.'

Amelie was impressed by the way Millicent showed such curiosity and eagerness to view copulation. She appeared to have her eye glued to the chink, and when Amelie got the chance to look she saw that Mr Ridley had his trousers down around his bony hips and was advancing on Mrs Tanner with his penis pointing towards the ceiling, a tear weeping from its single eye. She could see his weighty balls, no longer swinging in their wrinkled sac, but tight and hard as walnuts. It was not a pretty sight and Amelie withdrew, letting Millicent get an eyeful.

When it was her turn again she saw that Mrs Tanner was blatantly offering her juicy sex, and Mr Ridley had sunk between her legs, sucking, his agile tongue diving into her dark cavern then licking over the stem of her clitoris.

'When is he going to put his thing in her?' Millicent asked. 'Has anyone done it to you?'

'No, I've told you. I'm still a virgin there, though not in the other place.'

'What do you mean?'

'I'll tell you later. If you don't want to watch, then let me.'

She did, and then Millicent looked again, each fighting to capture the moment when Ridley's blunt-nosed dick pushed into the housekeeper. There followed a great deal of heaving and grunting, groans of pleasure and cries that resembled pain. At one point he rolled her over and administered a severe spanking that she seemed to enjoy immensely. Millicent's hand gripped Amelie's as they both tried to look at once, catching glimpses of the lovers reaching their apogee. Mrs Tanner was yelling that he was hurting her with his size and force, but her complaints were soon changed to whimpers of lust as his cock-root rubbed against her large nodule. He thrust and withdrew, his arse moving rapidly, propelling his penis till they both cried out in unison, and he collapsed across her.

Millicent and Amelie closed the wardrobe door and retreated to the wide bed. 'Heavens!' she exclaimed, red in the face. 'Whatever must it feel like to go with a man. I don't think I ever want to do it. It looks horrid.'

'And interesting,' Amelie interjected. She was in a ferment, knowing she could easily satisfy herself, yet wanting someone like Ralph to possess her.

Millicent lay back against the lace-frilled pillows and could not keep her hands away from her breasts. 'I don't think I can wait until tomorrow,' she said shyly. 'I'm all afire.'

Arrows of desire darted through Amelie. She appreciated Millicent's impatience. 'Shall I help you to undress?' she asked softly. 'This may ease you.'

Millicent stood while Amelie undid the buttons that fastened the back of her bodice, then slipped it off. Petticoats came next and she tugged at the tight lacing of the stays, eventually freeing Millicent from the restriction. All that remained was a semi-transparent chemise and cotton drawers.

'Oh, that's better,' Millicent sighed, rubbing her ribs and waist. 'Those corsets are so tight! Let me do the same for you, Amelie.'

It was a novelty to have a lady acting as her maid, and Amelie did not stop at underwear, but insisted in baring all, preening herself as she looked in the pier-glass. She breathed deeply and lifted her ribcage, her breasts standing out, the nipples like succulent cherries. Aware that Millicent could not keep her eyes off this display of naked beauty, she posed even more, parting her legs and fingering her russet pubes. Millicent, drawn like a rabbit to a snake, came up behind her and the mirror showed her slender arms slipping round Amelie from behind, and her hands finally resting on her breasts.

Amelie's heart swelled with affection. She placed her hands over Millicent's, holding them in place, her nipples reacting as if it were a man who touched them, or herself. Millicent's eyes, reflected in the mirror, were languorous. Gently Amelie disengaged herself, and taking Millicent's hand, led her to the bed.

There she leaned forward and kissed her. It was a honey-sweet experience, Millicent's lips as soft as a child's, tender and loving, without the hard possessiveness of a man. Only Ralph had been as gentle. Yet there was hesitancy there, and Millicent withdrew her lips to say, 'Is this sinful?'

'We are friends, aren't we, Milly? Let us lie in each other's arms and see what happens, shall we?'

Millicent hesitated no more. She rested back on an elbow, one knee raised, and Amelie explored her through the silken chemise, then eased it off. Now there only remained the knickers, and by mutual consent they were soon laid aside. Amelie half-sat, half-knelt on the quilt, admiring her. Millicent had a delightful body, her backside narrower than hers, less fleshy and voluptuous. Her skin was tauter, with an enviable sheen and a softer texture. She was alert and waiting, her rosy nipples puckered.

Amelie followed her instincts. She passed a hand over Millicent's body, caressing her waist, the slight swell of her belly, circling the dimple of her navel and down to stroke the curly dark hair at her apex. Millicent stiffened and gasped.

'I feel like I did with Mr Spollet. Oh, Amelie, has he unlocked the secret kingdom for me? Is this what you bring on for yourself? The same as he did this afternoon? Will you do it for me?'

'I'll try,' Amelie promised.

She wanted more kisses, sucking Millicent's lower lip

between hers, then opening it and tonguing the inside of her mouth. Millicent went limp and then Amelie felt the tiny, nervous movements of her fingers on her nipples. It was more exciting than the roughness of masculine hands, more sensual and lingering, giving Amelie time to relish the sensations flooding from her teats to her clit. Her inner thighs were bathed in love-dew.

'Is that right?' Millicent asked.

'Yes, it's lovely,' Amelie encouraged, and reaching out made Millicent's breasts tremble as she stroked them with the back of her hand. She then pressed her face to them and nibbled each pointed tip.

'Go on, do more to me,' Millicent begged. 'Look, I'm yours.'

Amelie could smell the freshness of her friend's arousal breathing from between her legs. It was like cinnamon and sandalwood and ocean spray. Millicent surrendered completely, and her delta opened as Amelie explored it. Soft, wet and smooth, it was as if she caressed herself, her fingertips transmitting sensations that quivered in her nerves, as well as Millicent's. Then Amelie could not resist dipping down and licking the other woman's cleft, finding her clitoris and sucking it. She felt the tiny organ throb against her tongue, while Millicent grabbed her by the hair, holding her firmly and crying out as she convulsed rapidly.

I've done it, Amelie thought proudly. I've given her an hysterical paroxysm, though I'm certain there's another name for it.

Aroused by Millicent shaking and moaning under her lips, her own passion was swamping her. Now it was Millicent's turn to give pleasure and she proved to be an apt pupil. She did as instructed, and added a few inventive moves of her own. Amelie pinched her own nipples, while Millicent's fingers joined her tongue, pressing each side of the clitoris, making it strain from its hood as she licked it steadily. Amelie reached that plateau from which there is no return, and then she peaked, achieving the acme of bliss.

At last they rested amongst the tangled sheets, legs entwined, clefts pressed together, breasts nudging breasts. They roused to make love again, caressing each other's parts, tasting their feminine fluids, inhaling those magical sea-fresh scents.

Amelie woke at dawn, and after kissing the brow of sleeping Millicent, crept to her own room. Dulcie would not snitch on them if she found out about this state of affairs, but Mrs Tanner was untrustworthy. There were some secrets it was better not to share.

'Buttocks bare, ladies,' Mr Spollet said, after he had welcomed Amelie and Millicent into his holy of holies, the consulting room.

Millicent noticed there were several pieces of apparatus absent yesterday. She eyed them apprehensively, for they were curious machines, bulky and strange, consisting of wires and pipes, wheels and phallus-shaped nozzles. She met Amelie's gaze, and her lifted brows showed that she shared her doubts. Now Mr Spollet's request was not reassuring.

'Do we have to, sir?' she asked, though nothing like as timorous as before. Her experience with him and the night spent with Amelie had convinced her that she was a person to be reckoned with after all.

'I'm going to treat you to a little taste of the whip. Miss Aston has already responded to this, both yesterday and, I suspect, on former occasions. I find it effective in some cases, allowing the patient to become submissive and thus enabling her to reach her beneficial paroxysm more easily.'

It was on the tip of Millicent's tongue to admit that her brother had already spanked her, but she kept silent. Though wanting to place herself in the physician's hands once more, she nonetheless removed her underwear reluctantly. Amelie did the same and soon both of them were lying across the couch, their heads hanging down over one side and their legs on the other. Spollet came up behind them and arranged their inert torsos to his liking.

He removed his frock coat and hung it on the back of a chair, then rolled up his sleeves and picked up a riding crop. There was something very intimate about a man in waistcoat and shirt. In the higher echelon it was considered to be bad form for a gentleman to appear thus in front of a woman who was not his wife.

But he was a doctor, Millicent kept reminding herself, so the rules didn't apply to him.

'Right, hold firm,' Spollet commanded.

There was a hiss and a crack and Amelie yelled as the leather thong landed on her. Millicent barely registered this before agony tore through her own bottom, a scalding pain that made her jerk and scream. Spollet directed a further whistling cut to Amelie's hinds, and Millicent, barely recovered from the first onslaught, felt a second sting. She was so concerned about receiving a third that she failed to be aware of Amelie's cry as she shuddered from head to toe when the crop bit into her again.

'Oh doctor, that's enough, surely?' Millicent pleaded, but something very strange was happening to her. It was as if she had reached a state of grace, soft and pliant, ready to submit to Spollet, accepting him as her teacher.

'It probably is,' he agreed, putting down the crop. 'The kiss of the lash usually works wonders in a short space of time. You may sit up now.'

They did so, groaning, and Amelie suffered most, for the new stripes had landed on yesterday's bruises. She reached round, lifted one hip and massaged her buttocks ruefully. Millicent was conscious of heat and soreness, but it was not unendurable, and she followed Spollet's actions keenly as he wheeled one of the contraptions towards her.

'What is it?' she asked, having never seen anything like it – a tall, solid cylinder with dangling objects that were a cross between an egg whisk and other labour saving devices found in the kitchen.

'A recent invention,' he said, fiddling with the wires that linked it to a box that, in return, was attached to an electrical power supply. 'We physicians are in much demand for the easement of diseases among women, mainly those brought about by hysteria. Some ladies come to us regularly once a week and this is fine for our bank balances but adds to our workload. We strain our wrists constantly massaging their privates. Now machines are available that relieve us of this burdensome duty. They can only be used by doctors and are not obtainable outside medical circles.'

The large black and chrome object was on wheels and could be raised or lowered as required. It had two attachments, one cock-shaped and the other resembling a wand with a rotating dish-mop on top. Spollet pushed down a switch and the machine started to buzz, both vibrators working in unison. He had stationed the unwieldy instrument between Amelie and Millicent. 'This enables me to kill two birds with one stone, as it were,' he said, smiling widely and displaying white teeth. 'Lift your hips a little… that's right… then rest back on your arms and enjoy, ladies.'

He touched the tip of Millicent's clitoris with the whirling mop-head. The sensation was extreme. She did not know whether to shriek in shock or whimper with pleasure. At the same time he caressed Amelie's sex with the smoothly vibrating penis substitute. Millicent supported herself on taut arms and thrust her pubis high, ready for the mop to rotate on her bud again. She wanted more! Her greedy clit was in heaven, constantly stimulated by an untiring automaton. Thrills ran up her spine, through her groin, belly and breasts.

The mop-head purred and so did Amelie's mock-penis, and Spollet held them in position after glancing at the surgery clock, judging how long this operation was going to take. It was seconds, not minutes. Millicent heard Amelie's sharp intake of breath, saw her legs stiffen and witnessed the ecstatic look on her face. And as she fell back and Spollet removed the attachment, so Millicent's crisis was on her without any warning. She convulsed as a fiery spasm shot through her, so acute it was almost pain. The spinning head was too much to bear and she pushed it away from her oversensitive bud.

'Finished, ladies?' Spollet said, and clicked off the machine, then wheeled it to one side.

'Oh yes, that was beautiful,' Millicent sighed. 'Such a pity one can't buy one to keep in one's own home.'

'Maybe,' he conceded, shrugging his shoulders into his coat. 'But you see, once you are married and have a husband to love and care for you, particularly in the area of the bridal bed, then you'll no longer have these distressing symptoms.'

'If this is so, then why do you have wives coming to you for relief?' asked Amelie, never one to beat about the bush.

'That is one of life's paradoxes,' he agreed, then shook his head. 'It does seem that women are romantic creatures and need something more. What, I can't tell you. I was taught to accept that the well brought up female is happy to do her duty and satisfy her husband, her reward being children.'

'Shall we visit you again?' Millicent said, stepping into her drawers and pulling them up, then lowering her skirts. 'It won't be easy, and I'm not sure that Mervin will pay for it.'

'May I make a suggestion?' Spollet replied, going to his desk and taking a business card from a drawer. 'I am sure you would benefit from a stay at one of England's leading spas, Westleigh, on the Somerset coast. I think you need a course of hydrotherapy treatment.'

'And what, pray, is that?'

'A wonderfully relaxing process by which you spend

your days in luxurious surroundings, with hot and cold baths, douches, sprays, massage and every refinement to cleanse the body and mind. You will bask in the warm mineral water that gushes from miles underground, and be pampered by nurses and masseurs and come away feeling renewed and invigorated. I highly recommend it, and help run the Westleigh Spa myself, training the staff personally,' and he gave her the card. It had italic print and a gold deckled border.

'I shall tell my brother,' Millicent declared. 'I want to go. I'm quite determined. There is no way I'll even discuss marrying Lord Balfour until he agrees.'

'No! No! No!' declared Mervin, whacking his crop against his jodhpurs with every word. 'I'm not prepared to spend any more money on your fads and fancies, Millicent.'

'But Mr Spollet says?'

'To the devil with Mr Spollet!' he exploded, and his spurs jangled as he paced the library floor. 'He's feathering his nest very nicely out of this craze for women to drivel on about their mysterious ailments, and demand special and expensive treatment.'

'I'll tell you this, brother,' Millicent said, pacing closer to him. 'You can forget all about an alliance with Nigel if you don't let me go to Westleigh before the week is out.'

Puce in the face, Mervin pointed directly at Amelie. 'This is your fault,' he roared. 'And it's cost me double because Millicent insisted on you going along. If I do consent to this foolhardy plan concerning hydrotherapy, then I can assure you that you won't be included.'

'She's my companion,' Millicent broke in with a firmness that rocked him on his heels. 'Where I go, she goes.'

'Tscha!' he spat, baffled by her coolness.

'And I'd like Ralph to come, too,' Millicent said, adding to her list of demands.

'Ralph?' Mervin blustered. 'Why him?'

'Just because,' Millicent retorted flippantly. 'And now that is all arranged, I shall retire to my room, there to check through my wardrobe and decide what new items I need for Westleigh. They tell me those who go there to take the waters are the cream of the beau monde, extremely wealthy and elegant. You wouldn't like your only sister to arrive there looking a frump, now would you, Mervin?'

He cursed and flung out of the room with a parting shot, 'Do what the hell you like, but I'm warning you, Millicent, if you don't accept Nigel after all this fuss, then you can get out of Kelston Towers forever.'

'Oh, brother, cruel one,' she cried, wringing her hands and pretending to throw herself on his mercy, just like a stage heroine. 'Does this mean you'll cut me off without a shilling? Our poor, dear mama would turn in her grave!'

He gave her a withering look and slammed the door. Amelie and Millicent clung to each other, stifling their glee. 'Seems like we can pack our buckets and spades,' Amelie said, wiping away laughter tears. 'My word, there's a vast change in you, Milly.'

'And it's all down to you, dearest friend,' Millicent said, and hugged her.

'Will you really, truly invite Ralph?'

'If that's what you want. You like him, don't you?' Millicent had a sudden vision of being chief bridesmaid at their wedding. Then Amelie would really be her sister.

'I must confess to harbouring a certain tenderness for him,' Amelie replied. 'But who knows what splendid fellows may turn up at the spa?'

'I'll write to him straight away,' Millicent said. 'Meanwhile, you promised to tell me about being taken in an unusual place.'

'I was sodomised,' Amelie explained, seated on the floor with her knees drawn up and her arms clasped round them. 'That's the proper term for what transpired.'

'And what does that mean?' Millicent wished she was not such an ignoramus.

Amelie looked down, as if the pattern in the carpet was of absorbing interest, and her cheeks were flushed. 'It means, Milly, that I was penetrated up my bottom.'

Millicent was confused. 'But how can that be? And who did this to you?'

'It was your brother, Lord Bessborough.'

'Mervin?' Millicent cried, wanting to deny it and defend him, but remembering the times he had spanked and humiliated her. 'How ghastly! I knew he was cruel but never realised... never guessed he could do something like that.'

'He is capable of much, much more,' Amelie continued. 'At first I was too tight for his organ to enter so he had Humphrey use butt plugs to stretch my anus. Then, not long ago, shortly after Ralph visited, he trapped me in the schoolroom, saying I must be punished for lusting after his brother. I was caned and then spanked, after which he stroked my bud until I spasmed and then he greased my bum-hole and worked his fingers into it. This hurt and I protested, but in vain. He used his penis instead and this was far, far worse.'

'Oh, Amelie,' Millicent sighed, unable to find words of comfort and hating Mervin with all her might. 'Oh, the merciless, vicious tyrant!'

'I know all that, but it was strange how gradually I accepted it and even began to find myself longing for his touch on my nubbin. But he forced himself into me violently and I retaliated, bearing down and succeeding in ejecting him. He was about to spurt and could not stop, covering my hinds with his fluid.'

'You poor darling,' Millicent said, tears very close. 'You shall have Ralph, if that's what you want, and never, ever have to endure Mervin's odious advances again.'

Amelie recalled these words when, after a fruitless struggle to escape, she was once more in the punishment chamber below the house. Mervin had struck after Millicent retired for the night. Thirsty, and not wanting to disturb the servants, Amelie had pulled her dressing gown over her nightdress and gone in the direction of the kitchens. A foolish move, as she now recognised.

Hardly had she reached the Great Hall when Mervin stepped out of the games room. She turned to flee, but he grabbed her, his grip like a vice as he held her to his chest. She was aware of Humphrey in the background and knew she was powerless.

'This is your doing, you troublesome bitch!' Mervin hissed. 'It's only since your arrival that Millicent has become so obdurate.'

'Not at all, she would have found you out eventually,' Amelie returned smartly, even though her heart was hammering. 'You couldn't bully her forever.'

'We'll see about that,' he snarled. 'Meanwhile, a spell at the whipping post won't do you any harm.'

And there she now hung, rough wood at her naked back, arms stretched and tethered to the crossbars, legs wide and taut and fastened to the lower struts. They had peeled off her clothing before stringing her up, and she feared that she must appear a rude sight, with her hair cascading over her breasts, her nipples taut and her cleft open.

'She's ready for you, Nigel,' Mervin said, and for the first time Amelie realised that Millicent's odious prospective bridegroom was lurking in the dimness.

'Why is he here?' she demanded, tugging ineffectively at her restraints.

'He often stays,' Mervin replied with his cold, sinister smile. 'Don't you, old chap? He's crossed in love and needs comforting.'

'Indeed, I suffer through Millicent's refusal to have me,' Nigel said, and came closer. Amelie looked into his red face and agreed with Millicent's opinion that he was most unattractive. 'May I touch this beauty instead?' he added, glancing slyly at Mervin.

'Of course, it's only right that she should provide you with relief, being an interfering slut who is influencing my sister,' Mervin said.

Amelie felt Nigel's sweaty hands on the insides of her thighs. They moved upwards and his fingers scrabbled about, combing through her bush and poking between her labial wings. She was wet there, but his touch was abrasive, far too hard as if he was attending to his own cock in that impatient way men have, unlike the sensitive treatment women need to rouse and satisfy them. It was all or nothing, it seemed, the male still a primitive savage compelled to insure the continuation of the species with all speed, lest a sabre-toothed tiger beat him.

She sagged in her bonds, her arms numb, her wrists burning, her sex vulnerable. He pinched her tender clit savagely and she yelped. It was excruciating. He tightened his grip, practically lifting her by her mons. Her strapped legs felt dislocated, her ankles chafed, and he was now positioned between them, holding a short-handled paddle that was more in the nature of a wooden spoon. At first she was not aware of his intentions, astonished and shocked when it landed with force across her lower belly. The breath left her lungs with a rush, and then he struck her again, lower this time, the spoon landing squarely on her helpless labia. She flung back her head and wailed, her body arching and twisting, trussed like a fowl and unable to defend herself.

Mervin stepped in and held her steady. 'You bastard!' she hissed through clenched teeth. 'What have I ever done to you?'

'Shhh, silly girl,' he answered icily. 'You don't have to "do" anything. This is for my pleasure, nothing more.'

Nigel was grinning inanely, flourishing the spoon. He struck again, just above her navel, and she launched into a fresh dance of agony, but the next ones aimed at her breasts were far worse, reducing her to a sobbing creature, begging for mercy. He stopped then, and she hung on the frame, crying brokenly.

She was hardly aware of Mervin untying her, taking her down and carrying her across to a divan with a crimson coverlet. She clasped her breasts, then shot a hand down to cradle her pubis. She was certain the lips were purple; they throbbed as if a dozen bees had attacked her there. Her inner thighs burned and her mound, too.

Nigel had followed, like a dog scenting a bitch on heat. He licked his lips, his eyes bulging as he scanned her, then at Mervin's invitation he occupied a wing chair near the bed. 'Is her cunt bruised?' he asked huskily.

'See for yourself,' Mervin answered with a casual lift of his shoulders, then yanked her hair. 'Get up, slut. Let Lord Balfour inspect your slit.'

There was nothing Amelie wanted less, but she feared Mervin more than she hated Nigel, and she got up and approached his chair. Every movement caused her pain. Nigel opened his legs and had her stand between them, then his fat fingers opened her swollen labia. She bit back a groan and he stopped gazing at her fork, lifted his eyes to hers and said, 'You are more obedient than Lady Millicent. Will you do anything I ask?'

'She will, if I say so,' Mervin put in, leaning nonchalantly against the bed's foot post, riding boots crossed at the ankles, a glass of whiskey in one hand. 'Ain't that so, Amelie?'

'Within reason,' she answered haltingly, Nigel's touch harsh against her sore delta.

'You have no choice in the matter,' Mervin returned. 'Do what Nigel wants, and I shall watch.'

Nigel needed no second bidding. He put his hands on Amelie's shoulders and pushed her down till she was kneeling between his legs. His hand was at the bulge in his trousers and he quickly unbuttoned, dipped into the gap of the fly and brought out his thick, dumpy phallus. It reminded Amelie of a pork sausage and she found this small male offering unappealing.

147

On her knees before him she was forced to bend forward, his hand on her neck. She could smell his sweat, the lustful heat that permeated his groin, and feel the brush of his wiry thatch against her nose as he pulled her ever closer.

'Hold it, suck it,' Nigel urged, sliding down, resting low on his spine in order to enjoy to the full this action on her part.

Amelie closed her eyes, finding it easier to open her lips wide and encircle the purple glans glistening with pre-come if she did not have to look at it. She felt it enlarging, filling her mouth, the helm pressing against her throat and making her heave.

This delighted Nigel who carolled, 'I say, Mervin old bean, my cock is too big for her. She's gagging!' His fingers tightened in her hair and she succeeded in enduring the fierce surge of semen that shot from him, filling her throat, making her gorge rise as he came in swift jerks. She swallowed, hating the vile taste of his spunk, and as he pulled out, feeling long strings of discharge spilling over her chin and dripping to her breasts.

'Good girl, good girl,' he muttered, sated and content. 'That deserves a present. What d'you want? Shall I order a piece of expensive jewellery?'

Mervin stepped in, slapping Amelie's haunches as she rose stiffly. 'Don't indulge her, Nigel. She was obeying my orders, that's all, and doesn't merit payment.'

Nigel sat there fiddling with his little dick, that had now shrunk back to coil in its nest of curls. 'Well, all I can say is that she's a damn sight more obliging than that sister of yours, old boy. Bugger me if she ain't.'

'No doubt that could be arranged,' Mervin replied coldly, and nodded across to where Humphrey had been watching the whole proceedings.

'Oh, come off it,' Nigel grumbled. 'You know I'm into fanny, not cocks.'

'You've not always been so fussy, as I recall,' Mervin

said, and handed him a tot of whiskey.

Amelie was kept waiting for dismissal, though she was permitted to don her nightgown and robe. By now she was shivering and her stomach heaved as she tasted the residue of Nigel's emission.

The gentlemen topped up their glasses and, 'Let's drink to the wedding,' said Nigel, slurring his words. 'There's the little matter of Millicent's dowry, too.'

'Don't trouble your head about that,' Mervin assured him. 'Papa left her a substantial sum which, when added to your own, should make you most comfortably off.'

'That's good news,' Nigel replied, swirling his tot and watching the movement of the golden-brown liquid. 'But I don't need a wife to keep me in style. I'm not poor by any means. There's all that land, coal mines, tin mines, shipping and I don't know what all, but I have several rather hefty gambling debts. I fancy your sister the most out of all the fillies that have been presented to me as prospective brides. I'll treat her well; give her my title and children. I've a feeling we'll rub along very well together. Has she agreed yet?'

'We're getting there,' Mervin said magnanimously. 'I'm allowing her to attend the Westleigh Hydrotherapy Centre, which is run by Mr Spollet, the physician who saw her in London. It seems his treatment improved her health and that a stay at this spa will complete the cure. All being well, by this time next year you and she will be married. Then she'll do her duty and produce an heir and a couple of spares, thus insuring the continuation of your line.'

Amelie could not keep quiet, her indignation boiling over. 'You're talking about a human being here, not a brood mare,' she snapped.

Mervin gave her a withering stare. 'Conduct her to her room, Humphrey. She's beginning to bore me.'

Marched upstairs by a back way, Amelie's arm was held in the valet's strong grip, released at her door and then pushed inside. She heard the lock snap as the key turned. She was alone in the lamp-lit warmth of her own room. It was comforting to feel its welcome, tired as she was and smarting from the beating she had received, but also by the uncaring manner in which she'd been treated. Candles were lit in sconces each side of the cheval mirror and she lifted her nightgown gingerly and examined her pubis. Fiery red showed through the curling hair, and when she used two fingers to hold back the labia, it was to find that area even redder and very sore.

She went into the bathroom, scrubbed her teeth and rinsed her mouth, but could not rid herself entirely of the taste and smell of Nigel. Then she started and turned off the tap, certain there was someone in the bedroom.

'Who is there?' she called tremulously.

'It's only me... Mrs Tanner,' answered the housekeeper, appearing in the doorway. 'Master sent me with this pot of balm. Says I'm to apply it to your sore cunny. Hop on the bed so I can get at it.'

'Am I to have no peace tonight?' Amelie complained, but did as Mrs Tanner instructed. 'It's my own property anyway and I should have the say in having it soothed... or not.'

'This is the genuine article,' Mrs Tanner assured her, holding up a jar made of green glass. It had a round gold lid.

'Why did he send you along with it?' Amelie asked suspiciously.

'I guess he desires to use you himself and wants you all healed up and ready to go,' Mrs Tanner said, leering.

'He's a monster,' Amelie sulked, shuddering at the thought of penetration in that tender portion of her that had been handled roughly.

'He's a man, and most all of them are monsters,' Mrs Tanner agreed good-humouredly. 'Now on the bed with you and up with your nightie.'

Sighing, Amelie complied, and after a little while was glad that she had. The housekeeper's hands knew how to

150

be gentle, and the balm seemed to be made from a magic formula that quickly took the sting out of her flesh. She relaxed, arms clasped behind her head, knees raised high, feet flat on the mattress. Mrs Tanner stuck her fingers in the jar and brought out a scoop of scented cream. When she applied this to Amelie's sex it was in the nature of icy snow, making her quiver and cry out. Then, miraculously, the pain went away.

'Oh, it's so much better,' she breathed, and Mrs Tanner's fingers continued to spread the potion over Amelie's clit and avenue.

'You want to come very badly, don't you, deary?' Mrs Tanner crooned, and exposed the hard bud that was the seat of all sensation. She crouched closer and stared at it, remarking, 'It's a fine one. You should be proud of it, my lass. Men think they rule the roost on account of that thing of theirs, but they don't understand that we women have an equally fine organ, that gives more pleasure than the men ever dreamed about. Isn't that so, my love?'

'Yes, oh yes... we have indeed,' Amelie panted, for pain had been superseded by pleasure. The urgent need to climax was upon her, nubbin shining like a pale pink shell, desire roaring through her womb till it was like a coiled spring.

She did not care for Mrs Tanner, thought her unkind, deceptive and cunning, but now the balm on her fingers and their clever manipulation was bringing her closer and closer to the brink. She was muttering obscenities as she stroked Amelie's parts.

'Are you coming, girl? That's it, my pretty darling, let me wet it more... let me run my finger from your gash to your button. There, that's right. Feels good, doesn't it? Nothing like a good frig. You can do it for me one day, sweetheart. I'm getting hot as Hades. I want you to burst as you come, fly up to the stars and back again, and know it was me who brought it on for you.'

Amelie was beyond caring who it was or why she was

there or anything, save the frantic urge to find release. She heard herself making animal noises, behaving like a farmyard creature in season.

Pain forgotten, she clamped Mrs Tanner's hand between her thighs and writhed against her massaging fingers. The passion grew, the feeling more intense, the need overpowering so that no matter who had come into the room then, were it Queen Victoria herself, Amelie would not have been able to stop. A huge spasm swept over her, so strong that she lost consciousness for a moment, coming to radiating heat and pleasure. Mrs Tanner slowly released the pressure of her finger, letting Amelie down gradually, tucking the coverlet round her and leaving her to sleep.

Chapter Nine

Westleigh was a popular seaside resort renowned for its bracing breezes and the miraculous qualities of its mud that was rumoured to cure anything from rheumatism to lung disease. This was Amelie's first visit there since she was a tot when she'd been taken on an outing organised by the church. Joseph Thacker and his family had travelled with his parishioners in a rare show of solidarity and hail-fellow-well-met. A horse drawn bus to the railway depot and a train had been the means of transport. All returned lobster-red and salty, with sand between the toes and repeated expressions of gratitude, saying what a fine time had been had by all. Thank you, vicar!

Amelie could remember snippets of this event, but try though she might, did not recognise landmarks at first. She, Millicent and Dulcie arrived at the station, and from thence took a hackney to the Royal Hotel, where the finest suite had been booked for them, facing the promenade and adjacent to the Winter Gardens. A balcony gave access to the view. The porter opened the double doors and Millicent and Amelie stood there, enjoying the warm sunshine and gazing at the vast area of sand stretching out to join an even larger expanse of pewter grey sludge. Light glinted on small, white-crested waves in the far distance.

'It's coming back to me,' Amelie said. 'I can remember trying to wade through the mud. It was fun, all squelchy and dotted with little coiled heaps thrown up by sandworms. It oozed between my toes as I headed towards the sea. I was wearing a navy-blue serge swimming costume. Charity and Agnes were dressed like it too, while Obediah and Caleb had striped ones. Aunt Harriet kept an eye on us from where she sat in a deckchair shaded by a large parasol, her cartwheel hat fixed firmly to her hair by pins and a chiffon scarf tied under her chin.'

'And where was your godfather while you were paddling?' Millicent enquired, leaning on the wrought-iron balustrade and looking down at passers-by.

'Leading the cricket team that had set up their stumps on a flat piece of beach,' Amelie replied, feeling guilty because she had made no attempt to contact her godparents since entering the Bessborough's fascinating world. 'He was always interested in the Kemble club. Still is, I imagine.'

The tide was in, flat and undramatic, needing a gale to whip it up, and brightly coloured bathing machines that resembled gypsy wagons had been drawn into the shallows by donkeys. 'I'd like to try one of those,' Millicent remarked. 'We could spend all day there, and it would be like a little house. Dulcie could arrange picnics. Couldn't you, Dulcie?' She addressed the maid who was busy unpacking, shaking the creases from gowns and filling the tallboy with stockings, underwear, nightgowns and headgear and shawls. No gentlewoman worth her salt ever travelled light.

'Certainly, your ladyship,' she answered briskly. 'But I've a notion that your days at the spa will be fully occupied.'

'And we were allowed to come without Mrs Tanner,' Millicent said happily, stepping back into the drawing room of the apartment. There was nothing vulgar about it, no modern fittings or overstuffed chairs and settees. It was perfectly in keeping with this large building whose origin stemmed from the birth of the century, when the Prince Regent was designing his Pavilion at Brighton.

'That surprised me and no mistake, her being left behind.

She was highly offended, I can tell you.' Dulcie nodded, the eternal gossip. If one wanted to know about anything that went on in and around Kelston Towers, then she was the one to ask.

'Ah, but you see, we are to be joined by Lord Ralph. He will escort us everywhere.'

'Is he taking the cure himself?' Dulcie said, arranging Millicent's shoes in a neat row at the bottom of the wardrobe. 'Sure and he doesn't need it. I never seen a bonnier man.' She turned to Amelie, adding, 'I'll do your things now, miss, if that's all right.'

'Of course, Dulcie,' Amelie answered, still admiring the scene from the balcony. 'But I can manage myself. I don't want you tiring yourself in the role of maidservant to both of us.'

'It's a pleasure, miss, it really is,' Dulcie averred, and it seemed that she meant it.

A visit to the Hydrotherapy Centre had been arranged for that afternoon and, as it was only a stone's throw away from the hotel, they walked there. Millicent wore elbow-length gloves and a Gainsborough hat, the broad brim an insurance against the ravages of the elements. A sunshade gave added protection, as did her floor-length skirt and long-sleeved blouse. Amelie, impatient with such tepidity, refused a parasol and pulled off her hat as soon as they left the Royal Hotel's stately precincts.

'I've warned you about freckles, miss,' Dulcie gloomed, bringing the hat along hopefully. 'Real curse they are. What man looks twice at a girl who is like a spotted roly-poly pudding?'

'Does it matter, as long as she has a sweet nature and a beautiful mind?' asked Amelie, ironically.

'It certainly does, miss!' vowed the maid. 'I've never yet met a bloke who has been keen to find out what goes on in my head, far too concerned about getting into my knickers.'

'What have I let myself in for?' Ralph groaned, slumped in a leather club chair in his studio.

'Go on, tell me, you're obviously dying to pour out your troubles to some unfortunate sod, and it happens to be me,' sighed the large man who was standing there with his hands on his hips, regarding him with amusement.

'It's not that bad, John,' Ralph confessed, giving a crooked smile and wondering if he could persuade him to pose as a Viking warrior. He fitted the part to perfection, tall and muscular, handsome and blond. He could just imagine him hefting a broad sword. 'Some people might find it enjoyable, even entertaining, spending days at the seaside with one's sister and her most delightful companion.'

'Ah ha, so there's a woman in it somewhere,' John said, with a cheerful grin. 'I thought as much. One of these days your sins will find you out, my boy. I thought you had enough to do keeping up with Maggie.'

'She's just a whore,' Ralph returned sharply.

'And a first-class model. Don't forget that. If you upset her she won't pose for you, and that means me, too.'

John leaned forward and added his name and the date at the bottom right-hand corner of the canvas he had just completed. It was a rather daring subject, with two naked ladies and two fully clothed gentlemen seated by a lake and sharing a bottle of wine. It was a contemporary scene, and one that could not be disguised as a classical composition. The men wore white flannel trousers, blazers and boaters. There was no evidence that these were legendary gods and goddesses, thus excusing the racy subject of the picture.

'There we go, I've finished it,' he said, 'and I'm not ashamed for everyone to know it was me, John Phelps, who did it.'

'It will cause a stink at the exhibition at the Royal Academy,' Ralph reminded.

'Good,' said John, dipping his brushes in turpentine and

rubbing them clean with a rag. 'At least that way it won't be ignored by the critics. What is it actors say? A bad review is better than no review at all.'

Ralph shook his head, studying his friend. He was so large, rather like a mastiff, and faithful like a dog, too. Ralph had been at Art College with him and they remained close, sharing the studio and the house when John was out of funds. This was a frequent event for although, like Ralph, he had a yearly stipend and sold the occasional painting, John never could save money. It simply burned a hole in his pocket. He was generous to a fault, extravagant and expansive, liking drink, fine food, living high and copulating with ladies. He adored them, rich or poor, harlot or unfaithful wife, and treated them well. He was extremely popular.

'Why don't you come to Westleigh with me?' Ralph suggested. He was rather annoyed with himself for Amelie was obsessing his thoughts. He felt like a lovesick boy and, while this was exciting, it was also exasperating.

'Can't afford it,' John said, taking off his soiled smock and throwing it into a corner. Beneath it he wore a white shirt with a soft collar, a loose tie, and knickerbockers that matched his Norfolk jacket and cap. He had developed a passion for cycling, such an easy mode of transport in overcrowded London. Knee-high socks and stout shoes completed the outfit.

'Let me take care of the bills,' Ralph offered, in great need of a friend around, confused as he was by his own emotions concerning his sister's companion. She was beneath him class-wise, but he did not want to simply seduce then leave her. A more permanent relationship floated in his visions of the future.

'That's mighty generous of you,' John replied, and went to the stove, took up the simmering kettle and filled the teapot. 'Tell me about the companion.'

'She's called Amelie and is very beautiful,' Ralph said, needing no prompting. 'Marvellous chestnut hair… it's natural and doesn't come out of a bottle. Eyes as green as can be. A figure to adore, and a strong personality.'

'You rogered her, of course.' John sipped his cup of strong brown tea.

'No, I didn't. She told me she is still a virgin.'

'And you believed her?'

'I did. I still do. She's had a rough time, orphaned young and brought up by her godparents, a vicar and his wife. The sons of the household attempted to corrupt her. She's been awakened to physical pleasure. Obediah, that's the youngest son, actually fingered her and brought her off during one of his father's sermons.'

'Ah, so she knows about reaching a crisis, does she? That's useful. So many girls don't.'

'She knows all right. I did it for her one day in the woods, but my brother's valet interrupted us. My brother who, by the way, has been whipping my darling Amelie and making her his slave.'

'Has he, by God? This gets more and more intriguing.'

'You'll join me? I leave tomorrow.'

John shrugged his wide shoulders. 'Why not? If you're footing the bill.'

'But you'll steer clear of Amelie,' Ralph warned. 'My sister, Millicent... now that's a different matter, but I wouldn't like you to break her heart. She is vulnerable enough, poor child, and needs tender loving care. That's what this trip to the Hydrotherapy Centre is all about. She's a bundle of nerves, subject to hysteria, or so the doctor says... weeping fits, general ill health and dark fears. Mervin is trying to marry her off to an objectionable oaf, Nigel Balfour, but she refuses. I hope she responds to the treatment available at the spa.'

'Shall we be expected to take part in the treatment?' John asked, wiping his moustache with his hand. 'I've heard about such places. It's all massages and exercise, isn't it?'

'I think so, but mainly for ladies. We'll be able to

entertain ourselves in other ways, while Millicent is having her daily sessions.'

'You mean finding one or two frisky little fillies?' John said with a wink.

'Not for me. I'm trying hard to keep myself pure for Amelie. I was thinking more along the lines of sketching. The scenery should be inspiring.'

'You're saving yourself? Practicing chastity? That I find hard to believe. Like most of us, you never have been able to refuse if it's offered you on a plate.'

There was a noise on the stairs outside, chattering, shrieks of laughter, the rap of high-heeled shoes. The door handle rattled and Maggie poked her head round, asking cheekily, 'Can we come in?'

'D'you see what I mean?' John said to Ralph, with a lift of one eyebrow. 'I'll bet you a guinea that your cock is in her within half an hour.'

'Done,' said Ralph.

Maggie was accompanied by another model called Bess. Ralph had booked them for a session. He was working on a picture with a Roman theme, Maggie and Bess posing as vestal virgins. Bess was black-haired, dark-eyed and gamin. She was no more than sixteen and had been on the game for years. Her Cockney accent was so thick it could have been cut with a knife. Her brain was not; she was streetwise and canny. No one ever cheated on her, and her customers held her in awe.

'Come in, girls,' Ralph said, and Maggie put down a hand and stroked his fly front in passing. His penis leapt and his resolutions regarding celibacy took a nosedive.

John had no such reservations, grabbing Bess and planting a smacking kiss on her lips, then tumbling her onto the couch, shouting, 'How about a free one? I'm out of funds.'

'Get off, you big lummox!' Bess retorted, giving him a shove in the chest. 'No pay, no play. I've told you that before.'

John shouted across to Ralph who was struggling to refuse Maggie's blatant offer, 'Hey, can you lend me a half a sovereign? If you don't you'll have to watch me wanking. My cock's fit to burst.'

'Go on, don't be a skinflint,' urged Maggie, tickling Ralph's nose with her feather boa. She then pulled in her ribs so that her big breasts bulged over the lace edge of her crimson satin corset. 'Get yer wallet out and we'll give you a treat. Won't we, Bess? You want to watch two girls doin' it together? You got it, mate. You want to join in and show us what we're missing? Let's see yer dick.'

She joined Bess on the divan and they treated the men to a view of black stockings, black and gilt suspenders, white thighs and pink gashes fringed by dark hair. Maggie was on her knees, her buttocks in the air, her skirt riding up, her hands on those well-rounded hinds, spreading the cheeks wide and displaying her amber-hued bottom-hole. Bess, meanwhile, was pinching her friend's breasts and parting the leaves of her own labia, playing with the shiny stem of her clitoris.

John was the first to crack. He leapt upon Bess and dragged her to the floor. There he positioned himself between her spread legs and plunged his engorged cock into her dark aperture. Grunting, he pushed and shoved till it disappeared, and his frizzy blond pubes mingled with her inky black ones.

'Jesus Christ!' Ralph muttered under his breath, smelling the pungency of Maggie's essences, and experiencing the pressure building in his balls.

Her very commonness acted like an aphrodisiac. He had no need to care for her, make sure she was satisfied, show affection or even liking. She was a whore, a hole in which he could let loose his spunk. What price poetry or love or gentle emotions now? She had wide hips and her skin was dimpled and pale as alabaster, having never seen the sunlight. A town dweller who had not visited the country, she was a creature who operated mostly after dark – like a vampire that stalked its victims.

Ralph despised her, yet his aching cock was straining to join her cunt. He tore at his trousers and it shot out like an engorged snake. Big, oh so big, and he was proud of it. Maggie's palm closed around it and she drew the ring of foreskin back and displayed the purple helm, then holding his testicles from below, squeezed them and inserted pressure on the area between, halting his orgasm.

'Look at this, Bess,' she called to her friend who was fully occupied with John. She waggled Ralph's penis and laughed. ''Ung like a bloody 'orse, 'ee is! I reckon I should charge twice.'

Ralph could wait no longer, pushing her hand away. He wanted to whip her, to see her rump turn fiery red under the lash. She never responded sexually, no matter how he tried to bring her off.

'I do this for money, not fun,' she always said. 'Men like fuckin' and women needs money. Don't try to kiss me. Don't tamper with me bud. I don't want pleasure. I don't feel nothin', though you're nicer than most of the dirty buggers.'

Now, even though his mind shrieked obscenities – slut, tart, draggle-tailed piece of filth! – so his cock, rigid as a spear, drove into her. This was all it needed. His thrusts were ferocious. He cried out in his extremity. Writhing, pumping, he was on the rack of unutterable pleasure, reaching the peak when he felt his semen shooting into the depths of her as he reached a shattering climax.

Just for a second he was washed with an overwhelming tenderness towards the woman who had just satisfied him. He collapsed on her momentarily, wishing she would love and caress him, but this was not Maggie's way. She had done her job and now wanted no more of him. Ralph removed his limp organ from between her thighs and wiped it on a square of paint-stained cloth. Then he sat up and looked across at John who, judging by his loud roaring, had just reached his climax.

'Well done, you baggage!' he exclaimed, slapping Bess briskly. 'Charge it to Ralph. Now, how about we go down to the Pig and Whistle for a pint of beer?'

'They are to pose for me,' Ralph said huffily. 'You seem to forget that is the arrangement.'

It was not John he was angry with, but himself. Once again he had been unable to control his lust. He loved Amelie, or was ninety-nine percent certain he did, but could not master his dick, that came erect without his permission whenever it scented pussy.

Mr Spollet was not at the spa, but a tall, fine-looking man with a reassuringly avuncular manner who introduced himself as Dr Robinson met Millicent and Amelie in the reception room.

There was a woman with him, wearing a plain grey dress with crisply starched collar and cuffs, a large white apron and a cap.

'This is Sister Mallow, who is a fully trained nurse,' he said, and Millicent could feel herself unwinding in the calm atmosphere. 'She will look after you and explain procedures.'

Millicent had been more than simply impressed by the building. It was palatial, not what she expected of a health hydro. Marble abounded, starting with the pillars that supported the large front door, and continuing on the floor of the magnificent hall into which they were ushered by a liveried footman. Rooms led off from this, and statues occupied alcoves, each one representing a perfect specimen of manhood or womanhood, almost nude and showing off their assets. Such physical excellence was presumably the goal of the patients who placed themselves in the medical staffs' care.

The reception room was carpeted and panelled and had high windows with brocade drapes. There was gilded furniture and fine china ornaments, a large fireplace and seascapes on the walls. Crystal chandeliers hung overhead, each holding dozens of electric light bulbs shaped like candles.

'Mr Spollet has written to me, describing your symptoms and setting out a programme,' Dr Robinson said. 'There's no need to be nervous. Sister Mallow will be with you and see that all goes smoothly. The treatment can stop if you find it offensive or uncomfortable, but I do suggest you give it a fair trial.'

'Very well, doctor,' Millicent agreed. 'And I would like my companion, Miss Aston, to share some of the benefits, too.'

'Certainly, my dear lady, whatever you desire,' he agreed, smiling at Amelie and asking, 'Do you experience similar maladies?'

'No, sir,' she answered truthfully and, to rid herself of any awe she might be experiencing due to his position, she imagined him naked. He would be strong and muscular, with a rounded belly, a hairy chest with wine-red nipples, and a greying bush from which a fine cock would protrude.

'In that case, you would probably find massage enjoyable,' he suggested. 'Now then, young ladies, Sister Mallow will show you where to go and tell you what to do.'

They followed the nurse's straight back, through the hall and further spacious rooms where ladies wrapped in towelling robes were resting after their treatments, drinking coffee, smoking cigarettes and chatting. There was a pleasant aroma everywhere that excited Millicent's nostrils; soap, sandalwood, and a strong hint of perfumed oils. She found herself revelling in these sybaritic surroundings that reminded her of a picture she had seen of a sultan's harem. She was eager to find out more.

'Miss Aston will be in a room next to yours, Lady Millicent,' Sister Mallow said, very formal and businesslike. 'You will be in here,' and she opened a door that was one of several leading from a wide passage.

'I'll see you in a little while,' Amelie promised, and Millicent went inside.

She was in a modest sized but lush room, its walls and floor glazed with blue Islamic tiles. There was a sunken bath, a massage table and glass shelves containing bottles of oil and jars of unguents. A curtained cubicle held a wooden bench and a long mirror.

'Please undress, your ladyship,' said Sister Mallow. 'I'll help you with your stay-lacing.'

Millicent did as she was told and was soon bare, coming under Sister Mallow's scrutiny. She was then handed a robe and told to leave the cubicle. Next she was instructed to sit in a hard-backed wooden chair that was set over a channel in the floor. Embarrassed to be watched by the nurse, even though she was so impersonal, Millicent reluctantly left the robe on the side and sat on the chair.

'Feet apart,' the nurse instructed. 'I shall leave you for a moment. The douche operator will be here directly.'

'I'm not accustomed to these terms,' Millicent plucked up courage to say. 'What is a "douche"?'

Sister Mallow pointed overhead to where a rubber shower hose was suspended on a hook. 'That is a douche,' she explained. 'When turned on it sends out jets of water, hot or cold, depending on the operator who is also a masseur. He will direct the current of water against the surface of your skin, or into the cavities of your body. This is a most popular form of treatment and very efficacious. I've seen many a lady leave here with a spring in her step and a smile on her lips.'

Millicent was agog. She could not wait, hoping to repeat the sensations given her by Mr Spollet and, later, Amelie. She felt so much better these days, but refused to tell Mervin lest he insist she marry Nigel. She could put off the evil day by a succession of treatments and, hopefully, would soon be confident enough to defy her brother for good and all.

Someone rapped the door and a pleasant male voice

said, 'The masseur, your ladyship.'

'Come in,' she quavered, reaching for her robe and dragging it awkwardly around her, thankful she had when he came in, smiling widely.

'I'm Peter,' he said immediately. 'I shall be attending you myself, or supervising others. Has Sister Mellow explained about the spray treatment?'

'Not exactly,' Millicent managed to say, taking a firm hold of her robe and her dignity. This was not easy, for he was a most personable young man, looking overwhelmingly masculine in a tight white cotton jacket buttoned to his throat and matching trousers that strained over the muscles of his thighs. He had slicked-back brown hair and was clean-shaven. His cheekbones were pronounced and his lips full, and his blue eyes sparkled as he looked at her.

'Well, you see, Lady Millicent, doctors have long decided that water is a great healer, relaxing tension. It is particularly beneficial in cases of hysteria, to which so many ladies are prone. The douche was invented, providing a powerful jet that trained people, like myself, can direct where we think best. I usually concentrate on the breasts, the navel and between the thighs. There is no need to feel any awkwardness, for I am completely impersonal and my attitude is that of a doctor. May I take your robe and we will begin?'

She handed it to him, nipples tightening, skin covered in goose bumps – not through cold but because Peter was looking at her, but only as a patient. He unhooked the hose and directed it towards her. His strong fingers controlled the nozzle and he said, 'Are you ready? We'll start without too much pressure.'

'All right,' she said, and tried to cup her mons and cover her breasts.

'No,' Peter said, shaking his head. He took her wrists reverently and bound them with silken cords to the arms of the chair. Then he spread her thighs, wound more cord round her ankles and tied them to the rungs. She felt heavy and voluptuous and more than ready for anything he wished to perform on her vulnerable body.

Then, taking the showerhead in his hand he tested the water. Satisfied, he let it play over Millicent's upper torso, concentrating on her breasts. She leaned her head back and closed her eyes. This was sheer bliss! Her nipples rose and strained, needing the little jets that cascaded over them and dripped from the peaks, then ran in rivulets over her ribs and down, down to where her throbbing clit yearned for attention.

Peter, judging her reaction to a nicety, increased the pressure a little. Millicent gasped with the joy of it. The shower wet her all over, cool and bracing. Peter let it grow warmer and faster, forming a pulsing jet. He moved it slowly, leaving her breasts and going down to her feet, playing over her ankles and insteps, soaking the cords and then letting the spray swirl up across her calves, her knees and thighs. The water pressed against her fork, danced across her labia and playfully teased her bud.

Millicent could not control her cries. 'Ooh, ooh! That's good. Go higher, please… please!'

Peter smiled but followed his set course. He repeated the path he had just taken, going at a leisurely pace and, when the jet returned to her labia, she arched her back, trying to catch its force on her clitoris. The machine that drove the douche was humming. She could hear it like a multitude of bees wanting to sup at her juices. Peter increased the pressure. Now it was driving, stinging, tantalising her bud with its closeness, making the little organ swell. Millicent shuddered and tried to chase the jet but she was at Peter's mercy. He turned up the power and the water shot out at speed.

It pulsed towards her, a surging tide washing over her labia. Peter turned it on full, thrashing her clitoris as she came in a rush of ecstasy so strong that she lost consciousness for a second. Spasms raced through her, each one a beautiful ache of satisfied desire. She returned to herself, realising that what she had just experienced was another hysterical paroxysm.

Peter released her bonds and wrapped her in the towelling robe, and then assisted her to the couch. He patted her dry, his hands as tender as a woman's, and then said, 'I shall now give you a massage.'

'I've never had that done to me before,' she murmured and stretched out on her stomach, face to one side, watching him pour a little puddle of oil into his palm. He placed a small towel over her buttocks, but left her exposed elsewhere.

He smiled again, and winked as if he knew very well what had just taken place. 'Lady Millicent, you've not lived until you entered our spa,' he said confidently.

Amelie could hardly believe her incredible luck. She was lying on a padded couch in a private room that was part of a luxurious hydrotherapy centre. Mother-naked, a man who, by his swarthy complexion, blue-black ringlets and fascinating accent, appeared to be of Mediterranean stock was massaging her body.

Not only this, but Ralph planned to join them at the Royal Hotel about teatime.

But now there was this new experience to be enjoyed. 'What's your name?' she asked.

The masseur's eyes lit up and he smiled, displaying perfect white teeth. There was the faint, exotic taint of garlic on his breath. 'Mario,' he said. 'I come from Italy. Have you visited there, Miss Aston?'

'Never,' she answered, responding to the novelty and spine tingling thrill of being touched by a foreigner. And such a one, too – an attractive Romeo.

'Ah, then you should go to my country – *la belle Italia*,' he said. 'Visit Florence and Venice and Rome. It is popular with English people. They love its antiquity, its warm sun and the music... ah, yes, the opera... so exquisite, Miss

Aston. It will speak to your heart and make you dream of love.'

How poetic, she thought, and lay prone on her belly, feeling a ripple of response in the area between her labia. Her little tyrant was stirring and wanted to be rubbed. Mario had part covered her with a sheet but she wanted him to remove it, anxious to present her buttocks and the dark valley between them for his inspection. He was dressed in white, even down to his canvas deck shoes, and this threw his olive skin into greater prominence. His sleeves were short and his arms dusted with springy dark hairs. As he stood beside her, his lower half at eye-level, she could see the outline of his penis under the neatly fitting trousers, and she longed for him to unbutton and take it out, letting her see and touch it.

He set to work and she lay as limp as a rag doll under his skilful hands. Her mound rocked against the linen-covered couch and she could feel the pressure. Mario's hands were sinewy and brown and she wanted them all over her, not just on her spine. He used the edges to hammer lightly up and down, then he kneaded the muscles and released the tension. He massaged the backs of her thighs, her calves, her feet, and all the time the thrumming in her bud increased and she thought she might come just by thinking about it, but found this impossible.

He slipped rubber pads over his palms. They were covered in nodules that chafed her skin pleasantly. They took away dry skin and stimulated every inch of her as he skimmed over her lower spine and traversed the rosy roundness of her bottom, dipping momentarily into the deep hollow between her lower cheeks. Amelie sighed and his dark eyes looked into hers understandingly.

'You are still tense, Miss Aston?' he queried. 'I can ease you. Turn over, if you please.'

She could not wait, rolling onto her back, glad she was entirely naked as he poured more oil onto his hands and then returned to her, getting down to work, moving over her body in long sweeps.

She trembled and he paused. 'Do you want me to stop, *signorina*?'

'No,' she said wistfully.

'But you are shaking,' he persisted.

'It's all right. Go on, please.' She felt she would die if he did not continue.

'I know,' he whispered soothingly. 'Don't worry, I will give you what you want.'

His hands shifted to her breasts, oiling the perfect globes and plucking the needful nipples. Her throat received attention, even her ears, and she loved the way he pulled gently at the lobes. He knew every one of her erogenous zones, and Amelie thought she had died and gone straight to paradise. She was shaking with desire, confident he would not disappoint her and leave her high, if not dry. All she had to do was lie there and let him take over.

She whimpered like a kitten while he roiled and rolled her nipples, making sure they stood up in peaks. She almost reached orgasm, but needed his specialist touch on her clit. He made her wait, tantalising her, paying attention to her ribcage and then circling the dimple of her navel. He lingered over this while she wriggled impatiently.

'Oh, Mario,' she whispered.

'Impatient one,' he chided, in that melting, lyrical accent 'We must not hurry this. Let me guide you to realms of pleasure you have never yet known.'

'But what about you?' she murmured, blushing madly. 'Don't you need satisfaction?'

Mario shook his head. 'This is not part of the treatment, *signorina*. If there is no union between the man and woman, then this is not viewed as sexual. The spa would be closed down if any such contact took place. It would be labelled a bordello. Most people believe it is only through intercourse that a woman can achieve a climax... when the man does.'

'I've never had a man, yet I can easily reach what Mr

Spollet calls an hysterical paroxysm,' Amelie returned, confused by this. 'And who says she is dependent on the male member?'

Mario shrugged. 'The medical profession... men in general.'

'Those lords of creation who imagine they have complete power over females?' Amelie huffed. 'Do you think this, Mario?'

Again he gave that typically foreign shrug. 'I am not paid to have an opinion. I do what I am instructed. Besides it being so bad for business if I transgressed, I am married, *signorina*, and would not be unfaithful to my wife. Shall we proceed?'

His hands moved to her pubic regions, feathering through her russet pubes and making them shiny with oil. He pressed with his thumbs each side of her labia, opening her. She could feel her nubbin ripening as he worked his fingers around her crest, circling, teasing, then finally concentrating on that overheated little bud.

So this was to be for her pleasure alone? He was not seeking gratification and this freed her to relax and enjoy everything he had to offer. Far gone now, it took but a few strokes for her to achieve an earth shattering climax. She cried out and convulsed and Mario did not abandon her clit at once, but rested his hand there till she fell back, utterly replete.

He moved away then after covering her with a towel, and she watched him washing his hands and replacing the oil on the shelf. Then he smiled, nodded and retired, leaving her to mull over this strange but immensely satisfying experience.

Chapter Ten

'Ralph, my dear brother, you're here at last,' Millicent said, beaming happily as she held out her hands to him. Then her eyes switched to the man who had come in with him.

Ralph made the introduction. 'And this is my good friend, John... John Phelps.'

'I am delighted to meet you, Lady Millicent,' this impressive individual replied. He was rugged and pleasant looking, not in the least formidable though very large. He took her hand and, bowing, bore it to his lips.

Millicent's breath came in a quick little gasp and icy shivers engorged her clitoris. She was becoming supersensitive to any half-presentable male she met theses day. Mr Spollet had indeed let loose an ungovernable force within her, with his fingers, his machines and his water therapy.

'John is a fellow artist,' Ralph explained. 'He's come to keep me company while you are having your treatment. Did you go today?'

'Oh yes, for the first time,' she answered, and could feel herself blushing, the memory of the douche and its attendant pleasures, including the excellent Peter, filling her with heat.

'And how was it?'

'Just fine.'

'You look well, doesn't she, John? Such rosy cheeks and sparkling eyes. Is it being away from Mervin that brings about this miracle?'

'A combination of that and the sea breeze and the spa,'

she managed to say, keeping her voice steady and peeking at John without appearing to do so.

She had liked the feel of his lips on her hand, even though her lace glove prevented skin contact. She liked his easygoing manner, too. It was all very well being brought to paroxysms, but she was anxious to find out about coition. There were limits, though, and marrying Nigel was one of them. It would be better to stay as unsullied as a nun in a convent than commit herself to him.

Amelie stood just behind her and she guessed she would be devouring Ralph with her eyes. She envied her. It must be wonderful to be in love. None of them could foresee what would happen, of course. There would be opposition should they desire to marry, if it ever got that far.

The gong boomed and taking Ralph's arm she walked into the opulent dining room. A table had been reserved for them in one of the great bay windows that looked out over the darkening promenade. Coloured lights twinkled, stretching the length of the esplanade and along the pier where they were mirrored in the sea. People were still strolling about, breathing in the balmy evening air.

Millicent was more content than ever before. The dining room was filling up with well-dressed gentlefolk, attended by smart waiters in black and their overseer, the lordly *maitre d' hôte*. Nothing escaped his eagle eye, the smallest misdemeanour dealt with on the spot. A string quartet played light music under a shell-shaped alcove verdant with potted palms. This added to the harmony that pervaded the room.

The menu was passed round and a waiter hovered on the balls of his feet, napkin over one arm. Ralph ordered for his sister and Amelie, and consorted with John regarding their own choice. It was all immensely civilised and Millicent found it difficult to equate this with the upheaval within her caused by Peter and his water jets. She could not help glancing at John's hands as course followed delicious course and the wine went down. Ralph ordered another bottle that arrived along with the most delectable puddings.

Had Ralph, Millicent wondered, engineered the inclusion of his friend especially for her? Did he understand how much she wanted to experience love, emotion and sex? Real sex, that is, not something brought about by water or fingers or lips, but actual penetration by a penis. John was such a large man. Did this mean his organ was to scale? Millicent sat there toying with her chocolate mousse like a true lady, while her imagination was full of rude visions of John's cock and balls.

He was seated next to her and her wayward fingers hungered to come to rest on his burly knee, hidden by the linen tablecloth. While her foot, in its dainty satin pump, moved towards his black shoe and it was all she could do to stop rubbing it against his instep.

He kept up a flow of conversation, witty, well-versed on subjects as diverse as politics, art, music and the theatre. Ralph chimed in and they were sometimes slightly too outspoken, using language and words that were hardly suitable for young ladies' ears. Millicent came to life, leaning forward and joining in, though ashamed at her lack of knowledge regarding worldly matters.

'Amelie and I went to see *The Mikado* when in London,' she said, after John had mentioned the operettas running at the *Savoy Theatre*. 'It was very amusing and the music is so tuneful.'

'I liked it, too, it's very satirical, Gilbert is a wizard with words,' John agreed, and pressed his knee against hers. By accident or intention? She felt the warmth of her arousal and wondered, almost desperately, if it was possible for them to be alone together somewhere.

That was not likely, for Chaperones were the order of the day where maidens were concerned. One could not even travel solo in a rail coach with an unattached male, or one might find oneself having to marry him. Her only hope lay in Ralph brushing aside convention in his desire to have Amelie to himself.

It was as if her guardian angel was sympathetic to her cause. Coffee over, with brandy for the men, and Ralph stubbed out his cigar and said, 'Shall we visit the pier? It looks so pretty and inviting,' and as he spoke, his eyes were feasting on Amelie.

Millicent followed her cue, answering, 'I'm rather tired. All this therapy, I expect. I'd much prefer to sit here and listen to the orchestra.'

'In that case, will you walk with me, Amelie?' he asked. 'I can assure you I'll be a reliable escort, and I trust John to guard my sister with his life.'

So it was agreed, and John snapped his fingers at a waiter, demanding more coffee, while Millicent, stunned by this turn of events that were the answer to her prayers, watched Amelie pick up her shawl and Ralph drape it gallantly round her shoulders. Amelie was a vision in oyster satin, her cheeks as pink as the band of feathers she wore instead of a hat.

John inched his chair closer to Millicent's and she could sense his desire washing over her in waves. The table was secluded, and they were reflected in the window glass, backed by the darkness without. He leaned over and kissed her softly on the lips. It was like a jolt of electricity down her spine. The feel of his moustache added another dimension. It was soft yet prickly, depending on how hard he pressed. She saw the couple in the glass, and it was as if she was set apart from them. It was not really happening to her, was it?

With an effort she roused herself, pushing him away. He took her rebuff like a gentleman. There was nothing uncouth about John Phelps. She was sure he would not force himself on a woman and placed her hand trustingly in his when he said, 'Shall we walk in the garden?'

She nodded and rose, and he held her pane-velvet jacket while she slipped into it, and then offered his crooked elbow so that she could curl her fingers round his arm. It was terribly daring but she did not care, feeling liberated as she left the hotel and strolled on the moonlit terrace with a man whom she had only just met, a single man, an artist, an unknown quantity. Perhaps he was the one who would initiate her into the union between men and women?

He looked up at the starry sky, then down at her, and said, 'I did not realise that Ralph had such a beautiful sister.'

'Flatterer,' Millicent chided, and tapped him lightly with her folded fan. This was all new to her, a game of flirtation that had yet to be learned.

'Not at all, Millicent,' he replied, and put his hands on her waist, drawing her up against his body. He was so tall that her head did not reach the pit of his throat.

She knew propriety demanded that she screamed, struggled or slapped his face – maybe all three. She could not bring herself to do it. There was too much aching and melting inside her, longing coiling in her womb like a fully wound spring awaiting release. The smell of him fired her, the strong combination of male sweat, shaving soap, hair pomade and the musky odour that always seemed to hang around men, stemming from their genitals. She swayed even closer to him, desire tingling to her nerve ends as he trailed a finger over her jaw, down her throat and over her taffeta-covered nipples. He moved from one to the other with a delicate touch.

She shivered and moaned, her pelvis arching to meet the bulge now distorting his evening trousers. It was hard, that organ she was yet to experience. His mouth captured hers again, closed at first, then prising her lips apart his tongue entered her as surely as he would soon take possession of her love-channel. She was overwhelmed by taste and touch, savouring his saliva with its trace of brandy and cigar smoke, the quintessential essence of John – manly, masculine. The words burned into her brain as she ground against him, wanting more.

Her nipples peaked, her bud pulsed and her moist virginal haven longed to have him enter it. John took his mouth from hers long enough to say, 'Are you ready for this? I am acting like a cad. You're my best friend's sister and I should be protecting your honour, not striving to rob you of it.'

'Hush,' she replied, laying her fingers over his lips, astonished by her own boldness. 'I want to lose my virginity. It is tiresome and Mervin will give me to Nigel Balfour if I don't do something drastic soon. I would like you to be my first lover. I know you will take care of me and make sure I don't have a baby.'

'I'll do my best. There are ways and means to prevent conception and, should it happen, then I'll marry you, Millicent. You have my word as a gentleman.'

'But where can we go? I can't take you to my room; Dulcie will be there. It's too public here, and I want it to be special, not some furtive, hole-in-the-corner fumble.'

'I thought we'd try the hydro. There must be nooks and crannies suitable for lovers.'

The massage rooms sprang to mind. 'We can try,' she returned.

The short walk to the centre gave her opportunity to think, though not very clearly with his fingers linked with hers. Would it be open? Was treatment carried out by night as well as day? Its mock Greek temple door was wide, light streaming from it, joining the flares set up on either side. They met no one as they mounted the steps. A cleaner was mopping the hall floor and gave them not a glance. The reception desk was unattended. A notice saying *To The Pool*, was placed at the head of a corridor.

'Have you been there yet?' John murmured.

'No,' Millicent whispered. Now that they were actually in the building, it did not seem such a good idea.

'Let us explore,' he said, and led her down the passageway.

He pushed open swing doors at the end and they found

themselves in a large construction with a domed glass roof, beneath which had been built an oblong swimming pool. It was tiled in turquoise blue and the overhead lights shimmered on its surface. It looked undeniably inviting, its starkness relieved by a tasteful display of small trees and leafy shrubs in pots, adding their scent to the hothouse warmth. There was no one in sight.

'Let's take a dip,' John suggested. 'Can you swim?'

'My nanny taught me. There's a lake in the grounds of Kelston Towers, but I must admit I'm rusty and haven't done it for years.'

'It's like riding a bicycle, you never forget,' he said jovially. 'Do you ride? Ralph and I do. It's capital fun. Tell you what, I'll hire a couple of bikes and we can tour Westleigh. What do you say?'

'I'm supposed to be here for the cure.'

'That will cure you, and what I'm about to do will be even better,' he whispered. 'Get undressed, Millicent.'

I must be mad, she thought as she took off her clothes in the changing room, having difficulty with her lacing but managing it, although her fingers were trembling. She left her undergarments in a neat pile and hung her gown from a hook on the wall. She had retained her chemise, too shy to strip completely. She crept from the cubicle, her feet meeting the coolness of the tiles. Every sound echoed.

John stood on the side at the deep end and a sudden bolt of desire fixed her to the spot. He was naked and the light reflecting upwards from the surface threw every angle of him into relief. He was proud of his body and had every right to be; broad-shouldered and narrow-waisted, with a muscle-ridged belly and neat flanks, long strong legs and a tight arse. Millicent had always been an admirer of art, nude male statues in particular, and it was as if one had come to life.

But it was his cock that drew her attention; it was large, curving proudly from a thicket of brown-blond curls, his balls hanging loosely in their hairy purse beneath it.

He was looking at Millicent and she tingled at his warm appraisal as his eyes flickered over her breasts, outlined by the thin chemise. It only just reached the apex of her thighs, clinging to the pointed triangle.

'Can't you bring yourself to take that off?' he asked gently. 'I've bared all, so why not you?'

'I will in a minute, have patience,' she replied, and walked to the pool's rim, sat down, the cold tiles making her bottom clench, and dabbled her feet in the water.

John gave a smile and lifted his arms above his head. Every muscle was stretched, each curve and plain sharply defined. Then he dived, cutting through the surface with hardly a ripple. The pool was ten feet deep there and he surfaced at once, tossed back his streaming hair and swam strongly towards the shallow end where Millicent waited.

'It's cold, isn't it?' she said, staring down at his wet face. His eyelashes were wet too, spiky and thick, and his moustache was beaded with droplets.

'Not too bad. I've known worse. Try it,' he urged, grinning up at her, fastening a hand round her ankle.

She tugged to free herself. 'Let go, John, I'll come in my own good time.'

'You'll do it now, my girl,' he said with mock severity, gave a jerk and she was in his arms under the water. She gasped with shock, then the chill turned to heat as her chemise floated upwards and she felt his hard cock pressing against her bare stomach.

'What are you doing?' she fumed, though it was more than obvious.

He chuckled and did not answer, and his hands coasted over her breasts. The neck of the chemise had come untied and she was bare there now. His fingers lingered on her aroused teats and they hardened even more. She could feel her juices joining the water that poked impudent fingers around her pussy. It was a lovely, warm, liquid embrace. She could bottom the pool easily there, and John towered over her, the water lapping his waist. Glancing down, she could see his impressive phallus bobbing as it strained upright, the helm brushing his navel.

'Millicent, let me,' John said, and his fingers found her clitoris and she rocked against the sweet friction she craved. She clung to his slippery shoulders and let herself go. Her climax arced through her and she could feel her inner muscles contracting, searching for something solid to clasp. John slid a hand under her buttocks and lifted her. She opened her legs and fastened them around his waist. He positioned his cock and pushed against the obstruction that denied him her vagina. He nudged against her entrance, then surged inside. He was large and she felt herself stretching to take him, agonised by that sudden, numbing thrust. For a moment she ceased moving, letting it happen as he slid in deeper and deeper and the pain eased. She waited passively, letting him in inch by inch, her cunt welcoming his shaft, the walls contracting around it.

John lifted her up and down on his rod, his body moving faster and she succumbed to the driving power of it, letting it happen, absorbing the new sensations – the pain, the tightness, the pleasure that radiated from her satisfied nubbin.

He moved faster and faster and she clung harder, sharing his tremors as he flung back his head and closed his eyes, grunting with pleasure. Inside her she felt his cock twitch several times, and her own warmth was joined by his heated libation. He remained there, his dick softening slowly, and Millicent drifted in the water like a babe in the womb, resting against him, quiet now. And he, it seemed, was content to hold her.

Sister Mallow braced herself against the rail of a secluded gallery that gave an uninterrupted view of the pool below. Few knew of its existence. She gripped the polished wood till her knuckles glowed white, as she took the full length and girth of Dr Robinson's cock in her arse. Her skirt was up round her waist, her legs splayed in their sensible black woollen stockings and, as was her habit, always ready to receive the doctor's tribute, she wore no drawers.

He was in charge of the spa, there was no doubt about that, but at times like these when he had his tool jammed in her deepest recess, she was in command. Then this autocratic personage was at her mercy, and she performed the same service for Mr Spollet when he came down to go over the books and see that his enterprise was showing a profit. Sister Mallow was no stranger to perverse means of intercourse. At least it was safe this way. She was still of childbearing age and had no intention of saddling herself with a brat. The crude condoms made of animal gut were unreliable and back street abortions hazardous. Anal penetration was safe and not unpleasant to someone like her, who had been doing it for years. She did not seek personal satisfaction, not with the doctors anyway; she liked lads and paid them handsomely, teaching them the art of cunnilingus and taking her pleasure from their lapping tongues.

She had been told immediately Millicent and John had entered the building and, guessing their intention, knocked on Dr Robinson's door and scurried up to the gallery. He followed behind, and when they watched John posing and diving and Millicent sinking into his arms, the doctor had bared his phallus, spat on his fingers and applied saliva to it. He then plunged into Sister Mallow's narrow aperture till his root butted with her distended anus. He had been in a frenzy to reach his convulsion of bliss, and she had taken her revenge, preventing his escape when he wanted to pull out then thrust in again. She tightened her sphincter round his cock, nearly cutting off the blood supply. She wanted to engulf it and show him who was boss. But he found this stimulating and ravaged her bum-hole anew. It was like a war game, with the nurse's rectum sucking at his member as if eager to tear it from his loins and cram it inside, and him determined to complete the act before she could carry out her dire intention.

Bearing the brunt of his powerful grip she observed the couple in the pool and, as they appeared to reach their conclusion, she felt Dr Robinson's scalding semen burst forth into the dark caverns of her body. Then he foundered, sinking across her back as if pole axed.

'They've done,' she whispered.

'And so, my dear, have I,' he groaned, and pulled away.

'I'll go down and express outrage, demanding recompense for our sacred pool,' she said, smiling at him, straightening her clothing and tucking stray strands back under her cap.

'Do that,' he said, willing to agree to anything now he'd shot his load.

With all the confidence induced by a wet arse that insured her of her power, Sister Mallow skipped from the gallery and ran down the stairs. She was feathering her nest very nicely, thanks to the nefarious activities taking place in and around the spa.

Millicent became aware that something was disturbing her peace, though she was still floating in John's embrace. At first she could not place it, then a voice spoke from the doorway and Sister Mallow came across to the water's edge, in her starchy uniform and crisp linen. Her face was expressionless and her hands were clasped at the waist of her apron. Millicent was alarmed, trying to pull away from John, but he stood his ground and would not let her go.

'Well, Lady Bessborough, and who gave you permission to use the pool at this time of night?' Sister Mallow asked frostily.

'No one,' Millicent faltered, feeling like the meanest criminal.

'Did you assume that your fee included the use of the facilities whenever you chose?' the nurse continued, though it was plain that she knew the rules and regulations all too well.

'I didn't think there would be any h-harm in it,' Millicent stammered, wanting desperately to reach her clothes, dress and get out of there.

'Did you not?' Sister Mallow said calmly. 'And did this include inviting a gentleman to join you and indulge in, what I can only call, a flagrantly immodest act?'

'I'm sorry,' Millicent blurted.

'Don't apologise, Millicent,' John said, his eyes turning to steel as he addressed the nurse. 'We are leaving now, and no harm has been done to your precious pool.'

'I can't be sure of that, sir, till it has been inspected, and this costs money,' she replied meaningfully.

'How much?' he asked brusquely, recognising her angle.

'Two guineas should cover it, sir.'

Before Millicent could dress and depart she had to wait till John had retrieved his wallet from among his clothing and dropped the money into Sister Mallet's greedy palm.

As they made to leave she was hanging about in the hall, all ingratiating smiles as she said, 'Should you want another *swim*, my lady, see me first and I'll make sure you are not disturbed.'

'For a price,' snapped John.

'Everything has its price, sir,' the nurse replied calmly, and it was infuriating to know that she had the upper hand.

Amelie was serenely happy. Ralph was at her side and they were returning to the seafront from a stroll along the pier. There they had viewed the sideshows, peered into the slot machine called *What The Butler Saw*, and been duly amused by the rather naughty film footage of a lady undressing.

'Ooh, how could she pose like that, with her clothes partly off?' Amelie had squealed, and then remembered that she had done almost the same during Mervin's Living

Pictures exhibition.

'I'm accustomed to seeing models in the nude,' Ralph answered, and the arm he had around her waist tightened a little. 'Will you pose for me, Amelie?'

'I shouldn't be able to sit still,' she prevaricated, while inside she was aching with want. She had the wild urge to undress for him on the spot, even though it was getting chilly now the sun had finally disappeared over the horizon.

'You would learn,' he assured her. 'Just think, Amelie, you would be immortalised on canvas, still beautiful when the years had flown and you were an old, old lady.'

'Is this what you tell all your models?' she teased, slanting him an impish glance.

'They mostly do it for money,' he replied carelessly. 'Unless of course, they are paying me to paint their portraits.'

'What a carefree life you lead,' she said, and some of her joy evaporated. This was nothing more than a mirage. It would disappear, leaving her with the reality of his position and hers, and never the twain should meet. But that was tomorrow, not now.

'I work very hard, and play hard, too,' he rejoined lightly, and helped her down the concrete steps that led to the darkened beach. 'Sometimes I'm in funds, but more often not.'

'But this isn't how I live,' she protested, feeling sand under the thin soles of her shoes and wanting to take them off. 'I rely on my wage from your brother, and have no other income. You, on the other hand, can always go to your bank if you get short, and your name will allow you to have an overdraft. Titles count, so do connections. I have none of these.'

'You have one of the greatest of assets,' he said, taking her hand and helping her over a tricky bit.

'And what is that?' she asked breathlessly, stepping into that ocean-scented darkness, where only the flickering promenade lights threw a faint luminance.

'Your youth and beauty,' he said simply, and her nipples crimped in response to the rich timbre of his voice.

The sea hissed in the background, the tide crawling up the sand, then retreating. Its scent reminded her of her own female essences. Night threw a mist over the water, and the moon sailed regally above, accompanied by stars that dusted the panoply of the heavens. In silence they traversed the firm damp sand, coming at last to a clump of rocks. Ralph settled his back against it, one leg braced to take his weight. Hers, too, as he drew her close to his chest. She felt the intoxicating brush of his fingers against her neck, and then undoing the top buttons of her dress, easing the rest from their embroidered holes till the bodice was open all the way down.

The cool air hit her, but she was far from uncovered. Her chemise lay between him and the sight of her breasts, and the edge of her corset lifted them, the nipples gleaming through the flimsy undergarment. She was thankful for the darkness that hid her. It spared her blushes and made her feel that she could show herself without fear. Suddenly and forcefully his mouth came down on hers, tongue diving between her lips and plundering the recess. She could feel her lower lips swelling and opening, juices dampening her knickers. He held her firmly with the flat of one hand, and with the other unfastened his trousers and set his penis free.

It was too dark to see it properly, but Amelie seized it in her fingers, relishing the warmth and strength of it. Would it be too big for her to take? She had made up her mind. This time there would be no hesitation and, please God, no interruptions. She was determined to have him. They had no need to speak. It was as if he read her mind and knew of her surrender. He slid his hand under her, pushed aside her drawers and foraged in the curly triangle of her pubic bush, finding the humid world of her crack. She wanted to cry out with pleasure as his lubricated finger made contact with her throbbing bud.

'Yes, yes,' she muttered. 'Stroke it.'

'Not quite yet, darling,' he grated, and with one agile movement he swept her up in his arms and laid her down on the sand.

The stars were wheeling madly overhead and the sand was damp, getting everywhere, but none of that mattered. She reached for Ralph, her legs spread wide, but her drawers were an obstruction. She sat up and pulled them off, the white bundle of cotton contrasting with the dimness below and around them. Now there was no barrier between her cleft and his cock.

He straddled her, trousers around his hips as he lowered himself. She enjoyed the weighty feel of him, firm but controlled, not crushing her but simply easing down. She lifted her hips but he remained poised over her, the tip of his cock at her entrance, no more. He trailed his fingers around her labia and the feeling of sexual arousal was extraordinarily powerful. Her clitoris was pulsing, the passage of air as he moved his hand almost enough to bring on her crisis. He rolled to one side, leaned over and lapped at her tender kernel with firm tongue strokes. She was rising higher and higher, climbing towards that precious peak from which she would plunge into ecstasy. She arrived there, hearing someone cry out and not realising it was her, so caught up in the waves of orgasm powering through her.

Ralph was at the entrance to her sex and she jerked as his helm met her hymen. She heaved upwards, meeting him, frantic to have that large member buried inside her. He gripped her, hauled her hips towards him and was inside her in one savage thrust. She cried out as its hardness shocked through her with a force she felt in every membrane and tissue. She had not expected so much pain, as the massive object ripped through her maidenhead and transformed her into a woman. He rested for a second, letting her get used to the feel of it, and he was considerate, kissing her nipples and caressing her body.

'You were telling the truth, sweetheart,' he whispered. 'I'm sorry that deflowering has to be so painful, but proud and glad it was me who did it. I'll go on now, press into you a little more, darling, for I can't hold back. I must... I *must* come.'

'Yes, I want you to,' she panted, clutching him to her. 'Go on, let me feel you spend in me. My first time ever.'

She took every inch of him, clenching her tight walls around his cock and exalting as he plunged in and out, finally coming into her in a fury of release. Amelie lay beneath this man who had filled her newly penetrated channel with his creamy spunk. She was proud of herself. No one could call her a girl any more. Ralph had done it, and she was thankful it had been him and not someone cruel like his brother. But even as she rested there with her lover's head on her shoulder and his penis still buried within her, so she saw herself in the punishment room with Mervin. He was thrashing her and tormenting her and buggering her, then bringing her to orgasm, that wicked man who made her call him master.

She kept these thoughts to herself, however, and Ralph was kind and courteous, helping her to rise and brushing the sand from her skirt and petticoats. Her hair caused her concern for it was dishevelled and she had lost some pins.

'Allow me,' he said gently, and drew her up the steps so that they stood under a streetlamp. There he rearranged her coiffure to the best of his ability, proving quite apt. 'I arrange my models' hair how I want it for a picture,' he explained. 'Yours is so soft and fragrant, Amelie. Ah, dearest girl, I do so wish I could spend the night with you, instead of retiring to my lonely bed in a room tantalisingly close to yours.'

'How long are you staying in Westleigh?' she asked, as they made their reluctant way to the Royal Hotel.

'Millicent is booked into the spa for a week, I gather,' he replied, and drew her closer to his side as they dawdled along. 'John and I have to get back to London the day after tomorrow. Let's meet in the morning and I'll teach you to ride a bike. You don't have to be with Millicent, do you?'

'I think not,' Amelie said, and laughed softly. 'From what she told me of today's activities when she was introduced to the douche and massage, she'll be quite happy to be alone.'

'And you? Were you treated, too?'

'Only to a massage, and that was most relaxing,' she said, refusing to divulge more.

The hotel was across the street and he kissed her fondly and deeply beneath the shadow of a large tree, then escorted her into the foyer. They found Millicent and John upstairs in the suite's boudoir, chaperoned by Dulcie. Shortly after the gentlemen retired to their own rooms and Millicent sent Dulcie to bed.

When they were alone, Millicent grabbed Amelie's hand and burst out, 'I've done it! I've lost my virginity! It was quite, quite wonderful.'

'Was it John Phelps who did it?' Amelie was more than a little relieved. Now she could confess to her own fornication with Ralph.

'Yes, yes!' Millicent cried, dancing round the room.

'I, too, have something to tell,' Amelie said. 'I'm no longer a virgin and it's all down to your brother, Ralph.'

This halted Millicent. She stopped in front of her, wide-eyed yet not expressing surprise. 'I thought he was fond of you!' she exclaimed, and clasped Amelie's hands in hers. 'Oh, I'm so pleased. Is he serious or merely toying with your affections?'

'I don't know for certain. All I'm sure about is that I've succeeded in getting rid of my tiresome maidenhead. I feel like a woman reborn.'

'So do I, and I'm not particularly worried whether John loves me or not. I've had my introduction and can go from there.'

187

There was a glint in Millicent's usually mild eyes and Amelie wondered at the change in her. 'What are you going to do?' she asked, fearful of the reply.

'Learn everything I can about sex. Arm myself with knowledge. We discussed earlier our experiences in the massage rooms. I have a plan to make myself powerful, the kind of woman who dominates men. I'm sure Peter, my masseur, can enlighten me.'

'And what do you plan to do when you are equipped with the information?' There was something wild about Millicent that Amelie found disturbing.

'Do, my dear? Do? Why, revenge myself on Mervin, of course, and Nigel and all the other men who have humiliated me. They'll never get the chance to do so again. From now on, I shall be in charge of my own destiny.'

Chapter Eleven

Mervin brooded, brows drawn, mouth almost snarling, like some disgruntled lion in his den. Millicent was back and he did not like the change in her.

Sea air, he thought, carrying on a monologue in his head, my arse! She's been tupped, I know it! I can sense it! Someone has breached her defences and borne away her hymen as a trophy. If I find out who it was, then I'll run him through, God dammit! Laws against duelling don't count down here, damn silly laws, anyway. Most gentlemen learn to fence as a matter of course; if not at their mother's knee, then at the first gentleman's academy they chance upon. That's what produces England's finest officers; swordplay, the ability to ride a horse and the inborn determination to defend family honour.

Millicent had not admitted to it, but she positively swaggered on her return from Westleigh. He met her in the hall of Kelston Towers. Acting streetwise, like a whore in some tuppenny-halfpenny knocking-shop! And he knew all about those establishments, having been a customer for years.

'Ah, sister,' he had said, glowering at her, distrusting this new radiance and confidence that surrounded her like a halo. 'The treatment was successful, by the look of you.'

'It was, I've never felt so well,' she rejoined smugly, working her fingers out of her grey kid gloves as she spoke. 'I'd like to continue using water therapy here. Order the groundsmen to clean out the lake. A daily swim wouldn't do you any harm either. You're looking haggard,

Mervin. You need exercise.'

'What do you mean? I ride. I fence. I lift dumb-bells in the gymnasium.'

'Tish! You do this when it suits you or if you haven't any other diversion... probably female,' she retorted acidly, turning on her heel and making for the grand staircase, but he called after her.

'Nigel is visiting, knowing of your return.'

She had swung round and paused, one hand on the carved newel post, staring at him as if he was something she'd scraped off the bottom of her shoe. 'If I see him, and I say *if*, then he'll have to conform to my rules.'

'What the devil are you driving at?' he roared, resisting the urge to hit her.

'You'll see, brother dear,' she answered loftily, and continued up the stairs.

'Will you marry him?' Mervin shouted, furious because she was ignoring him.

'I doubt it,' she called back over her shoulder.

All through this unpleasant meeting, he had been aware of Amelie in the background, Millicent's *aide-de-camp*, as he now referred to her – nothing as straightforward and simple as a companion. His rage had become centred on her, and fulminating in his opulent bedchamber he decided on a course of action that would bring her down a peg or two.

'Humphrey!' he bellowed. 'Tell Miss Aston that I wish to see her... *now*!'

He had to wait another hour, and when Amelie finally sauntered in she was not in the least repentant for the delay. By that time he had practically worn a hole in the carpet with his frenzied pacing up and down. He cursed all women and turned on Amelie, but she met his gaze steadily. She too had altered subtly. Ralph, he thought immediately. Has he been rogering her? Has she high hopes of becoming a member of this family through marriage? I'll soon put a stop to that!

'You sent for me, sir?' she said, her tone ever so slightly insolent.

'Brazen hussy,' he hissed, and giving her no time to retaliate, he grabbed her and twisted her arms behind her back.

'What have I done?' she spat, resisting him with feline fury, but Mervin was not deceived, knowing from experience that beneath this show of indignation she was as hot as Hades and probably creaming her knickers.

'Done?' he growled, implementing the word with a vicious shake. 'You have corrupted my sister, made her aware of matters that were best kept from her. Encouraged her defiance and disobedience towards me, her brother and guardian. That's what you've done, bitch!'

'It's not me, it's life and learning and Mr Spollet and the health hydro that have opened her eyes to her own self-worth,' Amelie retorted. 'You're nothing but a bully, my lord.'

'And you love it, don't you?' he whispered in her ear, and she became quiescent in his grasp, like a cat having its fur stroked. He could almost hear her purring. 'Confess, Amelie. Tell me in confidence, as if I were your priest, murmur your deepest desires and most sinful longings. Tell me that you reach greater heights of bliss when I chastise then pleasure you, than you have found in the arms of my milk-sop brother, Ralph.'

'That's not true,' she protested.

'You need a reminder, something that will make you think of me every time you touch your quim,' he mused, then turned to his valet. 'We'll move to the bathroom. Let Lord Balfour know where we are and what I'm about to do.'

The room beyond was bright with the sun's rays pouring through many windowpanes, perfect rectangles of glass forming prisms that made rainbows everywhere. The décor was white, contrasting with the bedchamber, that

191

mysterious, decadently furnished lair of her master. Amelie pulled herself up short, but the word had already escaped into and been accepted by her mind – master. She thought of Mervin as her master, even though she railed against her submission.

The valet returned with Nigel, whose little porcine eyes were all over Amelie, even though she was fully attired... but not for long. Humphrey wheeled a sparse metal couch from behind a screen, spread it with a linen sheet and stood to one side in readiness.

'Take off your drawers and shoes and get up on the table,' Mervin ordered, reminding her of Mr Spollet. Hadn't he used almost the same phrases?

'Am I not allowed to know what you are going to do to me?' she asked, though getting out of her knickers and sitting on the couch, her legs dangling.

'It's simple, my dear. I am going to pierce your labial wings and inserted little gold rings.'

She tried to get down but he detained her, pressing a hand to her shoulder and making her lie flat. By this time her skirt was tucked up behind her and her nude parts exposed to the gaze of Nigel, Humphrey and Mervin. He lifted her arms above her head and secured her wrists in steel cuffs fastened to a ring. Her feet went into stirrups, and the mechanics of the couch allowed them to support her upper thighs and the backs of her knees, spreading them wide apart. Her heart thumped and her sex clenched but there was no way she could avoid being vulnerable.

'Oh, sir... master... don't do this to me,' she implored, tears trickling back to dampen her temples and soak into her hair.

'Be quiet, slave. You will thank me for it. I'm about to shave off these unsightly hairs and insert golden rings through your sex lips. You will be able to hang gems on them as soon as you have healed, and a chain that loops them together. All at my behest, naturally, as I am your master and you are my creature.'

Humphrey brought over a shaving bowl and Mervin covered the end of a stubby brush with fragrant soap and applied it to her bush, from cleft to lower belly, turning her mons foaming white. She had been on the brink of hysteria, but now that the end result was inevitable a curious peace settled over her and she started to enjoy every swipe of the razor as he scraped the curly hairs from her pussy. He was extremely neat, taking off every stray frond but leaving a foxy arrow pointing straight down to her clitoris.

When he'd finished he laid a warm towel on her mound. This was soothing for she stung from the well-honed blade. She lifted her head and peered down the length of her torso to her pubis. Such baldness was shocking, pink flesh where russet hair had been, now shiny and smooth.

'You have a lovely crack, Amelie. I can see it so clearly now. Your inner folds are swollen and prominent. I have always found this to be the sign of a libidinous nature. Plump petals that ache to fold round a man's organ of generation. This pleases me. Nigel, your assistance.'

The fat peer needed no second bidding, settling himself between her legs and holding her avenue wide. Mervin took up a padded strut and inserted it there, nudging Nigel out of the way. Amelie was so open now she could feel air on her vulva. Mervin inserted a finger, pushing it far in and then removed it, shaking his head.

'Someone has been ploughing your furrow, Amelie. I'm disappointed in you. Tell me who it is?'

'No sir,' she said firmly, though very uncomfortable below. She was wet there, but Mervin had used unnecessary force.

'I shall question Ralph and find out,' he warned and slapped her thighs. 'You've been a dirty slut, haven't you, Amelie? Letting some man put his stiff cock into your cunny. What I'm about to do will make other lovers pause when they see it, a reminder that you have a master. Later I may brand you on the arse, using my seal with the

Bessborough crest.'

Her legs were beginning to ache, held and spread by the stirrups, and she could not see properly as Mervin took an instrument from a silver tray held by Humphrey. She felt it, cold on her heated parts and then, suddenly, pain shot through her as he punctured her right labia majora. She shrieked in shock but he did not pause, inserting a gold keeper through the hole.

'Ooh… that hurts,' she whimpered.

Mervin did not stop in his labours, repeating the piercing on her left labia, then he put the tray aside and scrubbed his hands at the washbasin, saying as he did so, 'Take care of your wounds. Cleanse them with salt water daily, and they will soon heal.'

'Is Millicent expected to join us?' Nigel asked eagerly, his cock out, massaging the thick stem and the fiery helm with its single weeping eye, but before Mervin could reply she appeared in the doorway, brandishing a whip.

'You wanted to see me?' she said crisply. She was wearing knee-length drawers with a split crotch, black stockings and high-heeled buttoned boots. Her purple satin corset reduced her waist to doll size, made her breasts bulge and exaggerated the swell of her hips. Nigel did a double take. So did Mervin and Humphrey.

'Well, I'll be a monkey's uncle!' Nigel spluttered. 'If this ain't the most rummish thing I ever did see!' And he stood there looking extremely foolish with his deflated cock in one hand.

'Millicent, go back to your room at once!' Mervin ordered, his face flushed and a vein thickening on his brow.

'I have come to learn from you,' she answered coolly, and went over to where Amelie was still on the couch. 'What is this you've been doing to my companion? Does it heighten sexual sensation? If so, then you shall do it to me.'

'Never!' Mervin vowed, disoriented by the topsy-turvy

world into which she had now plunged him.

She shrugged, just as she had seen Mario do, and said casually, 'In that case, I shall find someone else to perform the service for me. Meanwhile, how about a little practice with the whip? Nigel, you shall be my target. Stand over there and stop fidgeting. If you take it well I may let you masturbate to orgasm.'

'I want to be released,' Amelie said, aching all over, needing to pass water and distinctly uncomfortable.

'Do it, Humphrey,' Millicent commanded, and flicked him across his neat butt, the whip making a satisfying noise.

Amelie's wrists were chafed and she massaged them back to life as she made for the cubicle that contained the lavatory. As she urinated the piercing in her petals stung and she cursed Mervin with all her might, and every man who chose to show his supremacy over women.

She returned to hear Millicent saying, 'Get your trousers down, Nigel.'

Nigel shook his head, but unbuttoned and bent over dutifully and Millicent took a swipe at his backside. It was one of the most wonderful noises Amelie had ever heard. Millicent was smiling fixedly, fulfilling her vengeful fantasies as she welted Nigel's obese and quivering backside. He was grunting and rubbing his cock, and Amelie watched it extend to an almost unbelievable degree.

Crack!

'Ow!' Nigel whined, and then grunted, 'I'm coming!' And he did, a thick stream of spunk jetting from his purple-ended cock and spattering the floor.

'You disgusting little worm!' Millicent sneered, levelling a kick at him. 'Lick it up, every last drop, and off my shoes, too! I don't want them stained by your vile slime.' Her pointed toe caught him in the balls and he collapsed, clutching himself and moaning, then dragging across to lap up his emission from the tiles and Millicent's instep.

She made it difficult for him, moving her foot restlessly,

presenting him with the spiked heel and jabbing at him with her pointed toe. She looked across at Amelie, her eyes alive with mischief, as if the sun had shone into her life. She was going from strength to strength and nothing and no one would stop her now. Mervin saw that look, too.

'You think you're very clever, the two of you, but no one gets the better of me,' he grated. 'I expect you imagine you know all there is to know. But believe me, you have a lot to learn. You think females are all we men want. You are wrong. Humphrey, get down.'

In a trice the blond valet was on his hands and knees on the cold tiled floor. His trousers were about his ankles, his arse bare and turned towards Mervin in open invitation. Amelie said nothing, but accepted that her master was about to illustrate his last statement. Excitement tightened her loins as she saw him opening his trousers and cradling his dick in one hand. It was already huge and stiff and raring to go. Once, not long ago, he had plunged it into her fundament. She recalled the tightness, the excruciating pain and the strange, forbidden pleasure. Now he approached Humphrey with the same intention.

She could tell that the valet was accustomed to being sodomised. He showed no fear or reluctance, peeping coyly round as Mervin touched his bare backside. His cock was as rigid as a broom handle, and Mervin reached beneath him and gave it a squeeze.

'That's got me going, sir,' Humphrey squealed.

'Let us show these cunt-proud women how men really enjoy themselves,' Mervin growled, and wetted the valet's tight arse with saliva, then thrust his cock deep inside him till it disappeared from view and they were locked together, pubis to posterior.

To Amelie's surprise Millicent stopped tormenting Nigel. 'I want to join in,' she said to her brother, who was thrusting rhythmically in and out of the valet's backside.

'Men only,' he grunted, absorbed in his pleasure, trying

to prolong it, pulling out his cock to the tip, resting for a second, and then shunting it back in again.

'Nonsense,' she said, and grabbed Humphrey by the hair, jerking his head up. Holding it in both hands she straddled his face, forcing him to take her clit into his mouth. 'That's right, suck it,' she commanded. 'And then after you've licked me I'll rub your prick. I can see it's full to bursting with love juice and Mervin is too busy and too selfish to attend to it.'

Amelie watched and made mental notes. If the same opportunity ever presented itself to her, then she would know how to handle it, but the thought of being touched, given the soreness of her labia, made her wonder if she would ever be ready to have pleasure lavished on her again.

Nigel, seated awkwardly on the floor, was feasting his eyes on the threesome who seemed oblivious to anyone else. Mervin was reaching his climax, his movements rapid and uncontrollable, Humphrey's arse the focal point wherein he would deposit his come. Millicent stood still, with her feet apart and the slit in her knickers held wide open with Humphrey's face buried in the gap. She moaned and threw her head back and appeared to reach a climax, not once, but several times in quick succession. Then Merlin barked, face contorted like that of a tortured martyr, jerking and writhing as his phallus relinquished its pearly jet of semen.

Millicent was true to her word, seizing the valet's overexcited member. It took but a few rubs to have him ejaculating, a white stream arching out and spattering her.

Mervin, already wearied of this game, started to strip. 'The bath is big enough for several of us, even Nigel,' he said. 'Time for a plunge, but not you, Amelie. We have to take care of your sweet little snatch, now it is so tastefully ornamented.'

Amelie and Ralph had escaped to the grotto on the pretence of cycling round the estate. She wore one of those new, fashionable costumes designed for the bicycle. It had a smart jacket tailored like a man's, worn over a prim blue and white striped blouse, with a collar and tie. Stays were still *de rigueur*, and pinched her waist in tightly and accentuated her hips that were now displayed in pantaloons. These had been invented by a Mrs Bloomer who had given her name to them, a daring exponent of the two-wheeled conveyance. They were full and fastened with a buckle below the knee, where they joined thick stockings and sensible lace-up shoes. A skirt went with it, supposed to be worn over the breeches so that not too much leg was displayed, but Amelie daringly dispensed with this. It was hot and cumbersome.

She appreciated the freedom, and wished she could wear something like them all the time. Skirts were a bore, always getting muddy round the hem and picking up dry leaves and stray twigs. Maybe shorter skirts might be the mode some day, to the knee perhaps, so that one could walk, run, dance and swing along freely, like a man.

Three weeks had passed since her piercing and the hair was growing back on her pubis, rather itchy and prickly, but her labia had almost healed. Mervin had taken it upon himself to examine the area frequently and promised her that soon he would bring along a length of thin chain and link the rings together. It was as well that Ralph had not been able to get down before; she would have found sexual congress painful. As it was, she had been hesitant about mounting the bicycle, but the saddle was well padded and she experienced no pain in her pussy, in fact the pressure on her clit was arousing. She bowled along beside Ralph, keeping up speed and thanking heaven that she was a thoroughly modern woman. If only the Reverend Thacker could see her now! He'd have an apoplexy, or on second thoughts, he'd probably get an erection.

The transformation in Millicent was remarkable. When they went shopping she was now spending like a drunken sailor, and buying garments and accessories that she would have once found too flamboyant. Mervin did not say a word for she was still keeping him in suspense about Nigel. The peer had become her slave, obeying her sometimes outrageous demands and adoring her with dog-like devotion. Amelie had wondered if John Phelps would visit with Ralph, but Millicent hadn't invited him.

Amelie had voiced her disappointed, and Millicent said blithely, 'I may see him again in the future, but he served his purpose and I have other fish to fry.'

When Ralph and Amelie reached their destination they leaned their bicycles against a tree and he guided her down rough-hewn steps leading to the grotto. This had once been a natural cavern with a stream flowing through it, but a former Lord Bessborough, inspired by his Grand Tour of Europe in 1780 and the antiquities he had seen there, enlarged it on his return. It had been transformed into a fairytale cave, its walls inlaid with pebbles and shells and semi-precious stones. The stream had been redirected to form little waterfalls, which cascaded into a series of carved stone basins, culminating in a large pool where carp swam lazily round a bronze statue of Neptune who leaned on his trident, flaunted his phallus and ogled the large-bosomed nymphs disporting themselves in the water, eternally young, beautiful and alluring.

Light filtered from an aperture in the roof, a dim light, green as moss, and Ralph took off his corduroy jacket and spread it on a level plateau just above the pool. Then he held out his arms and drew Amelie down beside him. He kissed her deeply and his tongue was wonderfully fresh, yet familiar, too. She could trust him, and this was important. She might find Mervin dangerously attractive, but Ralph would always love and care for her. He was fully roused, his fingers clumsy with haste as he slipped the mother-of-pearl shirt buttons from their holes and laid her breasts bare. He leaned over and flicked the nipples with his tongue, and at the same time pushed a knee between hers and seesawed back and forth. Sensation stabbed through her at the harsh frottage that pleasured her clit but dragged at the rings.

She flinched and he stopped. 'What is wrong?' he asked, his eyes concerned, his fingers gently trailing across her brow.

'I'll show you,' she said; he would see anyway as soon as he had her knickers off.

She sat up, took off her shoes and undid her breeches, then wrinkled them down to her ankles. Her drawers came next and once they were removed she lay back and opened herself to his gaze. He whistled soundlessly and leaned closer. The light was eerie, as if they floated under the sea, but there was enough illumination to glint off the gold in the labial rings.

'My God!' he exclaimed in a low tone. 'Who did this to you? No, don't answer. Let me guess. It was Mervin, wasn't it?'

'That's right,' she replied, and let her legs go slack, covered in white woollen socks to the knee.

'But why?' Ralph shook his head, puzzled, and his fingers gently rasped through the foxy bush that was beginning to take over from the bareness. He landed unerringly on the arrow and followed it down to her clit.

'To make me remember that I am his and he is my master.'

'What nonsense!' Ralph barked. 'You don't belong to anyone. You are free, Amelie, free!'

'And if I don't want to be?' She was struggling with the paradox, yet could not really be bothered with it at that precise moment. More important was making love with Ralph.

'Then you are mad,' he responded, but could not keep his fingers away from her bejewelled delta. 'Oh, Amelie... dear little Amelie, let me take care of you. I'm leaving for Paris soon. Come with me.'

Paris? France? It was as if he'd invited her to journey to the moon. 'I couldn't,' she whispered.

He threw a leg over her, then knelt with her between his thighs, and he took his weight on his hands placed flat on either side of her. 'Yes, you could. What's stopping you? You have no ties here.'

'Millicent,' she said, though her pelvis was stretching up to meet the penis he now exposed. If this could only go on forever, just the two of them alone. The clarion call to adventure rang in her brain. It tingled in her blood, chased along every nerve, urged her to up sticks, throw caution to the winds and follow where destiny led her. Paris!

'You would love it,' he enthused, his enormous cock at the ready. 'All those narrow streets steeped in history... the flea markets, the high culture, the Louvre Museum, Notre Dame. I have an apartment in the heart of the Latin Quarter. My neighbours are poets, musicians and philosophers. We meet in the cafés and drink absinthe. We go to the Moulin Rouge and watch the girls dance the can-can. We carouse in one another's studios. We picnic on the banks of the Seine. It is a haphazard, glorious life, full of heartbreak, high times, happiness and success. Come with me, Amelie.'

As he spoke he gently touched her labia, and when she made no signs of discomfort he started to bring her off with his hand. She relaxed. There had been nothing to fear, not with someone as gentle as Ralph. He soothed her wings, working his fingertips slowly and luxuriantly between the protuberant inner pair and spreading her abundant juice up and over her throbbing bud. With his other hand he pinched one of her nipples and shocks of pleasure shot down to her womb and sent further floods of lubrication seeping from her vagina. He skilfully massaged her clitoris, stroking and circling, rubbing harder, then more slowly, prolonging her coming. She wriggled her hips, silently pleading for more, and in answer he increased the rubbing. Her second of bliss was approaching as he went faster and more boldly, and she spread her thighs wide and arched her back and screamed out her ecstasy as she reached the ultimate peak.

Ralph held her there, not interrupting her climax till she started to return to earth. Then he brought his penis to her wet centre and pushed. Amelie gasped and lifted her legs, resting her ankles on his shoulders and pressing against his shaft, drawing him closer and closer into her lush, wet, engorged opening. She was aware of burning heat engulfing her membranes and her body convulsed in the aftermath of her orgasm, the muscles contracting round Ralph's mighty organ.

He could not hold back any more, and she rejoiced to feel his absolute surrender to the dictates of his cock. He surged against her, pumped and thrashed and suddenly spent. She was bathed in the warmth of his seminal fluid. Tentatively she squeezed her inner walls, but he was already softening within her. He slid out and rolled over on his back, his penis limp as it rested across his thigh. He held out an arm and Amelie accepted it, her head nestled against his shoulder. She took a deep breath.

'So that's agreed, then,' he said sleepily. 'You'll come to Paris with me. We'll take the ferry from Dover and go across to Calais, and then it's a train ride to the capital.'

'I have little money,' she began, trying to avoid committing herself at this stage. 'And I don't like leaving Milly... and Dulcie.'

'Oh, darling, I have money,' he said, staring into her face. 'It's the wisest course of action, I assure you.'

'Suppose we fall out of love?'

He laughed and filled his hand with one of her breasts. 'We shan't. Well, not for ages anyway. I'll protect you and you can get work modelling. My friends will be falling all over themselves to paint you.'

'I don't want to become a whore,' she pouted, though her nipples were clamouring for his touch, and he did not refuse, subjecting them to tweaking and rolling, teasing and flicking.

'Dearest, would I see that fate befall you?' he answered earnestly, then licked her nipples, one by one. 'Trust me, Amelie, I'm more than simply fond of you.'

'I'll think about it,' she promised, but had already made up her mind.

'Paris?' Millicent screeched when Amelie broke the news to her. 'You're off to Paris? You lucky duck! This is Ralph's doing, I suppose? And how, pray, are you going to manage that? Mervin will have his bloodhounds on your trail.'

'Ralph says he will take care of everything,' Amelie answered, curled on the window seat in Millicent's boudoir.

'Oh, I'm sure,' Millicent said with heavy sarcasm. 'And has he taken into account Mervin's fury and the backlash it will have on all of us?'

'Come with us,' Amelie suggested impulsively. Millicent could see she was cock-struck, so happy that she was oblivious to difficulties that might turn her and Ralph into a pair of star-crossed lovers.

She reached out and caressed Amelie's chestnut hair. 'Not yet, my love. Later, perhaps. Mervin is talking of visiting Monte Carlo this year, and if he finds out where you have gone and with whom, it may galvanise him into action. Leave it to me. Now, dear thing, when are you leaving and are you going to tell Mervin?'

Amelie paled and fidgeted restlessly. 'Ralph goes to London tomorrow. He says I'm to follow next day and has bought my railway ticket to Paddington. I shan't unpack at the Chelsea house for we shall be leaving on the night ferry from Dover.'

'Fine, I'll arrange a shopping spree in Bath and this will be your cover. I will face Mervin with the news of your departure. Don't worry about money; I have plenty, and can't have you relying on Ralph for every penny.'

'He has promised to take care of everything,' Amelie stressed.

'No doubt he has, and no doubt that is his sincere intention,' Millicent said firmly. 'But he is a man, my dear, like all those of his accursed sex who think they are God Almighty. No, Amelie, you shall receive a monthly allowance from me, just till you see how your affair with Ralph is progressing. Oh, and by the way, don't tell him anything about it. Artists are notorious spendthrifts, and he is no exception. I dread to think how much he throws away at the card tables, to say nothing of wild parties and magnums of champagne. In all of which I shall wallow when I arrive,' she added, smiling at the thought.

'John may be accompanying us,' Amelie said, and Millicent saw through the ruse. She was trying to persuade her to run away too, but Millicent, though finding him a fine figure of a man with an impressive penis, had no intention of involving him further than as an occasional lover. Besides which she had to visit her bank and insure that her fortune was safe. When she finally left Kelston Towers she intended to be solvent and not dependent on Mervin for a single penny.

This is how a bride must feel when she and her groom are eloping to Gretna Green, Amelie thought as she boarded the train. Saying goodbye to Millicent and Dulcie was more painful than she had anticipated, but it had to be done. Millicent was prepared to bear the brunt of Mervin's temper, when on her return to Kemble she broke the news. She had maintained that she was looking forward to seeing his face, and Amelie was thankful she would not be there.

It was strange to be travelling alone. Her luggage was stowed in the guard's van, her reticule held firmly on her lap. Millicent had insured that she occupied a first-class carriage with a couple of respectable middle-aged ladies who promised to take care of her, the story being that she was her ladyship's young sister who would be met at Paddington by their brother, Lord Ralph. This was a suitably impressive lie, and the good souls fussed over

Amelie to the point of irritation. She sank behind the ladies magazine she'd purchased at the newsagent's stall and prayed that the journey might soon be over.

She could not believe it, and daydreamed to the rocking of the train, seeing Ralph's face imprinted on her inner eye and thrilling at the thought of crossing the Channel with him that night. Would there be the opportunity for love? Or would they be forced to wait until they reached Paris? She did not see how she could, so frustrated that every movement of the moquette upholstered seat beneath her stirred her clit and eager cleft. She could feel the juices wetting her vagina, and wanted Ralph with a hunger that was beyond reason, his cock stretching her, filling her, impaling her.

He was there on the station, waiting for her, a big box of chocolates in one hand. He ran to sweep her up and give them to her, shouting above the hiss of steam and the orders of the stationmaster waving his red flag and the hubbub and clatter and bustle that attended the famous terminus.

'Amelie! Amelie! Oh, darling, you're here!'

She was aware of the two ladies staring at her aghast, amazed no doubt at the devotion of the young man towards his sister, but she looked the other way and ignored them. There was a row of hansom cabs and hackney carriages and Ralph hailed one. Within a short time they were in Chelsea and the front door was thrown open by John, ready and waiting in his Ulster greatcoat, too hot for this weather but there was a sea voyage before them, of short duration but no matter. Amelie had hoped that she and Ralph might have snatched a few precious moments alone, but this was not to be. Keeping the cab on hire, they and their baggage were soon bundled in and heading for the station again and Dover.

Amelie was too excited to do more than follow Ralph's instructions to keep close to him and let him do the talking. Both he and John appeared to be seasoned travellers, and although she was very tired by the time they reached the docks, adrenaline was pumping through her. She mounted the gangway feeling like a child at Christmas, gazing wide-eyed at the lights, the smoking funnels, the crowd boarding and the sailors in their smart uniforms. She clung to Ralph's arm and they stood on deck as the anchor was weighed and the vessel moved slowly out to sea. John had taken himself off to the saloon, seeking a drink.

'Alone at last,' Ralph said jokingly, and he held her tight as the English shore gradually faded into the distance.

'I wish we were,' she said, nestling against his chest. There were people everywhere, mostly standing at the rail, as they were, saying farewell to their homeland.

Chapter Twelve

'*Bonjour, mademoiselle,*' said the petite woman who stood behind the counter.

'*Bonjour, Madame Renier,*' Amelie responded cheerfully as she entered the patisserie, her nostrils flaring at the gorgeous smells wafting from the bakery at the back.

This had become her morning ritual, rising before Ralph and wending her way down the narrow street that led from their garret at the top of a tall, lopsided house in Montmartre to the shops and cafés. There she purchased croissants for their breakfast, piping hot from the oven. Served with butter and honey they were a feast fit for the gods.

Two weeks into Paris and she already felt like a native. 'An illusion, darling,' Ralph had said, curled against her back, spoon fashion, when they lay in his rather lumpy brass bedstead. 'Like any English village the inhabitants of Montmartre and thereabouts will be polite, but you'll not be accepted for at least twenty years.'

This had not upset her. It was of no significance compared to the feel of him slipping his arms round her, cupping her breasts, his cock like an iron bar nudging her and searching for her vagina. Morning awakenings! With the sun pouring through the dormer windows, striking across the uncarpeted floor and making patterns on the ancient armoir and tallboy, the couple of battered chairs heaped with clothes and the trail of garments they had cast aside en route for the bed last night.

He had taken her sightseeing and she was stunned by the glory of the Champs-Elysées and the Grand Boulevard, wooed by the beauty of the Jardin des Tuileries and shocked by the boldness of the *dames de nuit* plying their trade in the Place Pigalle. As for the Opéra: Ralph had said that the only way to see the grandiose, gilded, white, blue, pink, red and green marble interior of that immense baroque palace was to attend a performance of ballet or opera. He had insured that they did. Amelie was in raptures, feeling like a great lady on her handsome escort's arm.

Paris, Paris. Amelie was in love with it, just as she was in love with Ralph. She had never been so happy.

Even John's intrusion into their Eden was of no consequence. He slept on a sagging couch in the studio, when he was there at all; many of his nights spent carousing with other artists, picking up women and going back to their rooms for sex. Amelie was glad that Millicent had not taken him seriously. He could charm the birds right out of the trees, but he was an unadulterated philanderer. Amelie did not mention this in the letters she wrote to Millicent. Dispatched almost daily, for she was missing her dreadfully, she had received several replies. It was heartening to be able to keep in touch so easily, the postal service a model of efficiency, but Amelie was too busy to be homesick.

Ralph, true to his promise, introduced her to friends and acquaintances, mostly from the art world and, as he predicted, she was much admired. Not all were pleased to see her, however; some of his models and, she guessed, former lovers, made no secret of their resentment, making bitchy remarks that sounded twice as offensive in French. It was just as well that she did not understand the full vehemence of these insults.

'Ignore them,' he said as he prepared for her first sitting, setting his easel at the right angle, squeezing oil-paint onto his palette and then positioning her beneath the North facing skylight, where he could see her best.

She had been nervous. He made sketches of her already when she was fully clad, fascinated by the way her hair fell across her shoulders, the tilt of her chin, the shape of her lips, but this was the first time she had posed naked. The sitting went swimmingly and she found modelling fun. It was tiring, of course. She became stiff, limbs cramped through holding one position for so long. Ralph was a hard taskmaster, but eventually he threw his brush aside and made a grab for her. Their coupling had been brief and passionate. He smelled of linseed oil, paint, and genius. She had no doubt that he had been touched by God and given this gift.

So Amelie became a Parisian. It was more exciting than even London; she copied the women's chic, shopped in little boutiques that sold exquisite trifles – lingerie, scarves, hats, fancy stockings and paste jewellery that looked like the real thing.

Ralph indulged her. The picture was almost completed, and when she returned with their breakfast that morning he sat up in bed, ran his hands through his tousled hair and said, 'Vicomte Henri Chartres is calling in. He is anxious to view the painting of you.'

She stopped dead in the centre of the room, the croissants in a paper bag in her hand. She could feel their heat penetrating it, leaving a residue of grease. 'He's what? Coming here? Oh, the place is so untidy.'

'Hey, calm down,' he said, laughing and throwing the quilt aside, rising to his full naked height and impressing her once again with his physique. 'You're acting like a bourgeoisie housewife, not someone who enjoys *la vie de bohème*. Don't worry about Henri. He's been here before, an old, generous and liberal-minded friend and he's going to adore you, and the picture.'

Needless to say, Amelie whirled round the place tidying up. A servant girl came in several times a week, but the garret was large and sprawling, composed of beams and rafters, with lathe and plaster walls, floors that sloped and worn steps that went up one way and down another. It was forever dusty and the artists were notoriously slovenly, except when it came to their creations. But Amelie had not met a vicomte before, especially one who was about to see a representation of her bereft of clothing, and she wanted the place to be clean.

John bellowed gleefully when she turfed him off the couch, piled up his dirty plates from last night's meal and stalked into the kitchen with them. 'Holy God!' he exclaimed, scratching his chest, and unashamed of his nudity staggering to the primitive bathroom. 'Henri won't be interested in anything but you and your divine bare backside.'

'We'll see about that,' she returned, affronted. She had cleaved to Ralph and he had not strayed, as far as she knew. She did not want any other man, yet an insidious maggot in her brain repeated Millicent's parting words.

'Be independent. Make sure you have your own money.' She had carried out her promise to provide Amelie with cash, arranging a transfer from her bank to one in Paris.

'This is my model, Miss Amelie Aston,' Ralph said, having opened the door to Henri Chartres.

'Charmed to meet such a fair English rose,' the vicomte said with a smile, eyeing her covetously as if she was a piece of bone china or some rare jungle orchid he wanted to add to his collection.

He was a tall aristocrat, and he bore himself well. Wearing an exquisitely tailored overcoat with an astrakhan collar, he carried a silk top hat in one gloved hand and a gold-headed walking cane in the other. His hair swept back in silvery wings from his temples, and he had a grey goatee beard and moustache. His eyes were dark and twinkled humorously. Amelie lost some of her awe. He might be blue-blooded but, like Mervin and Ralph, he was only a man, after all.

Ralph stepped up to the easel and whipped away the cloth that covered it. There was a moment's hush, and then Henri said, 'It is magnificent. *Lilith and the Serpent*.

I shall hang it in my saloon where all my visitors can view it.'

'You want to buy it?' Ralph asked, his face lighting up at the vicomte's praise.

'I do. What are you asking?'

'My agent will discuss the financial side with you, sir. This is his address, near Saint-Germain-des-Prés. I'll send a messenger boy with a note telling him about the transaction.'

'Don't bother,' Henri said, standing in front of it, chin in one hand, gazing at it enraptured. 'I'll call on him on my way back to my house. I would like the picture delivered at once.'

'Certainly, sir,' Ralph assured him. 'That can be arranged.'

'You have excelled yourself, *mon ami*,' he said in excellent English, over which he had great command. 'But then, what artist would not be inspired by such a breathtaking subject. So graceful yet sensual. A girl's face but a woman's eyes, a woman, moreover, who has tasted the heady delights of the flesh.'

He certainly was a striking man, mature and commanding without being arrogant, very different from Mervin, but with the same sexual attraction that carried a thrilling hint of danger.

'You are most kind,' Ralph replied, and his arm encompassed her as he said, 'You are right about my model. She *is* inspiring.'

'I am holding a fancy dress party tonight, please come along,' Henri said, and nodded at the painting. 'This shall be the star of my collection. My guests will be several shades of green beneath their masks. Oh, I forgot to tell you, it is in the nature of a Venetian masked ball, so bring a mask and your dancing pumps. Will you come, Miss Aston? You'll be my special guest.'

Amelie assumed a demure expression and accepted his invitation, though disconcerted when Ralph said, after

Henri had departed, 'He is a most influential person in artistic circles. I'd like you to please him, Amelie.'

'Please him? I don't understand. Of course I shall be polite and friendly. It's in my nature and he does seem a fine gentleman.'

'Do you love me?' he asked.

'I think so… yes, I'm sure I love you,' she answered.

'And you trust me? You will do whatever I ask?'

'I trust you, Ralph. I'm sure you won't do anything to hurt me.'

'Tonight, at Henri's soirée, he may want you to pay special attention to him. Will you do that for me?'

'You want me to flatter him. Is that it?'

'Yes, but there may be more. Along with his ambition to possess rare objects, he also has an insatiable appetite for women.'

Realisation dawned. A giant fist closed around her heart and gave it a squeeze. 'I hope you don't mean what I think you do,' she said slowly. 'Are you suggesting that I sleep with him?'

He had the grace to look sheepish, spreading his hands in an apologetic gesture. 'Well no, not exactly.'

'That's exactly it, isn't it?' she said coldly. 'If not spend the night with him, then make sure he's satisfied, fire his lust and put you in his favour.'

'It's not like that,' Ralph muttered. 'But this is a hard road I'm on. Nothing is for nothing, and if I can get Henri to be my patron then my worries are over. He'll help to sell my work everywhere, including America.'

'And I'm to be the bait, am I?' she said, fighting back the tears.

'Darling, it's a little thing I ask of you. He may not even want you and will help me anyway. I'm just saying… you could ease the way.'

'And if it turns out that I go with him, what will you do? Stuff one of the other models? They all seem keen on you.'

'I shall get drunk on absinthe,' he said darkly. 'I don't relish the idea of him having his way with you, but?'

'Ambition comes first.' She ended the sentence for him. 'Very well, Ralph, I'll do it, but for my sake, not yours.'

'What do you mean?' He looked genuinely worried.

'You'll see,' she answered, and walked to the bathroom where a decrepit boiler supplied hot water, when it decided to work.

'There's no need to be upset,' he called after her. 'Whatever happens, it won't make any difference to you and me.'

'That's what you think,' she muttered, and spun the taps. Tonight she would dress to kill, and let Ralph beware.

Henri's mansion was situated in one of the most prestigious residential quarters of Paris. Detached and surrounded by a large garden enclosed by spiked railings, it was more like a palace than a home.

When Ralph and Amelie arrived in a horse drawn cab, they found that the driveway was already filling up with private conveyances. The coachmen were either waiting patiently, maybe snatching a nap or imbibing in wine, or winging towards the servants' hall, there to converse with Henri's flunkeys or flirt with the parlour maids. Amelie had already formed the opinion that the French were an amorous nation, never letting an opportunity for dalliance pass them by.

Into the brightly lit hall they went, and Amelie wished she had worn something more exotic, rather than the costume Ralph unearthed from a trunk in the studio. It was vaguely Dresden shepherdess, with an ankle-length pannier skirt, a tight, revealing, square-necked bodice, a little beribboned hat and a crook.

'Aren't you dressing up?' she had asked as she shook the creases out and contemplated taking the flatiron to the skirt.

'Indeed I am,' he replied, and though keeping her in the

dark, appeared as they were about to leave wearing the guise of Mephistopheles, complete with red leather trousers that showed his rear, his muscled flanks and the fullness of his cock and balls with such clarity that it was as if he was unclothed.

He wore a doublet that was laced across the front where his chest hair poked between the thongs, a closefitting cap, two little horns on his forehead and a black mask from whose slits his eyes glowed with wicked fire.

Amelie wore a mask too, a glamorous affair covered in purple velvet flecked with diamonds and edged with spreading plumage, making her look like a mythical bird. The guests were milling about, some attired as fauns, Egyptian gods and goddess, knights and medieval damsels, or priests and nuns, novices and demure schoolgirls. With their faces concealed it seemed to give them the freedom to do as they liked. They chatted and admired each other's bizarre costumes and tried to guess the identity of those who remained anonymous, meanwhile touching each other intimately.

Holding Ralph's arm tightly, Amelie did not know where to look as they moved into the ballroom and saw couples, mostly bare, gyrating to a waltz. A few wore dominos, consisting of a black hood, a half mask and a cloak. Several of them were men, judging by the equipage between their thighs, though wearing flowing wigs and enormous headdresses and high heels and dancing with male partners. Breasts and buttocks, female pudenda and phalli; Amelia was confronted by them on every side. Her shepherdess frock seemed totally inappropriate, even though her breasts popped out of the bodice and the hooped skirt rose wilfully as she walked, and Ralph had forbidden her to don knickers. Any careless movement and her pussy was on display, to say nothing of the deep valley between her bottom cheeks.

A magnificent Eastern potentate stood in their path. 'Welcome, Ralph, and you, Miss Aston,' declaimed Henri, his skin darkened with walnut juice, his beard too, a turban wound round his head and kept in place by a huge ruby-encrusted brooch. A mask covered his eyes and nose.

'You recognised us,' Ralph grumbled. 'That's not fair.'

'Not so hard, especially you, Miss Aston, though your modest attire is a far cry from *Lilith and the Serpent*. Equally alluring, though, in its innocent girlishness. Come, help yourself to refreshments,' and he waylaid a footman, snatched two champagne flutes from the tray he held and handed them to Ralph and Millicent. 'And enjoy the entertainment, then later the portrait will be unveiled and you will be the belle of the ball.'

Amelie was overwhelmed. Not only was he ideally suited for his role as a pasha, but also it appeared that every member of his staff had been handpicked. The waitresses had black bustiers and pink gauze skirts that left their lower regions exposed to sight and touch, free to be used by anyone of either sex. The footmen were in powdered wigs and gold-braided uniforms and were chosen mainly for their bulging calves, upright carriages, handsome features and the size of their cocks. These protruded from openings at the front of their burgundy velvet breeches.

In the banqueting hall the long trestle tables were heaped with food; truffles, caviar, pyramids of fruit – oranges, peaches, grapes – all out of season and doubly expensive. There were trout laid out on beds of lettuce leaves, sliced beef, salmon in aspic, and a dozen more delicacies, all served up with artistic flair by the master chef who lorded it in Henri's kitchen. The band continued to play and the crowd grew as more and more people arrived, costumed and masked and aroused. The atmosphere was heavy with perfume and love juice, incense and roses, and other more mysterious smells.

'Opium or hashish,' Ralph informed her. 'Many people smoke it these days.'

'Do you?' she asked outright, somehow imagining that drugs were only used by the dregs of society, or sailors who had been to the Far East, not by upper class people.

'I have done,' he admitted. 'There's no more harm in it than in alcohol. "Everything in moderation" is my motto. Stick to this and you won't go far wrong.'

The tempo changed and with wild whoops a troupe burst on the scene from the back of the ballroom and flung themselves into the outrageous can-can. 'I hired them from the Moulin Rouge,' Henri explained, watching their antics with lustful glee. 'Did you ever see such high kicks? And look at that beauty doing the splits. She'll have landed on a bare cunny, for they don't wear drawers.'

They were dressed in tight stays, low bodices and flounced skirts, held up as they whirled and postured, and the audience roared as they glimpsed white thighs topping black stockings, the flash of gilt suspenders and the open invitation of bellies, arses and cunts, some shaved, others hairy. They shrieked like banshees and did cartwheels, postured and tempted and kicked up their heels, then finished their performance by facing away from the spectators, bending over, spreading their legs, whipping up their skirts and frothy petticoats and showing their naked posteriors. The audience burst into thunderous applause, especially when it was now revealed that several of the dancers were transvestites.

'Is this what they do on the stage in public music halls?' whispered Amelie. Ralph stood behind her and she leaned back against him and bore down on his middle finger that he'd inserted in her wet sex. She had almost forgiven him for wanting her to be 'nice' to Henri.

'Oh yes, that's what all the tourists want to see, but mostly they wear underclothes, except for special parties like this one. I always think they rather enjoy exposing their parts.'

'You've seen them before, under circumstances like this?' she asked, trying to keep the nagging edge from her voice.

'Once or twice,' he said noncommittally.

Her attention was on the dancers who were performing an encore, and this became inexorably mixed with her own impending crisis. She felt Ralph's warmth leave her for a second and almost protested, then he was back, finger on her clit, and now she could feel the bareness and heat of his cock, the tip hovering at her entrance.

Her senses swam and she was saturated with pleasure, but had not yet peaked. The finger fucking did not cease, continuing with unwavering strokes, the penis leaving a sticky trail wherever it rested against her rear.

'I'm nearly there,' she gasped, fireworks sparking in her brain. 'Oh yes, just a little bit more…' and her orgasm was so strong she thought she might disintegrate. The contractions went on, undulating through her and she ground her bottom against that penis and cried out in joy as its slippery length penetrated her convulsing vagina. He felt bigger, more forceful, and she suddenly froze, reaching round blindly. Her fingers encountered a silk robe worn over baggy pantaloons, a wide sash and a dagger in an ornamental sheath. This was not the satanic outfit adopted by Ralph.

'Who are you?' she gasped, her voice drowned by the uproar as the guests copulated freely and some chased the can-can girls who pretended to be reluctant until sums of money were exchanged.

'Don't be afraid, *chérie*. It is I, Henri. Ah, don't try to get away, for I have you fast, my manhood plunged into your juicy snatch, *mon petit chou*.'

Ralph had betrayed her. Her legs trembled and she wanted to push Henri away and pull down her skirt, but could do neither. She was trapped in a corner and this was not all – her body was enjoying the feel of the mature penis possessing her. He was going to complete the act standing on his feet. It made her feel like one of those hussies she'd seen in the Pigalle. They plied their trade brazenly, their pimps touting for money, on the lookout for trouble, ever ready with their fists and using them on whore and client indiscriminately. She hungered to taste the lowest depths of degradation, and yielded to Henri. Wasn't Ralph acting like the meanest of procurers, selling her, not for money, though this came into it, but for fame?

The noisy party continued at full stretch though it had not yet reached its zenith. There were gales of merriment and cries of ecstasy, the whack of the lash hitting tender flesh, and voices shouting in a mixture of foreign accents. The stalwart footmen joined in, obeying orders or perhaps seeking gratification. The masked ladies pounced on them, exploring their cocks and fingering their arses, pushing them back across couches and sitting astride them, wriggling into position with those hard batons buried inside them.

The maidservants were pressed against walls, their breasts rising out of their stays, nipples pinched and rolled and sucked by the ardent gentlemen. Tulle skirts were pushed high and neatly clipped or hairy clefts fingered. Rosebud anuses were a great attraction too, and the stripes that marked some fleshy white bottoms, their master's signature carved there by the flogger.

Henri lost control, entering Amelie with added force. He clasped her breasts and hauled her against him, and his penis felt huge, larger than Ralph's, a hard bough of solid flesh boring into her cunt. She would have lost her balance and fallen had he not held her so tightly, but this was for his benefit not hers, giving him greater purchase. He humped and bumped her and she was tiring. There was little pleasure for her being penetrated as she was by this outsized dick, almost lifted off her feet by the size and force of the thing plunging in and out of her tender passage. Faster and faster he went till she was sure she could endure no more, and at that moment he finally erupted, filling her with his spunk. He sighed, slowed down and slid out of her, his spent organ no longer threatening.

'Amelie, *mon enfant*,' he murmured. 'It is nearly time for your unveiling as Lilith, Adam's first wife who fornicated with the serpent.'

'Where is Ralph?' she wanted to know, trying vainly to cover herself with her skirt, but the hoops were unmanageable, especially as they had been squashed up while both Ralph and Henri explored her lower regions.

'Somewhere around, *chéri*,' Henri said soothingly. 'He will be there when his masterpiece is unveiled. Shall we join him?'

She followed where he led, to a podium overlooking the ballroom. He mounted it and held up his hand for silence. The crowd became quiet, the musicians ceased playing, and even those who were in the throes of ecstasy paused in their labours.

'My friends,' he began, although she could not understand what he was saying for he spoke in his native tongue. 'It gives me great pleasure to see you here tonight, and I have another treat in store. I have just purchased a painting to add to my collection. It is by a young English artist who you may already know, Ralph Bessborough. Now, if you will follow me we will go into the drawing room for the first viewing. In times to come you may tell your grandchildren that you were present when the famous painting, *Lilith and the Serpent*, was shown to the public for the first time.'

Amelie saw Ralph and ran to him. He was looking belligerent and not at all happy, a half empty glass in one hand, and she recognised the pale green drink as the absinthe of which he was so fond. He stared at her, screwing up his eyes as he tried to focus.

'Ralph, it's me, Amelie,' she began, and placed her hand on his arm. 'Come to the drawing room. The picture is about to be unveiled.'

'Did he roger you?' he asked loudly, and people looked round.

'Never mind about that now,' she prevaricated. 'All that matters is that your work is well received.'

He seemed not to hear, tossing back the remains of his

drink, then saying, 'I love you, Amelie.'

'I know,' she said, and strangely enough in the light of what had just happened to her, she believed him.

Who could put restrictions on love? He might be driven by his overpowering need to paint, even selling her down the river in order to satisfy it, but she knew that underneath it all he probably loved her more than any other creature on earth.

Hand in hand they went into the drawing room. It was already crowded and Henri had positioned himself near a splendidly carved Italian easel. This in itself was practically priceless as it was rumoured to have been given to Michael Angelo by one of the powerful Medici princes.

'Ah, there you are, Ralph, and the beautiful model too. Ladies and gentlemen, I give you Miss Amelie Aston,' Henri announced, his voice filling the room.

All eyes were on her and Amelie found it hard to face them, knowing that very soon they would be seeing her naked body depicted in paint. She tightened her grip on Ralph's hand, but Henri refused to let them sink into the background. He came forward and insisted that they stand with him to one side of the shrouded picture. It was now so quiet that one could have heard a pin drop. Henri throve on the theatrical and spun out the moment, keeping his audience hovering in suspense. Then, suddenly, he reached up and swept the cloth away.

'Oh!' came the cry, issuing from several dozen throats.

Amelie could hardly believe that the sultry siren making love to the giant snake was her.

Ralph, to amuse her while she was posing, had told her the tale of Adam's first wife, Lilith, who had been disobedient and finally left him to consort with Satan, who appeared in the guise of a snake. She was called The Mother of Demons, and God had been so angry with her that he created Eve to take her place at Adam's side. Amelie privately thought she sounded far more adventurous than the downtrodden second wife, and had been proud to represent her.

This portrayal of Lilith was that of a woman to drive men insane. Her naked body lit up the picture, making it difficult for the viewer to look anywhere else. Amelie recalled how Ralph had scoured the second-hand and bric-a-brac shops seeking a large stuffed python, and in the end had to pay full price at a taxidermist's for a magnificent specimen. It retained its sinuous grace, strikingly patterned. Ralph had draped it round Amelie's naked form that was bathed in shining light, her face slightly shadowed, the python's coils part covering her, sliding over one shoulder and resting its head on the other.

'Isn't it superb?' Henri crowed, and pulled Amelie forward. 'The model will now pose for you, as she did for Ralph Bessborough,' and he dragged her behind a screen and added, 'Amelie, take off your clothes. I borrowed the prop from Ralph. Drape the serpent round you and appear thus, standing beside the painting.'

His hands were in her hair, pulling out pins and having it cascade in a mass of ringlets down her back. Then he unlaced her and stripped her of her clothing. She made no protest; this was Ralph's hour and she felt of little consequence. Henri picked up the python, which had been so skilfully preserved that every bone in its spine was articulated and it moved in a lifelike fashion. Amelie shivered as its heavy, magnificently coloured length coiled around her. Henri arranged it in exactly the same position as the picture. He adjusted it here and there and then stood back.

'Perfect!' he murmured, and slipped a hand into her cleft, teasing the lips apart and fingering her clitoris.

Amelie started, amazed at the need his touch evoked, waves of desire coursing through her. And along with these feelings came the urge to show herself to the public. She was beautiful and bold, unashamed to portray Lilith. The men would look at her lustfully, their cocks standing to attention and she welcomed that, and the women would envy her, wishing they had the courage to bare all for the sake of art.

Henri led her from the screen and she was greeted by thunderous applause. In a flash she understood how stage performers must feel when the curtain is lowered and then rises again for them to take their bows. She was being worshipped. The men handled their balls and cocks, rubbing them and staring at her as if offering their genitals as a gift. The women did the same, standing with their legs apart, their hands moving down and massaging their nubbins. Then one by one the spectators fell to their knees before her. She was being worshipped as the embodiment of Lilith. They crawled closer, and in that instant Henri fastened a blindfold over her eyes. She felt his hand on one arm and Ralph's on the other, then she was lifted and seated on what felt like a smooth wooden toilet seat. It was comfortable but had a hole in the middle. Her ankles were shackled and her arms tied behind her back, her private parts exposed through the seat opening. There was a cold space where once the snake had rested. Someone had removed it.

Denied sight, her other senses were heightened. She sat motionless, her breasts jutting forwards. There was no way she could defend herself, neither by kicking nor lashing out. Such utter helplessness caused a dark warm glow to smoulder like coals in her depths. She imagined how she must look, with her legs open and her newly growing pubic hair on display. The gold rings would be glimpsed, threaded through her swollen labial lips. She felt someone pushing her thighs apart, and a solid male body standing above her. She could smell his musk and sweat, but it was an unfamiliar odour, not one she recognised as belonging to either Ralph or Henri.

A stranger was facing her with his cock on a level with her mouth. He grabbed her hair and wound it round his fist like a halter, yanked her face towards his pungent groin, then traced over her lips with his wet prick, using it like a paintbrush. It was overwhelming, robbing her of breath and giving her claustrophobia. She couldn't see it, but was judging the size of it and doubting she could take it all.

At the same time she felt a disturbance beneath her, and then interference with her pouting purse and parted rear. Lips were exploring her, slurping at her pussy, entering every fold, and a tongue was dipping into the sacred entrance to her most private parts. Fingers held her open, twirling the gold labial rings. Her clitoris was on fire and she was unsure whether to come or go, laugh or cry. Meanwhile the male holding his penis to her lips said, 'Give it a good sucking, you naughty girl.'

His words shot to the heart of her sex, and she obediently stretched her mouth over his hugeness. It filled her and plugged her throat. She choked, gagged, and he withdrew a tad. She worked on him, her cheeks drawn into hollows with the effort. The pleasure increased in her exposed genitals and she bucked against the tongue that persisted in lapping at her, lips nibbling her bud. A tempestuous orgasm beckoned her, but she could not reach it – not quite.

The cock was not her only preoccupation; one was pushed into her bound hand on one side, and another on the left. She closed her fingers around both, their owners grunting and panting, while the man in her mouth was speeding up, chasing his climax. The smell of lust was everywhere. There were hands on her buttocks and others on her breasts, stroking her nipples. Someone ejaculated over her, smoothing his emission into her skin. The tongue on her clitoris was persistent, determined to bring her to orgasm. And she wanted to, very much, but could not quite reach the blissful state that beckoned tantalisingly, hovering on the edge of her senses. There were too many distractions – the cocks in her hands, the one in her mouth that was about to jettison its load, and the person busy licking her sex. She needed something – but she did not know what.

She heard a swish then felt the burning pain as the whip struck her, cutting into the round globes of her bottom that hung so provocatively over the rim of the seat. She cried out more in pleasure than pain. Whoever it was brandishing the flogger let rip again and Amelie was close to swooning, fire spreading over her rear, her vagina spasming sharply and her mouth, hands and pussy being used by unknown others. She jolted every time the flogger struck, and she wriggled, wanting the tongue to make her come. The man in her mouth shot his spunk, wetting her face and hair. The cocks in her hands fell into a rhythm, faster, faster, then their owners groaned and sprayed her with seminal fluid. She leaned forward, almost begging the playful tongue to suck her clit with brutal friction. Whoever it was obeyed her need, and Amelie was hardly there any more, flying high, reaching the stars in an explosion that left her shaking and barely conscious.

She slumped in her bonds, quite alone now, all her lovers having vanished. Then she was unbound and lifted by familiar hands. The blindfold was removed, and blinking in the light Amelie looked into Ralph's face. The crowd were still there, but she was unaware as he pressed her against the wall, raised her onto her toes, then pulled out his cock and inserted in her wet channel, driving in and out until he was finished. He withdrew and Henri took his place. She was too dazed to resist, and part of her wanted to submit, watching Ralph watching her as the vicomte impaled her on his meaty tool and pumped relentlessly until he released a stream of milky semen.

This was not the end of Amelie's introduction into the decadent highlife of Paris. Henri, enchanted with her, had her conducted to his apartment that was even more lavish and spectacular. It seemed that he needed to perform in front of someone else, so invited Ralph along.

Beyond shame or embarrassment or sentimental

emotions, Amelie was taken to a neatly laid out games, massage and steam bath area. Henri was conscious of his figure and fanatical about keeping fit. He employed masseurs of Turkish origin, muscular men with olive skins and shaven heads who wore nothing but loincloths. He handed Amelie over to them while he entered the oblong pool and swam several lengths. Ralph did the same, and Amelie wanted to join them, but first had to lie prone under the ministrations of his silent, diligent experts.

She remembered Mario's cunning fingers that had eventually brought her to orgasm. These towering giants had no such intention, concentrating on kneading her back, shoulders, upper arms and thighs, then with one accord working a scented balm into the stripes bequeathed by the flogger. She felt utterly relaxed as one worked on her feet, massaging each toe until she squirmed with pleasure, then her ankles, arches and calves. She squinted sideways, trying to see if there was any action taking place behind their linen loincloths, but though bulky it seemed they were unmoved by her female form.

Henri saw her from where he rested, bobbing in the water. 'You won't stir their pricks,' he called. 'They are eunuchs. They come from Istanbul, sold into slavery and castrated when young, then serving in the harems. Young men are the only creatures who rouse their lukewarm passions, and even then they can't do a lot about it.'

Once Amelie was freed from the eunuchs' attentions she walked, weak-kneed and wobbly from so much manipulation of joints and ligaments, to the side of the pool and slipped in, enveloped in the heated water. It was lit by the warm glow from gilded walls and light filtering from crystal shades shaped like minarets. An erotic atmosphere reigned and became even more apparent when a trio of diminutive girls appeared, wearing the apparel of geishas.

They bowed to the half-submerged vicomte, so submissive that Amelie wanted to shake them. Their wide-sleeved silk kimonos were colourful, embroidered with chrysanthemums and fastened at the waist with wide sashes, and their blue-black hair was dressed high and held in place with bodkins and combs and flowers. Their makeup was extreme – chalk-white faces and crimson Cupid's bow lips and a lot of kohl round their eyes, rendering them even more mysterious and slanted. They put Amelie in mind of the Three Little Maids from the comic opera set in Japan she'd seen in London with Millicent, although the characters were innocent girls and geishas were little more than rich men's toys.

But what intrigued her most was the suggestion of the small breasts and narrow hips hidden beneath their clothing. They were like dolls, and she wanted to undress them and find out what they were like naked. Would they be brittle, so small that the average man would be unable to effect penetration for fear of snapping them in half? Did they, in fact, prefer a woman's caress, so close in age and stature that they might already be lovers?

One of them, a little bolder than the others, rested a tray on a low table and heated a container over it, then said in a curious mixture of Pidgin English and French, 'You will take a little sake, master?'

'Bring it here, Nami,' he said, smiling indulgently and then saying to Amelie, 'Come hither, little one. Have you tried sake? It is rice wine and must be drunk warm. How about you, Ralph?'

'I have drunk it before,' Ralph admitted, and Amelie was pleased when he swam over to where she clung to the rail, though well able to bottom it there.

She admired his lithe body, the skin already sun-kissed from his habit of lying on the roof of their garret and basking like a tomcat. She felt sure that she would always remember this scene, her first excursion into the underside of Paris society, where there were no holds barred and anything went. Who would have thought that the nicely reared orphan, more or less adopted by the vicar and his wife, would find herself naked in an indoor pool, with an attractive man on either side of her?

How daring and reprehensible – and thrilling!

The girls pattered across, bearing blue and white bone china bowls. Henri introduced them as Nami, Mimosa and Kiku. There was much giggling and bowing, but under the playfulness was a thread of sensual awareness as they handed the steaming bowls to the bathers. Amelie sipped hers and found it sweet and inviting and did not realise how intoxicating it was until she had drained the bowl and had Mimosa refill it.

The atmosphere became dreamlike and she drifted happily, with Ralph holding her from behind and Henri supporting her at the front. The water sloshed pleasantly at every movement. She could feel Ralph's cock hardening against her bottom, rubbing her anus. Henri caressed her breasts under the water. Her nipples stiffened, and she felt Henri's helm brushing past the gold rings and finding her clitoris. She rocked slightly and the friction was just what she needed.

She leaned back against Ralph's chest and felt the promise of his cock at her rear hole. Her groin became heavy and her nipples reacted to the water and Henri's coaxing fingers. Ralph's hands were on her hips, holding her steady. Then, still keeping up their tender caressing of her breasts and the nudging attentions of their phalli, they turned her so she could watch what was happening at the poolside.

The eunuchs, who had been standing near the golden walls, legs braced, bare feet apart and arms folded across broad chests, seized Nami, Mimosa and Kiku, stripped them of their garments and held them aloft as if they were puppets. Amelie watched, enchanted. The girls were as she had imagined, but even more delectable with slender limbs, conical breasts with protruding rose-brown nipples and the most beautiful quims, covered by a thatch of night-black curls.

The eunuchs lowered the geishas to the floor, and with firm grips on the backs of their necks had them kneel with their foreheads touching the tiles. Henri's cock grew larger and harder as he observed them, and Amelie closed her thighs round it, wriggling backwards and forwards along its length, her climax but a heartbeat away. Her excitement grew, and so did Henri's and Ralph's as the eunuchs took up pliable paddles covered in white leather and walloped the geishas' tiny rears. The skin turned from olive to dark rose, and the girls whimpered and implored but made no attempt to escape.

Released at last they ran to the draped divan and lay there entwined, still exclaiming and giggling, each rubbing the other's sore butt. They lay together voluptuously, thrusting forward breasts that were tweaked and aroused. Mimosa knelt between Nami's legs and burrowed into her delta, her busy tongue exciting her clit. Kiku was astride Nami's face, accepting the homage accorded her as Nami slurped. They made a lovely tableau.

'*Mon Dieu*!' breathed Henri. 'They are like something that has stepped straight down from a screen. Did you every see anything more piquant or arousing?'

Amelie felt him push then surge inside her, pool water and all. Ralph, equally erect and unstoppable, thrust against her anus and she moaned as she felt him succeed in inserting his helm into her. There it was, an undisputed fact – she was being penetrated in rectum and cunt by two men at once, and Henri was stimulating her clitoris with a thumb even as he worked his tool into her, thrusting deeply. She came, whimpering – then slumped, her body upheld by the rods of flesh penetrating her deeply. They jerked and lunged and she hardly knew which one was which or where she was feeling the most extraordinary sensations, her climax still shuddering through her.

The geishas sighed and moaned, seeming able to bring one another to orgasm again and again. The Turks stood impassive, the light gleaming on their shaven skulls. Henri gave a final great heave and the force of his come warmed Amelie inside. Ralph, whose member must have been restricted by Henri's possession of her channel, pumped his cock forcibly and finally reached his completion.

Amelie did not move, drinking in the sensations of their coming into her and the spasms radiating from her clit and womb following her own ascent into paradise.

Chapter Thirteen

Millicent was aware of straw in her hair, itchy bits poking into her tender flesh at its most exposed point, the smell of dung that hung on the air, and the scent of fresh young sweat belonging to Josh, the stable boy.

She had made him sweat, all right, and he had come back for more. He was a curly-headed gypsy who had a passion for horses only surpassed by his lust for her. At that very moment he was pleasuring her, his head between her spread thighs, tonguing her with catlike laps.

They lay at the back of a stall, hidden from preying eyes. Not that this worried Millicent a jot. She was like a woman reborn, empowered, confident and able to fend for herself. Mervin had given up remonstrating with her, and even stopped nagging about Amelie. Now she went her own way, joining him when he entertained but only if it amused her to do so. He never mentioned a betrothal to Nigel nowadays, but the peer was still enslaved, begging her to subordinate him, and she was only too willing to comply. She revelled in the dominatrix role, her repression caused by a lifetime of being controlled by males now finding an outlet through whips, canes and bondage directed at them.

Under her instructions the lake was cleared of duckweed and was used almost daily, by both herself and Mervin. She had taken up horse riding again, spending long hours in the saddle, feeling the wind in her face and the rise and fall of her gelding's withers under her, and the pressure of the pommel against her clit. Eventually she had taken to wearing breeches and sitting astride the broad equestrian back where the up and down movement very nearly brought her to orgasm. She had ordered Josh to accompany her, and this gave them ample opportunity for him to fill her with his virile cock and teach her his philosophy of enjoying nature and all her gifts, and never worrying too much about tomorrow.

Nonetheless, Millicent had no intention of burdening herself with a child, and as with all her other lovers she took what precautions were available. She went to see Mr Spollet for the express purpose of arming herself against an unwanted pregnancy and he advised her.

Now, languid with desire, she reached into the gap in front where Josh's breeches had wrinkled round his hips. She never tired of the sight of his curving prick jutting from its nest of raven curls. She took it out, its smooth knob poking from between her fingers as she rubbed it briskly, her almond-shaped nails grazing the shaft. Josh lifted his head from her crotch, fascinated to see her handling him in such an experienced fashion. She wanted him to go on sucking her, but was excited to have him eyeing her slim hands as they worked him to full erection. She looked at it lecherously and longed for him to fill the void within her that ached to be penetrated.

The horses rustled in the adjoining stalls, and she thought of the stallion who serviced not only the Bessborough mares but others in the county. She thrilled to see him nipping the backs of their graceful necks as he mounted them, and envied those beauties that took his mighty phallus without a murmur. I'd like to dress as a filly, she thought, drawing closer to Josh's penis, observing the slit in the dome that wept tears of need. I'd wear my hair in a mane and have a tail too, maybe thrust up my arse. I could prance and canter and pull little carts, or maybe have my submissives between the shafts and stand with feet spread to balance my weight, like Boadicea in her chariot, whipping them to greater effort.

The image was a powerful one and her avenue was

slippery wet from Josh's ministration. She wanted to come, not once but many times, and lowered her mouth to his pulsating cock-tip and took it between her lips. Josh jerked and groaned and threw back his head, his face wearing a tortured expression. Millicent withdrew, simply hovering over that needful helm, blowing on it gently and at the same time putting pressure on the space between his scrotum and anus, delaying his orgasm.

'Whoa there, who's an impatient pony, then?' she said sharply and slapped his quivering buttocks. 'Hold back until I say you can come.'

Josh groaned even louder and the sounds were music to her ears. There was no greater aphrodisiac than having control over a man. His chest heaved and he was obviously terrified that he might somehow offend her and she would refuse to relieve him of his spunk. This had happened in the past, and she had made him go off somewhere alone and masturbate.

'Lady Millicent,' he muttered, his dark eyes flashing, his sensual mouth petulant, 'you torture me beyond endurance.'

'What are you going to do, rape me?' she challenged, the thought of him using force causing such mayhem in her loins that she could hardly contain herself, let alone him.

'I might just do that,' he growled, and pushed her back in the hay.

Millicent had already taken off her breeches, her pubes bare between the lower edge of her corsets and the tops of her stockings. Her neatly clipped mound was framed by her suspenders, her labial wings sparkling with gems and her luscious dew, for she had followed Amelie's example and had them pierced. Her black riding boots were still in situ, and she thrilled at the thought of the lewd sight she must present, so aroused that she grabbed Josh by the shoulders and pulled him on top of her. He reacted quickly, rolling over and having her kneel above him. He heaved her up till her pussy was covering his face.

'Oh, oh, oh,' she whimpered, feeling him drawing her nubbin between his lips.

Her back arched, her breasts jutting from her opened blouse and he groped them, his thumbs revolving on the erect nipples. This, coupled with his busily working tongue on her love button was enough. The stable span and she came, yowling like a cat on heat and clawing at him. Josh moved her down till she was impaled on his shaft, grinding her cunt on this solid bar of flesh as its hugeness plunged inside and gave her inner muscles something to spasm around. She lunged against him, bounced up and down, remembered the sensation of riding astride, but this was far superior. It was as if they were fused together, until finally he roared and flooded her with his ejaculation.

'Oh, Josh,' she sighed, suddenly reduced to melting, lubricious womanhood.

'Was it good?' he asked in that superior way men have after copulation, as if they have given their partner the moon and stars, to say nothing of the sun into the bargain. 'Did I do it well?'

'You're learning,' she conceded, his replete cock slipping from inside her. She untangled her legs and lay with her head on his shoulder.

He was almost asleep, while she was wide-awake. She reached across and teased his limp prick, then cupped his relaxed balls, gently squeezing the velvety sac. Did she want more? It was true she was on fire most of the time lately, a furnace roaring within her, or at best reduced to a smoulder, like now.

She'd received another letter from Amelie in the morning post. Amelie wrote how wonderful Paris was, and launched into a graphic and somewhat lurid account of her latest exploits, nothing specific, but enough to whet Millicent's appetite. You must visit, Amelie had penned repeatedly.

So she might, Millicent thought as she woke Josh and angled her hips under his, ready for another bout of bucolic love, but just for now she was enjoying herself at Kelston Towers.

'I've not forgotten, Dulcie, nor have I forgiven your complicity in Miss Aston's departure without a by-your-leave,' Mervin said sternly, tapping his left palm lightly with the pliable cane held in his right fist.

'It wasn't nothing to do with me, sir,' Dulcie replied boldly, though there was the scared look of a trapped animal about her. This pleased Mervin. A spasm of lust moved his groin and his cock lifted its head and started to swell.

'Don't lie to me,' he said with forced patience, assuming his part as headmaster in the schoolroom that had recently become one of his favourite punishment areas. 'You may think it clever to flout me, my girl, but you'll pay dearly for your insolence. Over the desk and up with your clothes.'

'Oh master, no, have pity on me!' she implored, and tears coursed down her freckled face.

'Pity?' he stormed, pacing nearer. 'You ask for pity? Mrs Tanner doesn't think you deserve pity, neither does Mr Brock. I have a solemn duty to teach you the error of your ways.'

Hypocrite, he was thinking, wryly amused. It was true that Amelie's flight with Ralph had angered him greatly, but there were other girls, other slaves, and he would be able to grind her pride in the dust when she came crawling back to him after Ralph had finished with her. Meanwhile, he was in the mood for a little birching, followed by anal intercourse with this common slut, Dulcie, who had been getting above herself. If nothing else it was a means by which to wile away an hour or so on a wet afternoon.

'I'm sorry, master,' Dulcie quavered, shaking.

Mervin, mouth set in a grim line, gave the rod to her

234

and said, 'Kiss it.' With a sob she took it in her hands and lifted it to her lips. Mervin's fingers were at his fly and he quickly took out his tumescent penis, snatched the cane from her and pushed her down so that she knelt before him. Then he forced her face into his groin and commanded, 'Kiss this, too.'

The feel of her soft wet mouth closing over his helm was almost his undoing, but he exerted control and succeeded in retaining his spunk. Not yet, he told his impatient tool. He pushed Dulcie away and she fell at his feet in abject misery. Hoping to please him, she licked his shoes and he stood still, enjoying this act of servitude.

But it was not enough. He needed to feel the rod, an extension of his arm, landing on her quivering hinds. 'Up!' he ordered harshly. 'Up, girl, and over that desk at once, and no clenching of your buttocks or movement of your hips during your chastisement or I shall double the number of strokes.'

Dulcie lay across the mahogany surface and lifted her skirts. Mervin took his time, making her endure the rack of suspense. When he finally struck her the sense of power went to his head. She moaned at the first blow, but remained still. He delivered the next few at intervals, his pleasure enhanced by knowing she was clinging to the desk in fear and trepidation, while he let her experience to the full the agony surging to its peak. Only then would he administrate another cut.

The rain lashed the windows and the schoolroom was gloomy. Dulcie's ample white bottom was like a beacon, drawing him towards her, but he knew that the longer he resisted the temptation to sink his prick in her fundament, the more intense would be his climax when he finally yielded.

Dulcie could not keep still, moaning and writhing, her hands scrabbling at the hard wood. Mervin, an authority on chastisement, judged how much more she could take before fainting, and he did not want her to be unconscious when he sodomised her.

He cast the rod aside and pounced, ignoring her protests as he spat on his fingers and inserted them into her anal hole. This was followed by his cock, liberally larded by Dulcie's juice that, despite her protestations, was seeping from her vulva, betraying the excitement she was experiencing through Mervin's brutal treatment.

Then he followed his instinct to find a hole wherein to bury his weapon and release his seed. Dulcie's was tight, but he'd been there before. He put his arms round her, driving into her depths with such force that she would have scooted off the desk had he not been holding her. In and out he thrust, her smell, her coarseness, the sinfulness of the act bringing him to an almost immediate crisis. He was caught up in this force that was mightier than he was, raised to such bliss that he wished it would go on forever.

It never did, of course, leaving him feeling disgusted and jaded and less than he might be.

That night over dinner he said to Millicent, 'It's time we took a trip to Paris. See if we can find our runaway. There's much to entertain one; burlesque theatres, smoky dives, and a freedom that appeals to the libertines among us. You'll love it. Ralph lives in a Bohemian stronghold with artists, men of letters, and women too, who ignore the conventions. It's full of *estaminets* haunted by the demi-monde, gambling dens, and women everywhere; models, dancers, whores and rich ladies seeking rough, working class lovers.'

Millicent hesitated for a second, then took up her glass and sipped the red wine, looking at him over the rim and replying, 'You've changed your opinion. I thought you considered Ralph's friends to be scum. I'm game, but I insist on bringing my servants, Josh and Dulcie. And I shall not persuade Amelie to return, for it seems she is happy with Ralph.'

Mervin dabbed his lips with a snowy-white napkin. 'We'll see, my dear sister,' he said.

Amelie ran round the studio, clapping her hands with joy. 'Millicent is coming!' she cried. 'She's really coming!'

Ralph looked across from where he was lounging on the couch. 'So is Mervin, don't forget,' he reminded her.

'Oh, him,' she answered scornfully, and did a twirl, her skirts flying out. 'He can't harm me now.'

This was the truth. She had carved herself a niche in the Latin Quarter, accepted by artists and patrons alike, led by Henri. Ralph was doing so well that he was contemplating a move to a larger apartment, possibly buying a house. Now Millicent was coming to the city, and Amelie could not wait to show her around and introduce her to her large circle of friends, and maybe rekindle the fire between her and John.

Not long after a messenger delivered a note saying she had arrived and was staying at the James Hotel in the Rue St Honore, Amelie went to see her, braving Mervin who was bound to be angry with her. She was amazed by the palatial splendour of the hotel, almost swamped by the army of waiters and footmen, and the sumptuous details in the foyer with its high, *trompe l'oeil* ceiling and columned walls. She was shown up a staircase covered in fern-green carpet and reached a double cedar wood door with elaborate brass fittings. She thanked the porter and tipped him, then knocked.

Dulcie opened one of the doors and Amelie hugged her. Close behind came Millicent. 'Oh, my dear Amelie!' she exclaimed, and they embraced, both having missed the other woefully.

With their arms still wound round each other, they walked into the drawing room of the elegant suite, and Amelie recounted details she'd thought prudent to omit from her letters.

Millicent listened, her smile deepening. 'Well, well,' she

remarked. 'I should have come here before.'

Amelie, her tale told, looked round anxiously, asking, 'Where is Mervin?'

Millicent laughed, a brittle sound. 'He's already touring the Paris bordellos, and Nigel is with him.'

'Nigel? He has come with you?'

'He refused to be left behind, for he adores me and is my slave,' Millicent said nonchalantly. 'I have also brought along my stable boy, Josh, whom I have promoted to groom. I intend to ride whilst here.'

'Oh yes, in one of the parks... the Blois, I believe,' Amelie answered, her hands clasped in Millicent's.

'I wasn't planning to do it in public; I have other ideas,' Millicent replied mysteriously. 'But for this I need help from someone with a large house and, best of all, a stable block with an exercise ring.'

'Henri,' Amelie answered promptly.

'The vicomte you've just been talking about?' Millicent murmured thoughtfully. 'He sounds just the very man I'm seeking.'

'His parties are a revelation,' Amelie concluded. 'I've learned so much under his tutelage. He is planning one for this evening, another fancy dress theme where everyone can follow their fancies and appear as whomever they like. I shall see him at once and demand that you are invited.'

This proved to be no problem; in fact Henri was pleased to include the Bessboroughs on his list. This was a wise move on Amelie's part, as Mervin would be given no chance to bully her into giving up Ralph and returning to England if she was a guest at such an important man's establishment. She confided in Henri and he promised his help, pleased to promote the welfare of the young lovers and also to keep her by his side.

'You are an asset, *chérie*,' he said. 'You charm my friends and are the toast of Paris, the lovely Lilith of Ralph's so excellent painting.'

'And you will admire Millicent, I know,' she replied, and proceeded to recount all that had happened to them in England.

'Poor lady,' he said, a romantic at heart. 'So she was not sick at all?'

'No. All she required was an understanding of her own body, and for men to stop treating her like a halfwit.'

'I shall send her and her brother an invitation straight away,' he averred. 'I can't wait to meet her. Do you think they will accept?'

'I don't doubt it,' she answered. 'It is just the sort of event they will enjoy.'

Ralph and Amelie had a stock of costumes now, for Henri loved inventing themes for his gatherings and dressing up, having his guests do so as well. His parties were renowned, lavish, spectacular and scandalous. This occasion proved to be no exception and Amelie flung herself into Millicent's embrace when they arrived simultaneously at his residence that night.

They hugged and kissed and Mervin stood to one side with a face like a thundercloud. He was looking remarkably handsome in the dandyish outfit of a Regency buck. He had a waist-nipping tailcoat with wide lapels, a frilled stock wound round his throat, and the tightest of tight buckskin breeches that left little to the imagination. His hair was brushed forward and ruffled in the 'emperor' style favoured in those days, and he carried a high-crowned beaver hat under one arm.

He was smouldering with passionate anger and Amelie's nipples crimped beneath the draped Greek robe she wore, flimsy and transparent and showing off her breasts, bottom and fork to the best advantage. She could feel her lower lips moistening, her wings remembering the day he had pierced them, and shaved her pubic hair. She might have grown beyond this, but her wayward parts still regarded him as the master. He met her eye and she steeled herself not to avert her gaze.

239

He smiled ironically and said in those velvety tones that went straight to the heartland of her sex, 'We meet again, Amelie. Did you really think you could escape me? How beautiful you are looking. Paris obviously agrees with you.'

'It does, brother,' put in Ralph, standing close beside her. 'She is under my protection now.'

'Does this mean what I think it does... that she is your mistress?' Mervin replied scathingly.

'More than that. We are betrothed.'

Amelie clung to his arm to prevent herself from collapsing with shock. This was the first time he had seriously mentioned marriage. It was presumptuous of him, but she overlooked this in the flush of joy that radiated through her. Of course she would accept. He was possibly the only man she would even consider marrying, for she doubted meeting another who would be so tolerant, allowing her, even encouraging her, to carry on a liaison with the vicomte.

Mervin looked as if he wanted to strike them both down, but was prevented by the appearance of Henri, clad in a Roman toga, a laurel wreath on his head. He was introduced to the Bessboroughs and bent almost double over Millicent's hand, kissing the back of it.

'Amelie and Ralph have told me so much about you,' he said, flirting with her outrageously. 'And am I to be let into the secret of your costume, Lady Millicent? What lies beneath your enveloping cloak?'

She tapped him lightly on the cheek with her closed fan, saying coquettishly, 'You must wait and see, *monsieur*. Robes also conceal some of your other guests. Is there a given time when we must reveal all?'

'After supper,' he promised. 'When we have wined and dined and are ready to satisfy our other appetites, eh?'

He conducted them through the hall into the salon, and Amelie could see that the size and grandeur of the mansion impressed Millicent. The floors were highly polished and there was a scattering of Persian rugs, and much Louis-Quatorze furniture. Hothouse palms stood in large jardinières, and orchids and other tropical flowers cascaded from priceless Ming vases; there were statues from Greece, and countless Venetian mirrors that reflected the scene over and over.

Since their arrival there had been nothing happening that might offend delicate sensibilities, but Amelie knew this to be but the prologue. Music was playing and dancers gyrated to a waltz, but there was a tingling air of anticipation impossible to ignore. Henri's parties usually commenced in this sedate fashion, a far cry from how they ended. More and more people entered, accepted flutes of champagne and sampled the delicious canapés.

Now even the most reserved was opening up, cloaks cast aside to reveal leather or silk costumes, all extravaganzas designed to expose breasts, nipples, buttocks and genitals. As on former occasions, the liveried flunkies were provocatively attired, and on every side one could not avoid being confronted by naked equipment belonging to both sexes. Every taste was catered for; middle-aged ladies who fancied young meaty cocks; older gentlemen who yearned after the saucy breasts and tight quims of maidens; and those who preferred members of their own gender to bring them to completion. It was all a matter of taste, and Henri was entirely without prejudice, as open-minded as he was open-handed.

The master of ceremonies, resplendent in the rig out of a ringmaster, clapped his hands and immediately the band struck up and a group of acrobats came tumbling in. There were lithe girls, bare apart from tassels twirling from their nipples and minute sequinned cache-sex that barely hid their mounds. They yelled and somersaulted, did handstands and the splits, then their handsome male partners entered, clad in baggy Eastern pants, their well-developed torsos bare. They danced with the girls, every movement beautifully choreographed, forming shapes to stir the senses and rouse the passions. The jewelled pouches were torn off and thrown to the audience, some of whom seized them and bore them to their noses, inhaling the scent of sweat and female essence.

The music became wilder and the couples were soon joined at the genitals. The strong men lifted the girls and held them with their hands under their bottoms. Their lissom partners hooked their legs round muscular waists and moved in time to the music, faster and faster, crying out as the climax broke.

Amelie was transfixed, holding Ralph's hand and feeling the answering pressure of his fingers. The dancers ran off and were immediately replaced by half a dozen small men dressed as hussars. Amelie was struck by their size, just over four feet tall, their bandy legs and little, stubby hands. They were not ugly, and only slightly grotesque, the latest in generations of dwarfs who had carved a niche for themselves in theatre-land by becoming entertainers.

They went into their routine, clever jugglers and clowns, and some of the women in the audience had to be held back, so intrigued were they by these miniature men, demanding to see if their phalli and testicles were normal. When the manikins had completed their act the women were allowed to satisfy their curiosity. Flunkies had the dwarfs stand in line and take off their coats and open their breeches, exposing their balls and cocks that were out of proportion with the rest of them. The spectators were in uproar. The footmen let the women choose which midget they wanted. While their escorts watched and rubbed their pricks or amused themselves with the dancers, the ladies lay back and enjoyed the efforts of the little men who were bursting with energy, and only too happy to oblige.

'Isn't this amusing?' commented Henri, and Amelie was becoming aroused as she saw the manikins on top of the women, or crouched between their legs, bringing them to orgasm with their fleshy tongues and short fingers.

'Very amusing,' Millicent agreed, answering for her. 'But I have something to offer by way of a diversion that I think you may enjoy even better. Pray excuse me while I prepare.'

She was being evasive, refusing to tell even Amelie what she had planned. Mervin glowered in the background, but she could now ignore him, protected by her knight in shining armour, Ralph, who had attired himself in a Renaissance costume with tights and a bulging codpiece. More than anything she wanted to slip off with him to somewhere private, inspired by the sight of the dwarfs rubbing their cocks and pleasuring the ladies. She could not stay still, moving her hips in small circles and slipping her finger into the groove between her thighs, opening further and getting wetter.

Ralph saw what she was doing and whispered, 'Let me,' then his finger took the place of hers and he drew the fragile silk into her cleft and used it as a means of massaging her love-button.

The fabric was soon soaked; the friction was arousing yet stabbed her with even greater need. Her legs trembled, her pubis lifted and the chiffon-covered finger delved deeper, then returned to its insistent palpating where she wanted it most. She was flying, chasing the sensation that swept her ever higher. She came, shuddering and racked with pleasure, unable to control her moans.

'Dirty slut,' said a voice close to her ear.

She turned to see Mervin staring at her, and the front of his buckskins was distorted by the size of his erection. Ralph had left her momentarily to fetch more champagne, whilst she was trying to calm down and assume a normal mien. Not that it mattered as almost everyone had lost control by now, all struggling to achieve gratification in one form or another.

'Go away, sir,' she said, stumbling over her words. He still had the power to make her feel like a hen hypnotised by the fox ravaging the chicken-coop.

He was carrying a riding whip and slashed it against his leather-clad thigh. The noise brought back a rush of memories and Amelie's bottom burned. She looked up and saw Henri watching them, a curious, lustful smile curving his lips. Her heart sank. Did he want to witness Mervin punishing her? He, too, could sometimes become the dominator. Yet she hoped this was not so, after all she had told him. But human nature being what it was, the hour was growing late and the guests were full of wine and passion and brushing aside their inhibitions. Might he not do the same? Was not this what his parties were all about?

The master of ceremonies, who had claimed the space used by the dancers and dwarfs, saved her. He ordered two of the flunkies to bring on a young woman, who had been stripped. She was slender and shy, her straight blonde hair falling like a curtain over her blushing face. They led her to the centre of the area, fingering her lewdly, much to the crowds' delight, then snapped metal, fur-lined cuffs round her wrists. A length of chain linked these unusual bracelets, and the hefty footmen attached it to a hook on a rope they'd pulled down from somewhere in the ceiling.

Amelie flinched as she saw how the girl's tethered arms were drawn up and stretched high above her head. The muscles and sinews tightened as she scrabbled to touch the floor with her bare toes and thus avoid the relentless pain. Her rounded breasts were lifted, the nipples two brown-red cones. The servants twirled her on the rope, displaying her to the spectators. The vision of her flat belly and taut buttocks brought forth a cacophony of hoots, guffaws, whistles and raucous comments.

Henri walked up to her, a three-thonged whip with a plaited handle in his hand. 'Go on!' urged the crowd, speaking in several tongues. 'Beat her! Show the tart who is boss!'

'Anything to please my guests,' he said. 'Your wish is my command,' and he flexed his arm and let fly, the force of the blow spinning the girl, the thongs wrapping around her body.

Amelie did not want to watch, but there was a sick fascination about the spectacle. It was as if it was a faked stage performance, not really happening. But the girl's sobs were real enough, as was the way her body jerked at every stroke, and how her knees lifted in a dance of agony. One of the lackeys manipulated the rope. The girl twirled, presenting her legs, golden-flossed pubis, flat belly and globular breasts for one blow, then was spun round so that the back of her thighs, her trim buttocks and her slender spine were hit next.

Henri was not a cruel man and the whip had been carefully crafted for this express purpose, and he moderated the force of his blows so that, though leaving a dramatic crisscross of scarlet welts, no real or lasting harm was done. Even so, Amelie was thankful it was not her receiving such severe punishment. Yet, at the close of this display of mastery, Henri dropped the whip and moved in closer, his arms holding the dangling body, his face buried in her hotly throbbing bottom cheeks. He kissed them tenderly, his tongue moving into the deep crack, his hands opening it wider, seeking out her clit.

Then Amelia felt a pang of envy. The girl would be treated like a queen, sleeping in Henri's seigniorial bed, spoiled and pampered, till he tired of her. Then she would be presented with a purse full of francs and allowed to keep all the jewellery and clothes he'd bought her. A public flogging such as this was almost worth it.

The girl was released and fell into Henri's arms, only to be wrapped in a robe and escorted off stage by the footmen. Her part was over. More food was served and the guests were disporting themselves in every room, the conservatory and garden, anywhere suitable for fornication. But where was Millicent? Amelie wondered and began to fret, the champagne doing little to lift her worry regarding her friend.

'Where is she, Ralph?' she fretted. 'Where? Where?'

'I know, and can take you to her,' said Mervin, who had been watching the whole proceedings from where he leaned against a marble pillar, arms folded over his chest, booted feet crossed at the ankles.

'Don't even think about it,' warned Ralph.

'You can come as well,' his brother said ungraciously. 'Although, of course, it is my intention to bugger Amelie.'

'In that case you can sling your hook,' Ralph retorted angrily.

Mervin shrugged and sneered. 'You seem upset, old boy. Could it be that you doubt her ability to refuse me?'

The question was never settled because the stage was now set for Millicent's entrance. Henri made the announcement himself. 'It is my great pleasure to present Lady Millicent Bessborough as Queen Boadicea.'

The orchestra, under their conductor's baton, broke into a rousing march. The glass doors to the conservatory were suddenly opened wide, and with the rumble of ironbound wooden wheels, a chariot bowled through it. It was a carved and gilded vehicle, light and bouncy and pulled by a human steed, not a horse.

The light sparked off polished straps and brass buckles, and illuminated the charioteer who balanced there with the reins bunched in one fist. In the other she flourished a long whip and applied it mercilessly to her slave's naked, red-striped rump. The crowd went wild, cheering Millicent on, and Amelie glowed with pride. It was a magnificent turn out, and she recognised Nigel between the shafts, but did not know the powerfully handsome young barbarian who strolled along at the chariot's side, wearing the trappings of a Celtic warrior.

Millicent cracked the whip again. 'Oh, thank you, goddess, thank you,' Nigel mumbled through the bit wedged between his teeth.

'Stop, you wretched apology for a horse,' Millicent shouted and hauled on the reins, her command augmented by another resounding meeting between the leather and Nigel's bare flesh.

He halted and stood in his harness, trembling and sweating and awaiting her orders. He was naked, apart from the straps that crossed his portly frame, and the collar round his neck with chains that were linked to the rings threaded through holes in his nipples. A wide belt spanned his girth, attached to the harness that bound him to the chariot. A crupper passed through the crack in his fat backside, spreading open the cheeks. It circled his balls, thrusting them up and forward, his cock too, though it did not need any help, it seemed, his situation keeping him in a permanent state of arousal, his tool stiff as a broom handle. He not only wore nipple rings, but one had been threaded through his foreskin and chained to another in his navel.

His head was adorned with a closefitting leather cap decorated with brass discs, and he was blinkered too, condemned to tunnel vision while being a horse. He wore a flowing roan-coloured wig beneath his hat, and had a matching tail rooted in his anus. His bonds were tight, and if it pleased her to do so, Millicent could make them tighter. None of this distressed Nigel, and he wore a happy expression, gazing at her with drooling adoration.

Amelie was entranced. Millicent held them all spellbound, wearing her bizarre costume that consisted of a corset moulded to look like chain mail, which covered her from pubis to just below her jutting breasts. Her nipples were rouged, and she had a wide gold necklace and armbands and a helmet that made her look like a Valkyrie, and every bit as fierce. Her white tunic barely covered the apex of her thighs, and her lower legs were protected by chaste metal greaves, and she wore toe-post sandals on her feet. She was magnificent; a queen, a goddess, and Nigel's worship was understandable.

'My lords, ladies and gentlemen,' Millicent began, not even attempting French, but sticking to English. 'It is my pleasure to introduce you to my horse, and to encourage you to take up this alternative to pony riding. The vicomte has given me his kind permission to use the exercise ring in his stable outside. There I will demonstrate my skills at handling this chariot, and put my steed through his paces. First of all, however, I would like to show you that it isn't necessary to go to these lengths. All one needs is a stalwart and willing slave. Look upon this one as my stallion.'

She snapped her fingers and Josh came forward and helped her alight. Then he picked her up as if she weighed no more than a feather, and set her on his shoulders with her legs round his neck. Her crotch was pressed hard against his upper vertebrae and she wriggled her hips suggestively. With a hand on each of her thighs he trotted round the salon. The crowd were overjoyed at the sight, the women admiring his smooth biceps and the package barely concealed by his short kilt that rose tantalisingly at his every step. The men were concentrating on Millicent and Amelie was so proud of her, remembering how she once was, a shrinking violet bullied by her brother and having no sense of her own worth.

Henri applauded and led the way to the stables, getting into the chariot himself and having Nigel draw it. His guests had reached the stage where anything went, and all seemed wildly enthusiastic about the idea of becoming steeds or taking the part of drivers. Several of the women were already discussing costumes that would turn them into spirited mares ready to be serviced by someone like Josh.

Much later that night, when most of them had departed or fallen asleep on the floor or ended up in bed, Mervin went to round up Josh and Nigel, and Millicent and Amelie had a few precious moments alone together.

'I have no intention of going back to England,' Millicent announced. 'It's boring and dull. I want to be the owner of a high-class establishment that caters for all sexual requirements, be it horse training, like tonight, or any other type of play. Will you come in with me?'

'But I have no money to invest,' Amelie said, as they sat on gilded chairs in the hall, waiting for the return of the wanderers. A few dazed couples were threading their way to the entrance outside where their carriages had been waiting all evening. 'And what about John? Don't you want to see him?'

'Not particularly. Don't worry about money. I have plenty, and I'm sure Henri would approve and give you a loan. I want to meet up with him and pick his brains. He'll know all there is to know about the pleasure induced by slavery, and the pain that brings about a state of ecstatic euphoria. We can have dungeons and torture chambers. And what about water-play, like we did at the hydro?'

'And the vibrators that Mr Spollet used,' Amelie chimed in, warming to the idea.

'Exactly. We can encourage male prostitutes, and escorts too, so that women no longer have to endure frustration. It is so unfair when their husbands can resort to whores.'

'You're not about to become a suffragette, are you?' Amelie asked, alarmed.

Millicent smiled and stretched her legs out before her, relishing the freedom of movement that could be enjoyed in a brief tunic and sandal-boots. 'I might,' she said. 'But when I'm older. I think they are too earnest for me at the moment. I want to enjoy to the full my newfound freedom, fuck when I like and with whom.'

'Milly!' Amelie exclaimed, shocked by her language.

'Don't bother about it,' Millicent went on, so lovingly that Amelie looked on her as the sister she never had. Charity and Agnes should have fulfilled the role, but were too narrow-minded and jealous. Her life at the vicarage now seemed as if it had happened to someone else, many years ago.

'But I do worry,' she answered, and shared the cloak that Dulcie had brought along to drape round her mistress. Dawn was not far away and it was chilly.

'We shall be together if this project is successful,'

Millicent assured her. 'Ralph won't mind, will he? We can buy a large property, and you and he can live in half of it, while the rest is turned into our funhouse. We shall make a fortune, and maybe there will be others. We can expand. Oh, say you'll do it.'

'I shall talk it over with Ralph.'

'And I'll tackle Henri; he'll be putty in my hands,' Millicent replied, radiating confidence. 'Oh, Amelie, I bless the day you came to Kelston Towers.'

'And so do I,' Amelie said to Ralph as they lay in bed in their garret, while the sun rose over Montmartre and they heard the sounds of a great city awakening. 'I was nothing until I met her.'

'That's not true, I'm sure; your personality would have risen above your early disadvantages,' he murmured in her ear, and they were so comfortable together that she was sure he did not mind at all that she was proposing to open what, for want of a better word, could be called a brothel.

Her heart soared and her future seemed to spread out like a bright carpet before her. She had been fortunate, she knew. So many women did not have her advantages and, best of all, she had Ralph, and there was a wedding to plan in the not too distant future.

More exciting titles available from Chimera

***

The full range of our wonderfully erotic titles are now available as downloadable ebooks at our great new website:

www.chimerabooks.co.uk

All **Chimera** titles are available from your local bookshop or newsagent, or direct from our mail order department. Please send your order with your credit card details, a cheque or postal order (made payable to *Chimera Publishing Ltd*) to: **Chimera Publishing Ltd., Readers' Services, PO Box 152, Waterlooville, Hants, PO8 9FS**. Or call our **24 hour telephone/fax credit card hotline: +44 (0)23 92 646062** (Visa, Mastercard, Switch, JCB and Solo only).

To order, send: Title, author, ISBN number and price for each book ordered, your full name and address, cheque or postal order for the total amount, and include the following for postage and packing:

UK and BFPO: £1.00 for the first book, and 50p for each additional book to a maximum of £3.50.

Overseas and Eire: £2.00 for the first book, £1.00 for the second and 50p for each additional book.

*Titles £5.99. **All others (latest releases) £6.99**

For a copy of our free catalogue please write to:

Chimera Publishing Ltd
Readers' Services
PO Box 152
Waterlooville
Hants
PO8 9FS

or email us at:
chimera@chimerabooks.co.uk

or purchase from our range of superb titles at:
www.chimerabooks.co.uk

Chimera Publishing Ltd

PO Box 152
Waterlooville
Hants
PO8 9FS

www.chimerabooks.co.uk

chimera@chimerabooks.co.uk

***

Sales and Distribution in the USA and Canada

Client Distribution Services, Inc
193 Edwards Drive
Jackson
TN 38301
USA

***

Sales and Distribution in Australia

Dennis Jones & Associates Pty Ltd
19a Michellan Ct
Bayswater
Victoria
Australia 3153